I0619224

Ideal

Ideal

Lydia Osborn

Copyright © 2018 Lydia Osborn

All rights reserved.

ISBN:978-1-7322661-0-0

CHAPTER 1

*E*vil isn't born, it's made.

Broadcast over the whole country of Atherian every night at sundown, this reminder from the High Chairman keeps all the up-and-coming Witch Warriors on the alert. You aren't born evil, but everything and everyone has the ability to change you... for better or for worse.

The wide, dark brown eyes of her professor stared the girl down. "One more time, Cyania, and you'll be suspended from class," he warned. She had just blown her seventh pigeon out the window of the classroom and now the school board was getting seriously annoyed. Being spontaneously pelted with dead pigeons was not the way to gain favor with the most powerful Witch Warriors in the country.

"Mara, listen to me. You're raw talent, totally uncontrolled. Just because you can obliterate almost everyone in the school doesn't mean you're ready to graduate." Professor Erros was a reasonable man and one of the best defensive magic teachers in the land. Mara knew she was lucky to have him, but while she was one of the most promising and powerful students in the school she still hadn't quite mastered her easy little short-distance transportation spells. Move the pigeon to the other side of the room; that's all she had to do and still she overshot. If only she could use her manipulation of gravity it would be so much easier. But now, at the expense of all the spare pigeons in the school, she was getting no better. For Mara, not being able to do the easy stuff was infuriating. She could do things at sixteen the eighteen-year-olds weren't even dreaming of, but what was being taught in class… not so much.

"You have to lay the foundation if your building is ever going to stand." Professor Erros repeated this to his students every single day, rather like a substitute for saying the Atherian pledge. Mara cast a glance over at her twin sister (whose full name was Katalina, but everyone called her Kat). Kat was one of the most popular students in school and, while she was also good with magic, her real strength was socializing. Competitive from early childhood, the sisters had always raced to stay ahead of each other in every area of life. They also shared a pretty interesting history, including the fact that they didn't know who their real parents were.

Their adoptive parents, Aerick and Etta Cyania, had been obsessed with education ever since they adopted Mara and Kat. When the girls turned three they were enrolled at the Academy, the huge magical school where all young Witch Warriors in Atherian went to train in magic and warfare.

The first requirement of all Academy students is that they study their heritage – the unique history of their planet and their country. They learn that the planet of the Witch Warriors, called CSO-244, was created by the CSO (Compatible System Overload) program designed by inhabitants of planets located outside a black hole as a response to the overpopulation of their homeworlds. Four planets that they thought would be inhabitable were located inside a black hole 70 million light years away, so they sent out a ship filled with Humans. Legend has it that some Humans were affected by the black hole's energy when they passed through it; most of the travelers remained Human, but others mutated into Witch Warriors, a few became Quirks, and some changed into werewolves, vampires, or other magical creatures. The Witch Warriors, Quirks, and other magical species formed a secret society, creating a country called Atherian that was located on the same land as the Human world but was invisible to anyone who did not have magical blood.

The Academy, the sole school for all young Witch Warriors, was created when the problem of Gone developed. Before Humans arrived the only things inhabiting the CSO planets were demons, ferocious black-blooded creatures dredged up from the bottom of Hell itself. They were beaten back by the first Witch Warriors and have been in hiding ever since. It has been centuries since anyone has seen a demon; therefore, they are commonly thought to be extinct.

At first the only goal of Witch Warriors was to exterminate demons and to ensure the safety and maintain the ignorant bliss of the Humans. They accomplished this, but then their numbers dwindled because they didn't have anything left to do. However, a splinter faction of the WW population adopted the slogan "Survivors write history" and decided to create an all-powerful race of WW that would never die, and that would one day reveal themselves to the Human world and take over. They had heard tales about a Fog of Souls, a place where all demon souls go to be stored once their host demon is killed. Since the WW had killed so many demons there was an abundance of souls in the Fog. The splinter faction set out on a quest to find the Fog and they succeeded. They took hundreds of demon souls from the Fog and implanted those souls into the dead bodies of WW, expecting them to turn into immortal all-powerful beings.

Instead they turned into Gone, mindless black-eyed killing machines who could multiply ten times faster than WW. The population of Gone soon got out of control, and the leaders of the splinter group had to reveal their actions to the High Chairman, head of the Council of WW. They were afraid of what their creations would do to the world, and they were right to be worried. WW have now been fighting Gone for centuries but their numbers continue to grow uncontrollably. That is why the WW have evolved into what they are today, and why the Academy is so vital to the protection of the planet.

Mara and Kat started early, learned quickly, and were naturally powerful. By age seven they had both graduated from being Novices to Learners When their parents first sent them to the Academy Mara had asked for a peregrine falcon and named it Mamba. Kat, who didn't like birds, asked for a red spitting cobra which she named Venus. Your pet becomes your companion and your helper as you grow older in Atherian.

In the world of the WW there are three kinds of magic – Basic, Talent, and Specialty[1]. Mara's Talent was gravitational manipulation, controlling the gravity around any object to a limited extent, which meant she could bring things toward her or repel them as long as they were small and moving fairly slowly. Her Specialty magic was fog. She could turn into it, control it, create it, even condense it into water if she had a large enough supply. She could move at the speed of sound when she turned into fog, but she could only hold that form for a few minutes, less if she was fighting or otherwise exerting herself. She could also turn things she touched into fog, even people, and bring them with her wherever she traveled in that form.

Kat's Specialty was very different. It matched her personality – fiery and not inclined to follow rules. Kat could transfer pressure from herself to something else, making it explode. She could cause air, earth, or people to explode; she could even use it to propel herself and to fly. Her Talent was one of the things that made her popular because she could turn into a tiger whenever she wanted to and give piggyback rides around the Academy between classes.

Once young WW complete their training they are assigned to small battle groups with missions to go out and fight Gone, attempting once again to ensure the safety and ignorance of Humans. When Mara and Kat turned thirteen they were assigned to a group with two

---

[1]Basic magic consists of the abilities everyone has, such as minor control of objects and enhanced senses, reflexes, speed, and strength. Talent is specific to each WW, lying between Basic and Specialty. And Specialty is the strongest, the one area where you can do anything. In most WW, Specialty magic emerges the day they are born.

other students, one another Warrior and one still a Fielder.

Hazen Luthuk, Warrior, had the Specialty of lightning and the Talent of sticky goo. She was half Glukon, a species that could could stick to anything they wanted to. Their skin produced a sticky slime coating that they could turn off and on, so they could climb straight walls or jump randomly and stick to whatever they landed on. Full Glukons could also whip this sticky slime around and use it as a shield or a whip-like weapon, but Hazen, being only half Glukon, could not. She was the same age as Mara and Kat and was their lifelong friend. A pretty blonde with long spiky hair that always looked electrified, Hazen was also very tall and one of the best fighters in the school.

Mara and Kat were both tall and dark-haired, though Kat's hair was more of a light chocolate brown and Mara's was a deep rich chestnut. They both had tanned skin covered in scars. Kat's emerald eyes were slightly lighter than Mara's. They were both pretty, but Mara wasn't concerned about her looks and almost never wore makeup. Kat, however, was the lead popular girl of the Academy and always wore makeup except for training periods where it was strictly forbidden.

The fourth member of their team, the Fielder, was Chase Hathaway. He and Kat had an ongoing flirtation that had never really amounted to anything, but they were the two most popular people in school and they sort of had to like each other. Chase was tall with platinum blonde hair and blue eyes. He had shallow cheeks and a personality to match. He was the perfect stereotypical jock and everyone (well, almost everyone, Mara *not* included) loved him. His one shortcoming was that he was rather awful at fighting, magic, and anything academic. It didn't help that he had been handed one of the worst Specialties there was and that he still hadn't discovered his Talent. His Specialty was that he could control krill, the tiny shrimp-like creatures that whales eat, and could make them come up on land if he wanted to. However, krill die after more than thirty seconds out of water so this proved to be less than useful. The only real thing he could do was exterminate all whales, and that was strictly forbidden. Another thing that had resulted in him staying in the Academy longer than any student on record was that he continually failed all his classes. Apparently the stress of controlling krill had fried his brain. He was 24, old enough to be a veteran Master, perhaps a leader of an elite Gone-fighting team, or a teacher, but he was still in the Academy with several years left to go at the pace he was moving. Safe to say the administration had pretty much given up on Chase.

CHAPTER 2

"Mara, get your things! Chase is meeting me at the café and I *can't* be late!" Kat shouted.

"I'm three feet away, Kat, and I'm not deaf." Annoyance, as always, leaked into Mara's voice as she scolded her sister. Picking up her sleek black combat boots, she shoved them onto her feet and did a kip up onto the revolting barf-colored carpet of the school powder room. Kat tossed her a food pill, which Mara immediately popped into her mouth and swallowed. Kat looked at her in annoyance.

"You have to *savor* your food! You always eat it like you don't care what it's doing for you," she said, reproachfully.

"You're the one all whiny and eager to get to Chase. I'm just being a helpful sister," Mara retorted, plastering on a look of fake sweetness before letting it morph into an eye roll. Walking towards the door Mara sensed Kat following her and purposefully pushed the door closed quickly behind her. Kat caught it, of course, and shot Mara a nasty look once she got outside.

"You could have *ruined* my hair! Do you know how long I spent doing this?" she asked, gesturing dramatically to her perfect curls.

"Much longer than I spent caring," Mara shot back, not missing a beat. Kat looked at Mara with something in her eyes that could only be described as pity. Pity that Mara would never know the world of the popular because she didn't seem to care about her appearance or what others thought of her. She could become popular, of course. She was naturally pretty and was good at *everything*. Everything, that is, except socializing. Mara saw no point in having a social life.

"Katalina Cyania?" Mr. Rosten asked. He was Mara and Kat's infamous history teacher. Infamous not for being mean or giving the most homework but for being the most dreadfully boring person in the history of the CSO planets, probably even in the history of the world outside the black hole.

"Present," she said. Mr. Rosten nodded slowly at her. The wrinkles around his face moved sluggishly as he talked. *This guy has got to be three hundred years old*, she thought, not daring to voice this in front of him.

"Mara Cyania?" Still the bored, tired voice that was normal for Mr. Rosten.

"Present," came Mara's voice from the other side of the classroom. Mr. Rosten and all the other teachers at the school had learned long ago never to let Mara and Kat sit next to each other. Another name was mumbled by Mr. Rosten, followed by another muffled reply. It took a good twenty minutes of class time just for Mr. Rosten to call attendance every morning, and since they had him first hour it was *every* morning. No weekends off at the Academy.

"Can you believe this?" Kat quietly asked Hazen, who was sitting next to her. "We have to study vamps today. They're *all* in hiding and not giving us any trouble and yet we still have to memorize almost everything about them."

Hazen turned to look at her, smiling patiently. "Do you have to complain about *everything*, Kat? Yes, we have to learn about vamps, and yes, we're not getting any younger while we're doing it. But just think ahead. Think to when you'll be kicking all the boys' butts in third hour Weapons Technique." That was sufficient to cheer Kat up. Smiling broadly, she focused her attention back to the front of the class and Mr. Rosten.

"... and to extenuate this thought the vampire's culture took a surprising turn in the middle of the 30th century towards more of a fantastical governmental system. They also implemented new laws that would one day form the foundation for ..." and boom, Kat's attention was back on anything but the lecture. Looking across the room she spotted Chase's perfect face, his eyes also unfocused and staring at something a little to the left of her. She looked up and saw a cute black-haired girl winking and smiling at him. Looking back at Chase, Kat saw that he was responding, smiling back in that irresistible way of his. *Ughhhh. Disloyal jerk!* Under her desk Kat reached her hand out towards him; instantly a bit of air right in front of him crackled and exploded like a tiny orange firework. He looked quickly and, Kat thought, guiltily over at her. Shooting her a desperate but still adorable smile, he had a look in his eyes that is common in raccoons caught eating the cat food. She made a face at him and exploded a larger chunk of air directly in front of him, this time loud enough to draw Mr. Rosten's attention.

"Cyania!" Mr. Rosten's voice still wasn't loud and Mara wondered if he was capable of anything above a raspy whisper. "I do expect that you are paying attention to today's lecture instead of doing petty tricks for your fellow classmates."

"Of course, Mr. Rosten." Kat flashed him her signature smile, and even though he was a teacher she could see him melting. "I was just pondering the effect of the vampire revolution on the general werewolf population. I mean, they're enemies, right? Which side would the werewolves have been on? Or would they have stayed out of it entirely, not wanting to risk casualties in such a bloody conflict?" Mr. Rosten smiled back at her, a sight that was not pretty, and turned his attention back to the class. How Kat was able to do that, Mara could never figure out. She herself was a top notch student, several years ahead of the rest of her age group. She and Kat were both in the final year before graduation even though they were only sixteen. Hazen was the only other sixteen-year-old in their class. There were a few seventeen-year-olds and many who were eighteen. Mara looked at the ancient clock that historically ran three hours twenty-seven minutes and eight seconds behind, and calculated that it was 7:19 AM. *Yes! Eleven more minutes until third hour.* Mara loved third hour. It was Talent Development for the eighteen-year-olds, and she, Kat, and Hazen had again tested into the highest skill level. She loved having things thrown aloft by students who possessed strength talents and then getting to pull the objects back to her as quickly as she could. No one was super strong in their talent, and she was no exception; she could only control gravity on objects that weren't moving or were moving slowly, but she could repel stuff pretty well. The most practical use of this talent was repelling people.

Suddenly, she felt a soft tap on her right leg. Looking down she saw Kaeli, Hazen's pet gibbon, looking up at her with her adorable big brown eyes. With one hand Mara scuffled Kaeli on the head, then touched her gently on the ear. One of Kaeli's magical enhancements was that she could carry a message in her mind from one person to another. In Mara's head she now heard Hazen's voice. "Just got an assignment. When class ends we need to round up and head out immediately. You're the leader, and you're the only one who has legal control over Chase. Meet outside in ten. Oh, and P.S. Try and leave your Device on so you get the assignments, too." Removing her finger from Kaeli's ear, Mara looked around at Kat and saw that Hazen had already conveyed the message to her. Kat nodded slightly at Mara, then looked back at Chase.

Her brain is scrambled from dating so much. Mara turned back and pressed her finger again to Kaeli's ear. She thought out her message and transferred it to Kaeli.

"You shouldn't be using your Device in class. You can get the assignment afterwards; it's not an emergency. Yeah, I'll get everyone out to the pavilion ten minutes after class in full gear and weapons. We need the practice, even if sometimes we run out of Gone to fight and end up slashing at trees." Hazen looked over at Mara and laughed when she got the message. Then she nodded and petted Kaeli on her head.

CHAPTER 3

Mara, Kat, Hazen, and Chase all stood in the pavilion outside the main entrance to the Academy. As planned, right after first hour had ended Mara had gotten everyone out and into full gear and weapons.

"Okay, minor assignment down east of the capitol building," Mara announced. Kat and Hazen nodded. This was a routine thing. Gone were multiplying faster than the government could monitor, and they were always attacking somewhere, although rarely in large organized groups.

"Ooh! Ooh! What it is? What are we doing?" Chase asked excitedly. Hazen and Mara exchanged looks. This happened *every time* they got an assignment. It was always to fight Gone – that was all that WW did. But despite being by far the oldest in the group Chase still didn't have a solid grasp of the assignments.

"It's fighting Gone, Chase. It's always fighting Gone," Kat explained half-heartedly. Mara found it hard to believe that after so many of these displays of his utter uselessness Kat still managed to have a crush on the guy.

"Move out. Chase, you're with me," Mara said. Chase, the only WW in the battle group who couldn't magically transport himself faster than a Human, always had to share magical transportation with someone. Kat morphed into a tall, beautiful tiger and took off running at ten times the speed of an unenhanced tiger, disappearing past the tree line in a flash. Hazen raised a hand to the sky and harnessed her power of lightning, pulling it down into her. She sizzled out of existence leaving only the disturbing smell of roasting meat, and the bolt of lightning that took her place shot off in a blinding flash. Mara turned to Chase and reached out her hand. Chase gripped it tightly, his knuckles whitening. Sometimes traveling as fog with Mara could get bumpy, mostly because she didn't really care about Chase; she figured if he cracked his head open it would only spray confetti and sawdust everywhere and no real damage would be done.

Mara focused on the internal sense of the fog. Her fog. She let the fog seep into her body, then morphed it into something bigger and better. Turning herself and Chase completely into fog she took off at the speed of sound toward the rest of her team.

Trees and brush rushed by with the whistling sound that Mara loved. Occasionally there were animals whose expressions seemed to be frozen in time for the split second Mara could see them. A tiny red and brown robin was perched in a tree, carefully adding a twig to her nest. A herd of deer was immobile, one mother gently leaning over her tiny white-spotted fawn. The animals never heard or saw Mara, but she saw them and wondered what it would be like to live such a benign life – eating, sleeping, occasionally hiding from predators. All Mara did was run *toward* predators.

After traveling only twenty seconds as fog they reached their destination. Flipping upright Mara condensed the fog back into the shape of her body. Landing hard as she always did, she bent her knees and leaned forward to keep from breaking something. Looking back at Chase as an afterthought she saw that he had landed on his back, legs up in the air, squealing, horribly resembling a large spider in its last seconds of life. Suddenly realizing that everyone was looking at him he scrambled up and brushed himself off, striking a pose that Mara suspected was supposed to look like a hero coming in to save everyone but that ended up looking more like someone who was about to throw up. Mara joined Hazen, who had already sizzled into existence with that unnerving smell of grilled meat. Both girls shook their heads slightly and walked off in the direction from which their Gone detectors were picking up the most radiation. Kat walked over sympathetically and took Chase by the arm.

"Come on, we've got to complete our assignment now. You can go with Hazen on the way back," Kat told him, using a smooth, reassuring voice that she hoped would calm him down. Nodding, Chase appeared to feel better, and he followed Kat like a loyal dog as she walked away. Mara, looking back, was convinced that she saw his tongue hanging out a little bit. *Gross. My sister is half-dating someone who is equal in intellect and occasionally in appearance to a dog.* Hazen had noticed Mara looking back and did so, too, letting out a derisive snort when she saw Chase's ridiculous expression.

"That boy will never learn, will he?" Hazen only half-asked, already knowing the answer.

"No, no, he will not," Mara muttered as she shook her head.

It took only a few minutes of walking before their Gone detectors spiked. They dropped into fighting stances and pulled out their specialty weapons, the weapons they had come to prefer ever since they started at the Academy. Kat, who had never really liked weapons and who would rather do hand to hand combat, was given custom gloves and shoes that had hidden claws. Push one button and the claws would emerge on every finger and toe. Boom! She became ten times deadlier still only using her hands. This was a very unusual specialty weapon and she was constantly mocked by people who didn't know what she could do with it. When she was five and fell off the roof of the Academy she had to get her front teeth replaced, and she asked for retractable fangs. Her brain controlled the neural chip inside the fake teeth that told the fangs when to pop out. Her lower lip had frequently been mutilated by the upper fangs but she eventually learned how to use them. This added credibility to her fighting style. She was now just as deadly as any other WW with a traditional specialty weapon. Pushing the button on the back of her hand Kat felt her claws slip out and "*Sni-i-ck!*" – there were her fangs.

Hazen summoned a ball of lightning in her palm and rested her free hand on a deadly butterfly knife near her hip. Since they were still inside the borders of the hidden WW country, Atherian, they were qualified to use magic whenever they wanted. Once they stepped out into the Human world they weren't supposed to use magic while fighting Gone unless absolutely necessary, for the purpose of keeping their secret society secret. Trying to be discreet, Chase moved closer to a nearby tree while casually resting a hand on his knife. Along with being below average at almost everything else, Chase was dismal at best in the area of fighting. Everyone knew that he wouldn't be any help at all in this assignment; Mara only forced him to come because, legally, she had to.

Mara herself dropped her hand to her waist and pulled out a small rectangular piece of grippy, hard rubber. It didn't look like much, but this was one of the deadliest specialty weapons at the Academy. There was a button at one end and another button at the other, easily accessible with the first finger and the pinky. Mara pressed the top button and "*shlick!*" out came a long, shiny, deadly silver blade. Although she didn't do so, she knew that pressing the lower button would trigger another blade to come out the other end, just as long and deadly. The automatic double sword was a very prestigious specialty weapon and had earned Mara the respect of WW three times her age once they saw how well she could use it. With her other hand she reached into her boot and slipped a throwing knife out. Positioning it in her hand she clicked her tongue once which was the order to "scan area." Chase stayed right where he was, and Kat, for once abandoning her instinct to protect him, walked in the opposite direction. Hazen went to the left, eyes furtively scanning the dark corners under and between trees that were the favored hiding places for Gone. Mara went straight forward, sword at the ready, senses heightened and scanning for the smell of pure evil that Gone usually emitted. Pure evil, like milk that had been left outside a year too long.

Kat was walking through prickly underbrush trying to avoid stepping on the odd squishy things that usually graced the forest floor. A branch caught in her hair and she impatiently sliced it off with her left hand claws. *Ughh. Love killing Gone but do* not *love the scenery.*

"Aaaauuughhhhhhhhh!" The scream came from where they had all separated. *Chase! He must have stayed instead of going off and scanning. Oh, why am I surprised.* Kat took off at a run, jumping over and crashing through the underbrush that she had been so careful to avoid earlier. *Now I'm going to have to get a new pair of boots. These will be so covered in mud and leaves I wouldn't be caught dead in them.*

A few yards before she came back into the clearing she heard the distinctive sounds of Gone. Soft snuffling and snorting accompanied them everywhere they went. Slowing, she walked the next few feet and peered out into the clearing. There was Chase, cowering against his tree with his knife brandished in front of him, completely surrounded by Gone. She did a quick mental count. *Nine.* She looked over and saw Mara's face framed by greenery on the other side of the clearing, the high braid she always wore for missions draped over her shoulder. If let loose, Mara's hair would reach all the way down to the floor, but it never was. It was *always* up in the same style. *Boring*.

Mara must have heard Chase's scream, too. Kat gave a slight nod to Mara and Mara nodded back. Kat kneeled and stretched her arms out, holding her palms at a thirty degree angle so they faced the ground underneath the Gone. Purple waves radiated out of her hands and into the ground, like purple sound waves. This was the physical form of Kat's specialty. Once the pressure entered the ground Kat could decide when to release it in a monumental explosion. She held the pressure back and poured still more into the ground. *You mess with us, you fly sky high.*

The purple waves stopped emanating from Kat's hands. A rustling of leaves caught her attention and she knew it was Mara making her way closer to Chase. At that moment Kat released the pressure stored under the Gone and a mountain of fire and earth erupted where a second ago there had been nine Gone cornering Chase. Kat ran forward, careful to avoid the blast crater, and stopped in front of the tree which was blown to smithereens. A few feet away fog was condensing into the forms of Mara and Chase. Kat walked forward and hugged Chase. Then she turned around and gave Mara their team handshake – fist bump, up down high fives, wink. Mara loved working as a team and especially loved vanquishing Gone. These assignments had the effect of turning her into a more lively and fun person.

A crack reverberated through the forest as Mara and Kat were celebrating their small victory. Both turned to look at the noise and saw the flaming tree falling straight towards them. "Look out!" Mara screamed, diving towards Kat and Chase and placing her hands on them. Instantly turning all three of them into fog she raced them away to the other side of the clearing as the tree came crashing down. Materializing again, Mara and Kat landed gracefully and watched as the spreading fire jumped from the tree to the underbrush around it. Smoke billowed up, looking like giant grey pillows.

Chase, once again sprawled on the ground, got up slowly. "Can you please stop doing that, Mara? We were having a nice celebration," he whined in the tone of a five-year-old denied the right to eat all his Halloween candy at once. Both Mara and Kat spared a second to turn and give him a disdainful look.

"That's gotta be Hazen," Kat said, turning to look at Mara. She nodded and they both took off in the direction the tree came from. Chase threw up his hands.

"Didn't even have the decency to tell me what's going on. *Girls!*" he muttered, and turned back only to notice the fire rapidly spreading towards him. "Oh, look. Fire! Why didn't they mention *that*?"

Hazen had been scouting the area east of the clearing with no remarkable findings. Coaxing her lightning into amusing shapes as she walked, she didn't hear the snuffling and snorting of Gone. Kaeli did, however, and became restless loping alongside Hazen. Sensing her pet's anxiety Hazen let the lightning return to its original shape while she looked around. Then she heard it. Pulling out two of her trusty butterfly knives she dropped into a low hunter's crouch and looked around warily. Gone were deadly, mostly because of their numbers and because Humans didn't really know what they were or how to deal with them. The professors had said that becoming Gone fries the logic, emotion, and decision-making parts of the brain. Gone were not known for their intelligence or strategic planning. They attacked with no plan; their only motive was the need for blood.

With a roar worthy of an ancient warlord four Gone burst out of the shadows and sprinted toward Hazen with deadly, demonically enhanced speed. Kaeli pushed off with small muscular legs and caught a nearby tree branch with her fingers. Swinging as only a gibbon can she took less than three seconds to cross the distance from where Hazen stood to a tree directly behind the Gone. Meanwhile, Hazen had flung a butterfly knife at the nearest Gone, piercing his carotid artery; she watched as he collapsed to his knees. His scarred, deformed hands went to his throat, desperately trying to stop the pumping of the thick dirty-brown blood that was soaking his clothes. Hazen's other hand reached up towards the sky and connected with the source of lightning. She pulled a bolt down and directed it at a female Gone on her left who was charging at her with a short sword raised high. The bolt hit its target, surrounding the Gone with tendrils of intense white light; she fell twitching to the ground, her eyes the only things still moving of their own accord, a black patch spreading across her abdomen. A bit of the bolt hit a nearby tree, burning away the trunk in a matter of seconds. It started to fall, missing Hazen but dropping flaming branches everywhere. *Oh drat. Now I'll have to clean that up, too.*

Turning her attention away from her fallen adversary, Hazen focused on the remaining two Gone. The closer one swung at her with a large piece of metal pipe sharpened to a point. She ducked, coming up and grabbing the weapon, placing her thumb on the skin between the second and third fingers of his hand and bending his arm backwards while pressing down as hard as she could. His hand automatically released its hold on the weapon, letting the pipe fall to the ground. She slammed her knee into his gut; when he doubled over she brought her free elbow down on the back of his neck. Releasing his hand she swung her leg around behind her in a large arc and slammed it hard into his back. The force of her whip kick shoved the vanquished Gone directly at the only one still standing. The remaining Gone's eyes widened as he saw his partner hurtling towards him. They crashed together and fell on the pine needles. Hazen drew another bolt from the sky and aimed it at the prone figures. "Crack!" the bolt struck, and they began twitching helplessly on the ground.

"Hazen!" a shout came from the other side of the clearing. Startled, Hazen saw Mara and Kat running towards her. They stopped when they saw the vanquished Gone.

"Nice," Kat said quietly after a few seconds. She turned and gave Hazen the team handshake.

A second later, so did Mara. "Nice going, girl," she commented, looking proud of the youngest member of the team. Hazen drew herself up even taller and straightened her gear. They were all wearing casual, sleeveless spring-and-summer gear that suggested "we're not really trying, we're just naturally awesome."

"Hey, I picked up some meter readings from the west while we were running here," Mara said, looking back the way they had come. "I could use the thrill of kicking a few more Gone butts." Smiling at each other, Kat, Hazen, and Mara headed west at an easy jog, grinning as if they were going to a birthday party.

CHAPTER 4

*B*ack at the Academy it was time for seventh hour, Specialty Defense and Offense with no padding, taught by Professor Erros. Ahdrien Erros was one of the most respected, and definitely the most loved of all the teachers at the Academy despite being only twenty-five years of age. He was, as Mara and Hazen liked to call him, Atherian's Golden Boy. Good-looking, talented, charismatic – he had everything. He was one of the most gifted magically and physically of all the WW, and High Chairman Kurthian had already given him many recognition awards. No one knew why he had opted to become a teacher; everyone thought he would put his expertise to use out in the field, but they were certainly grateful to have him at the Academy. Of course he taught the most fun class in the entire school – Fighting with Magic – where you didn't have to worry about trying not to hurt your opponent. By Mara's calculations an average of 6.82 people went to the infirmary with mid-level to serious injuries per class. Even though there were plenty of healers and everyone was back to normal in no time it was still funny to watch the unfortunate loser wheeled out of the room on a gurney.

"I. Can't. WAIT!" Kat half-screamed. The look of excitement on her face matched the look of someone finding out they had won the lottery, or perhaps a three-year-old discovering marshmallows.

"Kat, that's gross. He's, like, twenty-five. And aren't you supposed to be dating Chase anyway?" Mara asked, giving her sister a sidelong glance.

"Well, yeah, but that doesn't mean I can't look at other boys. Besides, which girl in our class do you know that *doesn't* like him?" Kat gave Mara a mock questioning look.

"You're looking at her," she replied, pointing overdramatically to herself. Kat rolled her eyes.

"*Other* than you. For some reason you don't like *anyone*." After sixteen years of living with her sister, Kat still didn't understand how she wasn't romantically inclined at all.

"That's because no one here is worthy of my love," Mara said, looking at Kat with an air of superiority.

"Keep telling yourself that," Kat responded, shoving Mara playfully on her shoulder. Mara shoved her back and they both started laughing. "But no, seriously, I actually do like him. And he's single! I can't imagine why."

"Probably because the youngest unmarried female staff member here is eighty-three. And I only say unmarried because her last three husbands all died. Rumor has it the last one committed suicide," Mara chuckled.

"Why am I not surprised," Kat said. "Come on, if we're late Professor Erros will think I don't care about his class." They dashed out of the room, racing each other to the west wing and the class of the celebrated professor.

Fog. Person. Fog. Person. Mara switched back and forth, throwing blows then turning and letting the other kid punch through fog. Flying up above the kid's head Mara condensed again and dropped onto his back, reaching for his right hand and pulling it up behind his head till he tapped his knee twice, a common Aikido practice that means "that's enough, I feel pain." Letting him go Mara stood up and turned back to the group of students on her right waiting for their turn.

"Ashley and Kat," Professor Erros called out. Ashley, a fine-boned, unassuming, dark-haired girl with enhanced speed stepped into the center of the floor with Kat. Ashley was a very small person, and despite being two years older than Kat was still a head shorter. She squared herself off facing Kat and brought her hands up to guard her face and core. Kat copied her, dropping low into a hunter's crouch and bringing both hands up.

"And… begin!" Professor Erros shouted and a beep echoed throughout the large room. Ashley immediately lunged forward in a blur. Kat sidestepped and shot out her hands. Purple waves emanated from them into the ground around Ashley's feet. By alternating her control of the pressure on each side of Ashley, Kat allowed it to rock the ground back and forth, each time letting it almost explode before she drew it back in again. Ashley, fast but not great at balancing, quickly tumbled backwards. In a flash she arched her back and pushed off from the ground, landing back on her feet and coming straight at Kat. This time Kat aimed her waves at the ground directly below her own feet, not loading the ground with pressure but simply using it to propel herself higher into the air. On a good day she could hit fifty miles per hour just using pressure for propulsion. Rising to about seven feet, well out of Ashley's reach, Kat aimed one hand at a support beam on the ceiling, loading it with pressure and then letting go. The beam cracked in two places and fell. Ashley was, of course, quick enough to dodge it, but it did distract her long enough for Kat to drop back down and swing a high crescent kick that connected with Ashley's temple. Ashley fell to the ground. She skidded several feet before stopping and reaching her hand up groggily to touch her head. Kat's kicks were powerful.

Looking very proud of herself, Kat turned to see Professor Erros's reaction. He looked at her with that half smile that *everyone* fell for. Kat smiled at him and then strolled back over to the group. Ashley was getting up very slowly, looking murderously in Kat's direction. Ashley was considered very good for her age and was near the top of her class in everything. Seeing that someone two years younger could beat her up so badly was rubbing her fur the wrong way. Kat flashed her a model smile and flipped her hair around, seemingly without a care in the world.

On the other side of the room, Hazen, Chase, and a boy named Tobias were working in a group practicing double attacks. Professor Erros had pitted Hazen against two others in the third round and, after seeing how well she did, had assigned her to help some of the struggling students. Tobias was Chase's number one minion. Also good-looking but a complete airhead, Tobias was the second most popular boy in school, and had also been voted most likely to ruin your weekend four years running. This was especially impressive because you're supposed to be in your last year to be considered at all.

"Okay, Tobias, Chase and I are going to attack you," Hazen said, looking at Chase for confirmation that he had understood.

"Hey, I can't do that. He's my best friend," Chase said with an offended expression on his face. "I can't believe you'd try to make me do that, Hazen."

"Chase, the whole drill here is to attack the person and see how they deal with it. It's not for real. It's just a game." Hazen put on the face she used when talking to really little kids and trying to convince them that everything was alright. Chase nodded and whispered to himself 'just a game, just a game' over and over. Hazen lowered herself into a fighting stance and came at Tobias with a right roundhouse elbow. He sidestepped into the live side and brought both hands up to knock her elbow away. Hazen brought her left knee up, expecting him to go into a low x-block and parry the blow, but there was no block and her knee went right up into his ribcage. Tobias doubled over and backed away, looking up at her angrily.

"I thought you weren't supposed to get hurt in this drill," he said, glancing over at Chase to back him up. Chase nodded with Tobias, both looking at Hazen accusingly.

"You wouldn't if you knew what you were doing," Hazen shot back. "If you had paid attention to your training you would be prepared for a rapid fire attack." She shook her head. Why was she even trying? These popular boys would never learn. At least Kat knew how to be popular *and* stay on top of her classes. Turning her

31

attention back to the boys in front of her she motioned for them both to attack her. Looking at each other as if they were getting the keys to their first car they both charged at once, each with one hand chambered at his side and ready to throw a punch. Chase arrived first. Hazen dropped down and slid across the floor under him, and because he didn't know how to measure the power behind his strikes his fist barrelled into Tobias, punching him instead. Turning back around Hazen ran a few steps and launched herself into the air, swinging her back leg around in a flying spin kick. It caught Tobias's left arm which was tangled with Chase's from their collision, and sent him spinning off to one side. Chase, pulled off balance by the blow, fell hard on his right side.

"Ooooohhhh," Chase groaned. Hazen, landing by falling into a left side roll, popped back up onto her feet and brushed off her shirt sleeve.

"That's called a double attack. You both attack me, I take you both down. After so many years here that should be second nature for you," she said, trying not to sound superior. Reaching down to help the boys to their feet, she straightened up and steeled herself to begin the long and arduous process of explaining every little thing to Tobias and Chase until they understood and could at least complete the exercise.

Professor Erros walked around the training stations observing each student's progress. He liked to begin class with a few one-on-one or two-on-one fights while the whole class watched. Then he would split them into groups, depending on what each student needed to work on. A few students, such as Mara, Kat, and Hazen, were doing quite well in his class, so he almost always assigned them to teach some less exemplary pupils. He knew that the three girls loved fighting, especially when they got to use magic, and he also knew why – they were quick learners and they had all started ridiculously early at the Academy. He felt that the twins, Mara and Kat, showed a lot of promise, especially if they were to take private lessons to help them discover just how far their specialty could go. A lot of WW, he thought, didn't know the full extent of their powers. *If only people were brave enough to try to push the limits, then this society would grow strong enough to eradicate Gone forever.* Ahh, if only. Even if he couldn't change the minds of the Council he could definitely shape the country's youth so they would become more powerful than any before them.

"That's good, Maybelline!" he called out to a wiry girl with dirty blonde hair who was practicing her hopping back kicks followed by an uppercut. "Try to get more reach on the uppercut. You want to make sure you connect with your opponent every time." She nodded and turned back to her partner. Professor Erros completed the rest of his circle of the room in silence, a far off look on his face. The bell to end seventh hour rang loud and clear, cutting through his train of thought.

"Good job, everyone. I look forward to seeing you tomorrow. We're going to be working on fighting in pairs with bo staffs, so everyone bring their own staff. The school won't provide you with any when you're this experienced," Professor Erros announced, smiling at all of them as they left the room. Mara, Kat, and Hazen walked past him in a bunch, arguing about something to do with flying hook kicks, which foot you should push off with for maximum propulsion or something like that. He thought, *These girls will be the future of our race. I must train them well.*

CHAPTER 5

*I*t was Friday, the best day of the week by far because all classes were shortened and students were released at 2:30 instead of the usual 5:45. Mara, Kat, and Hazen were going down to a popular café and hangout area in the Human world right after school, mostly so Kat could talk endlessly to Mara and Hazen about boys and the other two girls could half listen while sending messages to each other through Kaeli. Kat had wanted to bring Chase along but Mara stood firm and forbade it, solidly backed by Hazen. But, before the excitement of hanging out in the Human world and pretending to be normal girls, they had to survive first hour magical history with Mr. Rosten.

He started by taking attendance – that was always twenty minutes out the window. No one was ever absent. The food pills that all WW ate prevented diseases from entering their body, and no parent in their right mind would let their child blow off school even for a day. Because of this complete waste of time, no one ever paid attention. One of the things that had made

Mara momentarily popular was that she had created a device that would record everyone's voices saying "present" and play them back at the exact speed that Mr. Rosten always took attendance. That way everyone could space out for the first twenty minutes of class while the device convinced Mr. Rosten that they were all alive and listening.

After that he delved into the subject for today – ancient folklore of CSO-153 that closely relates to documented sightings of mythical creatures on CSO-244.

"How much more boring could this class possibly get?" Mara whispered to herself. It wasn't that she didn't care about history; she did, but it was Mr. Rosten's teaching technique and the fact that they had covered all the interesting curriculum by age twelve that really put her to sleep. Mr. Rosten droned on in his lecture and Mara could see kids slumping and their eyes glazing over. Occasionally Mr. Rosten would let them do a lab class, which meant they'd actually get to use equipment and experiment to prove his point about some biological or genetic flaw in the history of magical species. Those classes were fun; even the kids who hated school agreed on that. But most classes were lectures, the type that made even the kids who liked school wish they were buried alive.

Suddenly, Mr. Rosten stopped talking. It took a moment for Mara to realize that there was no droning coming from the front of the class. She looked up, surprised, and saw that Mr. Rosten was just staring at a point on the wall behind the students, his eyes glazed over the same as theirs. But now other people were waking up too, noticing that the lecture had stopped and looking curiously at Mr. Rosten's unmoving form. Then she felt it. The slight, almost unnoticeable pull that meant someone was using magic. She scanned the room and her eyes locked on a boy she had never seen before. He had dirty blond hair and a slim face. She could just make out his deep green eyes from across the room. He was focusing almost lazily on Mr. Rosten, but still focusing, his eyes never leaving him. This was the giveaway of someone doing magic; for most types of mind magic you have to maintain direct sight for it to work. Mara stared at him hard. She was sure she hadn't seen him before, but she knew everyone at the Academy. How could someone have just walked in unnoticed? As if he sensed her looking at him, his head snapped around and his eyes focused on her. Mr. Rosten swayed slightly but didn't start talking again. Somehow this boy was maintaining his magic without direct sight. He looked at her, not in any way mean, just curious, as if asking what she was staring at. She maintained eye contact for a few more seconds, then swiveled her head around and leveled her gaze onto a book sitting on a shelf near Mr. Rosten's right shoulder. She stretched her fingers out under her desk and, making sure no one could see her, connected to the gravity surrounding it. She pulled the gravity around the book forward, making the book move off the shelf and float in midair. Pulling it little more Mara made the book collide with Mr. Rosten's right shoulder. He stumbled slightly to the left and then shook his head slowly as if waking from a deep stupor. He looked confused for a second, then seeing all of the students sitting up and actually paying attention he smiled slightly and returned his weary eyes to the book in front of him. The bee buzzing sound returned and all the students again slumped over in their chairs.

First hour, which felt a lot longer than an hour, was finally over and the students were filing out of the classroom. Mr. Rosten, being a rather small person, had had his classroom designed with a tiny door that fit only one normal sized person at a time. Everyone, especially the larger people, had to squeeze out looking quite silly. Mara glanced around after class and saw the new boy standing against a wall, facing the opposite direction from her and looking at a small piece of paper. She walked up behind him, careful not to make a sound.

"You do know that messing with teachers using magic is against the rules, right?" she asked. He spun on his heel to face her, looking very startled. Seeing her he visibly relaxed and cracked a small smile. He was about three inches taller than Mara but didn't have to look down to talk to her.

"Really? Well, in the case of that man I think the school should make an exception," he said, looking around as if scared that someone else would hear them. "Leif Morsvant, by the way," he said, sticking out his hand.

"Mara Cyania," Mara said, shaking it. He had a firm grip, but not one common with people rescued from the traveling freak shows that WW sometimes got trapped in in the Human world. Those unfortunates usually had scars covering every inch of skin, but this guy only had the visible scars of a normal WW. "Are you a transfer student or something?" she asked, even though she knew that the Academy was the only WW school in the country.

"No, I come from the Human world. My dad's Human, but I'm full WW so my mom must have been from here. Anyway, the scouting agents found me and brought me here," he said, his eyes giving something away that Mara recognized all too well. She knew he was lying to her, at least partially, but she decided not to press it. After all, she had just met him. She couldn't expect him to spill his heart to her, and frankly she didn't want him to.

"So how do you know how to fight, or to use magic at all for that matter?" she questioned. He gave her an odd look.

"How do *you* know I know how to fight? I've only been here for one class." She smiled at him with a slight air of superiority and opened her mouth to explain.

"Your hands. They have all the right calluses that show that you use weapons a lot. Also, no one who couldn't fight would be allowed in any of the advanced classes." She looked at him with an expression that suggested that *everyone* knew that. He looked down at his hands self-consciously.

"Yeah, I play with weapons now and again," he admitted. *Why does he sound ashamed?* Mara wondered. *Being able to fight is one of the key characteristics that will make you successful in this life.* "Hey, can you help me get to my next class? I have no idea where to go, they didn't even give me a tour before sticking me in class," he asked her, looking hopefully at Mara's face. The small slip of paper he was holding turned out to be a printed schedule. Mara traced her finger to second hour. *Specialty Magic Enhancement, room 709, Mrs. Graciet.*

"Sure, you can come with me. That's my next class too," Mara said. "Oh, and watch out for Mrs. Graciet. She thinks she's French and her name is pronounced Grah-see-ae. It's really Graciet, but if you ever say that she will flay you." Leif held his hands up in mock surrender.

"Good to know," he said, looking around as if this was the weirdest place he had ever been.

In Mrs. Graciet's second hour Specialty Magic Enhancement class, Leif proved to be the hot new subject of conversation. Apparently, his dad was the local drunk of a small town in the Human world and they had brought Leif here because he had discovered his magic and kept it a secret while learning to control it and fight with it. This sounded reasonable enough. Mara had detected a small note of disapproval in Leif's voice when he talked about his dad, but there was also a rumor that his mom was a zombie from CSO-97, so Mara had no idea how credible the sources were. Leif had said his mom must have been a WW, which meant that she was either dead or estranged from the family. Mara guessed dead – there were a lot of WW women who lived in the Human world and who ended up dead.

"Okay everyone, let's move it! Line up along the wall and shoot out some magic!" Mrs. Graciet shouted with a very fake sounding French accent. Mara and two other girls that Leif didn't know lined up next to each other, laughing about something that he couldn't make out. He moved in besides a boy who was a little shorter than he was but who seemed to be very popular. Walking to class Leif had seen this boy surrounded by girls and boys alike, all trying to talk to him. The boy turned and saw Leif looking at him.

"Hey, what's up? I'm Chase Hathaway, resident popular kid," he said, a wide smile spreading across his face. He winked at Leif as if that was the normal thing to do.

"Leif Morsvant," Leif said, not sure of whether to wink or not. He decided not to – that seemed to be Chase's thing and he didn't want to encroach. "So... what's your specialty?" he asked. It seemed like a lame thing to say – everyone probably knew what everyone else's specialty was – but he was new and he had an excuse.

Chase didn't seem to think it was lame, he only smiled and said, "I can control krill. You know, those tiny pink shrimp in the ocean. I know, it's not a very impressive specialty, but I make up for it in every other way." Leif nodded as if he believed him, but inside he was collapsing into fits of laughter. *Krill? Now I really want to see what Chase can do.*

"Well, let's see what you can do," Leif said, gesturing toward the wall. Chase shook his head a bit, leaned down low, and focused. Raising his hands he held them up in the air and closed his eyes. Nothing happened.

"Umm... do you need some water to get the krill out of?" Leif asked, at a loss but still wanting to help. He had never encountered a specialty magic that seemed so useless.

Chase's head snapped up. "Right, I almost forgot! Someone get me my bucket please!" he shouted out across the room. About eight or nine girls shot their hands up, as if this was the opportunity of a lifetime. He looked over at Mara and the other two girls. None of them were raising their hands, and Mara and the blonde girl were looking at the hopefuls and rolling their eyes. The other brunette girl, who looked fairly similar to Mara, was looking at Chase with the kind of expression that suggested she owned him. *Girlfriend, maybe.* Chase was looking over the crowd of girls like a powerful emperor would look at possible wives. He raised his hand and pointed at a tiny but strong-looking girl with cropped white-blonde hair.

"You there, you can go get my bucket," he said, looking very proud of himself. She jumped up in the air, giggled slightly, then ran off to the closet. All the other girls slumped and cast dejected looks at one another. When the tiny girl came back with a large bucket of water, the others directed their envious and angry looks at her. Setting the bucket down in front of Chase, the tiny girl went back to her place along the wall. Chase again hunkered down, raised his hands, and closed his eyes. This time, out of the water came tiny squirming pink things. 'Things' was the most descriptive word Leif could think of at that moment because they really didn't look like anything he had ever seen before. Drawing his hands in towards his body Chase pulled the things with him until they were hovering right in front of his face. Stepping aside he allowed Leif to come up and look.

"These, my friend, are krill," he said proudly as if introducing his friends who had very high status. "They come in very handy in a battle, as long as I have some water nearby. They make really good shields."

Leif shuddered to think of having a squirming pink mass shielding him from Gone, but nodded anyway and tried to look impressed. He got the idea that everyone wanted to be on Chase's good side, and he wasn't about to alienate him.

"So Leif! You haven't told us what *you* can do. Could we get a demonstration?" Chase asked, looking expectantly at Leif.

Leif's hands clenched at his sides, but quickly returned to their natural position. Chase didn't notice. "Umm... my specialty's kind of hard to demonstrate. It's a weird specialty. I can, well, control other people's minds if I want. Change what they're thinking, put new thoughts in or take them out. I don't want to hurt anyone here." He looked at Chase for understanding but Chase just turned to the rest of his friend group with a very excited expression.

"Awww, we could totally use this! Leif, you've gotta show us what you can do. That sounds *so* cool!" one of the other boys said, and everyone else quickly nodded agreement.

"Ooh, ooh, ooh, Leif, do that girl," Chase said, pointing to the brunette next to Mara. "This is gonna be a blast!" he said, his eyes widening at the prospect.

Facing the girl, Leif reached his mind out and touched hers. There were mental barriers everywhere, walls upon walls upon walls that he couldn't break down. Breaking his line of sight he shook his head and turned back to Chase.

"Her mental defenses are beyond anything I've ever seen. It'll take a lot of time to break through that," he sighed. He would have liked to show these boys what he could do. Even though it wasn't a traditional specialty, it was still cool and he had the feeling it would have gained him favor with the "popular group." Chase and the rest of the boys slumped down and turned away, dejected. Leif was about to follow them and attempt to re-engage when he felt a sudden blow to the back of his head. He stumbled forwards and fell onto his hands and knees, seeing faint black spots around the edges of his vision. He was back up in a second, though, flipping off his hands and onto his feet. Spinning around, he saw the brunette girl he had tried to control standing in a low fighting stance.

"No one tries to break into my mind," she said, not in the usual tone of a girl's voice but in a low growl. She ran forward, aiming a punch which Leif grabbed with his left hand expecting to stop its momentum, but instead the girl pushed through and twisted her hand out of his grip. Grabbing his wrist, she flipped him over. He landed on his back and she pressed her high-heeled boot into his throat. Now everyone in the class was watching the spectacle. Even Mrs. Graciet, who was supposed to keep order, was standing watching with the rest of the students. Leif lay there for a second, then brought both his feet up and connected with the girl's abdomen. She flew back a couple yards but landed squarely on her feet. Flipping her hair out of her face the girl looked at him with a clearly defiant expression. Leif stayed still for a moment, then launched himself into the air and spun around, coming down hard at the girl with his right leg extended. She sidestepped and flung out both hands, knocking his right leg off course. Leif swung his left leg around and still landed, but slightly off balance. The girl came at him with a left side kick which he blocked, and then a right back roundhouse elbow. This caught him in the cheek and sent his head snapping to the other side. He kept his feet planted and brought his opposite hand up for a right uppercut. The girl didn't even try to block it but let it connect with her chin. She fell to the ground.

"Stop. I'm hurt!" she cried out. Leif took a step back and began to stoop over to check on her. Planting her left hand on the ground the girl pushed off faster than Leif could see and swung both legs around, sweeping his legs out from under him. Landing on her side and using her momentum from the sweep to spin back up onto her feet, the girl stood over Leif and again declared, "*No one*tries to break into my mind." She stalked off to retake her position next to Mara.

Slowly and painfully getting back to his feet, Leif walked over to Chase and the group of boys. They were all smiling at him as if he'd won the state championships.

"Dude, that was sick! You totally almost won!" Chase said, slapping Leif on the back a bit too hard.

"Ow," Leif said. He was pretty sure he had broken at least one rib from falling after the sweep kick.

"Oh, sorry, man. We'll show you where the infirmary is," Chase said reassuringly. While they had been talking a group of girls had gathered around. Leif assumed they had all come to talk to Chase, but instead they focused their attention on him and started bombarding him with questions. Leif held his hands up to signify that he didn't want to answer right now. His right side was really starting to hurt. *Maybe it's two or three ribs.* Chase held his hands out and gently pushed back the girls.

"Not now, ladies, we have to get this guy to the infirmary. This is Leif, by the way, and he's *awesome*!" Chase said. The girls giggled slightly, waved, and walked off in a group to the door. Mrs. Graciet rushed them all out of the room. Chase and several other popular boys flanked Leif as he walked out.

"We're going to the infirmary, Mrs. Graciet," Chase informed her. She nodded.

When they finally got to the infirmary – it was on the other side of the school from all the classes that people got hurt in – Leif thanked the boys and tried to walk through the doors alone, but Chase followed him and all the other boys followed Chase.

"I think I can handle it from here, guys," Leif said, a bit worried that they were going to keep following him around.

"Nah, man, we'll stay with you. You're part of the group now," a boy named Tobias said. He seemed to be Chase's best friend, the second most popular boy in school. Leif pondered what he had said. *Am I popular now?* He shrugged and walked over to the woman in a sterile white gown who was motioning for him to come over.

"What have you boys gotten yourself into now?" she asked, looking disapprovingly at Chase. He plastered on an expression of innocence and smiled.

"I think I broke a rib," Leif said, wincing. The medic felt around his rib cage and with every press an arrow of pain shot up Leif's body.

"Yep, that's several broken ribs, mister. You better sit down," she motioned to a nearby chair. Leif eased his weight into it and the medic kneeled down next to him. He had heard of healers, but never actually seen one. She placed her hands on his right side and relief flowed through his body.

"Don't move," she scolded. "I'm not done yet."

Leif stayed put and watched as her hands moved down slightly. After another twenty seconds she removed them. Leif stood up and poked his side experimentally a few times. No pain.

"You're good to go," she said, waving him out the door. Leif managed to squeeze in a quick "thanks" before the door closed behind him.

CHAPTER 6

*T*he deep mahogany wood shone in the harsh lighting of the dining room. Mara and Kat sat down next to each other as they always did at their dining table, with their parents directly across from them. The dining table was about twenty-five feet long and seated twenty people, twenty-five if everyone squeezed. It was traditional for well-to-do people to have large dinner parties, but the Cyanias never did. They simply liked the look of the ultra-long table.

They were all waiting for the first course to be brought out when a loud clanging sound resounded throughout the house. The doorbell.

"I'll get it!" Mara and Kat said at the same time. They both hated formal dinner with the family just because there was always so much food and so little to do. They preferred eating quickly with friends and getting back to whatever they might be doing. Mara and Kat both jumped up from their seats and rushed out the dining room door, leaving their parents slightly ruffled and confused. Running along the endless hallways through the twists and turns of their very elaborate house, Mara and Kat finally reached the front door. It was a double door, tall, with gold and mother-of-pearl inlays and a large door knocker in the shape of the WW symbol.

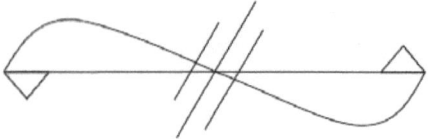

Their door knocker was never used, it was extremely old-fashioned, but Aerick and Etta had it put in just for show. Reaching down for the carved door handle Kat opened the door and looked outside. No one was there.

"Mamba!" Mara whispered. Her beautiful blue peregrine falcon swooped down from her perch above the door and landed on Mara's right arm, her talons fitting perfectly into the many deep scars forever engraved into Mara's skin. She had learned how to handle Mamba without wearing a glove, and she still didn't use one. In the early days Mamba would cut her arm to pieces, forcing Mara's parents to take her to healer after healer. It was only when they finally got used to each other that Mamba learned to land more gently and Mara learned to move in ways that avoided injury.

Mamba folded her wings and looked at Mara with intelligent yellow-brown eyes. She squeaked and looked at Mara curiously as if to say, "What? What do you need me to do?" Mara ruffled her feathers affectionately and whispered, "Go and see who's out there. Don't attack without me." Mamba's eyes widened signifying she understood and pushed off of Mara's arm, spreading her wings. Catching a current, she flew out and glided up to make large circles around the yard.

"Kak, kak kak kak, Kaak!" Mamba's alert cry was easily heard. Mara rushed outside, calling to bring Mamba in. The falcon closed her wings and dove straight at Mara. At the last second her wings opened again and caught the air, slowing her enough so she wouldn't hurt Mara. Landing, the bird straightened herself and called again, pointing her beak in the direction of the street. Looking over from her porch, Mara could see a figure. It was very late at night, she now realized. Kat appeared beside Mara with her red spitting cobra, Venus, wrapped around her arm. Venus's forked tongue flicked out and her head weaved gently back and forth. The figure, about twenty feet from them, had been walking away but turned around and slowly began to jog back. It was either a boy or perhaps a girl with short hair.

"Go," Mara whispered to Mamba. The falcon took off gracefully and, letting out a battle cry, dove for the figure. Mara watched as the figure put its hands up. Mamba didn't hit it, she just circled around it.

"Mara?" a voice came from the figure. Mara stared. She knew that voice.

"Leif?!" she asked. *How does he know where I live? Did the school give him the directory of all Witch Warrior families in the area?* "What are *you* doing here?"

Kat dropped her arm and let Venus slither off. One of Venus's magical enhancements was that she could move at five times the normal speed for a snake. She shot over to where Leif stood and wrapped her tail around his arm. Shooting back, she dragged him along with her. He stumbled over in front of Mara and Kat. Mamba came in again and landed on Mara's arm while Venus, letting go of Leif's wrist, slithered back around Kat's arm and up onto her shoulder.

"Aahh!" Leif half-shouted upon seeing Kat. "You... you live here too?" He looked worried and glanced over at Mara as if pleading for protection.

"Relax, dimwit, I'm not going to attack you again. I already proved I can kick your butt," Kat said.

"Kat!" Mara rebuffed. "He's new, cut him some slack." She looked apologetically at Leif. "Sorry about her. This is my twin sister, Katalina, but everyone calls her Kat." Leif looked slightly less worried but still regarded Kat fearfully. Mamba suddenly reached out and poked Leif in the arm with her beak. He jumped back, falling into a fighting stance and staring at the bird.

"Don't worry, she's just curious. Sorry about her attack earlier, but she's trained to eliminate anyone she doesn't recognize," Mara explained. She put her hand on Mamba's head and said gently, "This is Leif, Mamba. Be nice," then turning back to Leif said, "She won't attack now unless I tell her to."

"So, new kid, what are you doing here? This isn't the grocery store," Kat asked. She had a tendency to be a little rough with strangers, especially those who tried to control her earlier in the day.

Leif made a face at her. "No, I wanted to talk to Mara, but if she's quarantined by her overprotective sister at the moment then that's just fine." Kat scoffed. In only the light of the black hole they looked remarkably similar. "Are you guys identical or something?" he asked.

Mara and Kat both looked horrified. "Oh, God, no," Mara said. "Fraternal twins that look similar, that's all. Hey, if you actually want to talk to me, you better come inside. In about fifteen seconds the home security system will be set off and you'll most likely be chopped in half."

"Oh, okay then," Leif said, looking around trying to spot their so-called "home security system." All three of them ran up the path to the front doors. Swinging shut automatically behind Leif, the doors made a loud clanging noise as their several locks engaged. Looking around, Leif felt his jaw drop but, remembering his manners, he snapped it closed again and tried to pretend like this was the normal type of house he got invited into.

Aerick and Etta Cyania had made a huge amount of money in their industry – blower manufacturing. They were the only company in all of Atherian that made government certified blowers, and everyone bought from them. Blowers were a fairly common specialty weapon largely due to their convenience. They were tiny, portable and easily hidden, but packed a lot of punch. You could press one button and a stream of either fire or ice would come out, depending on the type of blower. Mara and Kat both knew how to use them, of course, but they weren't super into them.

Using their fortune, Aerick and Etta had done everything they could to provide for their kids. They had paid extra to start Mara and Kat early at the Academy, had given them an entire wing of the house, had bought them the best equipment and trainers. Of course, Mara and Kat didn't actually use their wing of the house, but they appreciated it anyway. They lived in the quarters they had built themselves out in the backyard, starting back when they were just six or seven years old and believed that they needed to know how to live in the wild.

Leif tried to notice landmarks and remember which way they had come as Mara and Kat led him through endless passages and corridors and out one of the many doors of their self-built house. It was nice, of course, but nowhere close to the extreme luxury that their parents lived in.

"So, welcome to our humble abode," Kat said, gesturing around the spacious entryway.

"Are you kidding?" Leif asked. "This 'humble abode' is *way* nicer than my dad's place will ever be." Mara deposited Mamba on a perch near a pile of logs, and Kat aimed her hands at the wood. A second later the air around the logs exploded and they caught fire. Soon there was a pleasant crackling sound coming from the fireplace.

"Don't you guys have heating?" Leif asked. A house as nice as this would definitely have the luxury of a heating system.

"Yeah, sure, but we don't like to use it. Especially at night. Our neighbor, Mr. Gravenstein, always plugs a cord into our heater and uses it for himself, so we figure if we can go without it's worth it to torture that old pig. He is one of the rudest people you will ever meet, I guarantee you," Mara said, waving her hands to demonstrate her annoyance.

"Oh," was all Leif said at first, followed by "So… I kind of wanted to talk to Mara alone." Looking at him suspiciously Kat nodded and left the room, closing the door with a thump. Mara glanced at Leif expectantly, but for a moment he didn't speak.

"Um… I need to borrow some money," he finally murmured, looking down at the ground, clearly ashamed.

"Oh," Mara said, taken aback. "Money? Why? Don't you live in the student dorms at the Academy?" Leif shook his head.

"No, I still live in the Human world, at my dad's place. He thinks I got tuition to go to some private Human school but still expects me to come home on weekends. Anyway, my dad, he's not the best role model. He's a drunk and a gambler." Again Leif paused.

Mara scooted a little closer to him and said, "You don't have to be ashamed. Nobody's family is perfect." Leif nodded and continued.

"My grandfather was a good man, and a hard worker. He made a lot of money and lived very frugally because he refused to spend any of it. He was saving it all to give to his only son – my dad. And then he died and all the money went to my dad. He wanted my dad to get a good job and build on the family fortune, make a good life for me. Obviously, my dad didn't. We've been living off the money ever since my grandfather's death, and now it's almost run out. My dad is sick and we don't even have a penny to find out what's wrong with him."

Mara looked at Leif, her heart filling with pity. She knew she was lucky to have been adopted by such a well-off family, and she knew it didn't happen to everyone, but the situation Leif had just described to her seemed especially horrible.

"So you need a loan?" she asked, already knowing the answer but needing confirmation.

"No," Leif said. This took Mara by surprise. Why would he tell her everything about his family if he didn't want a loan? "I'll never be able to pay you back. I guess, well, I guess I'm asking for more of a donation." He looked down at his hands. All in a rush he started explaining and apologizing. "I'm really sorry to ask this but I heard you were well-off and I thought 'why not?' I understand if you think it's ridiculous, it is. Maybe I should just go." He stood up quickly and started to leave with a miserable expression on his face. Mara jumped up and vaulted over the couch to block the door.

"No, no, I understand. My parents have more money than they could ever use, and so do I. I don't see why I shouldn't give you some," she said, shrugging. His face lit up.

"Really?" he asked. His face expressed what he wouldn't say in words – *I need this.*

"Yeah," Mara said, shrugging again. "On one condition." Leif's smile faded again, but only slightly.

"I'll do whatever you want," he said quickly as if he was afraid that she would change her mind in the next few seconds.

She smiled at him with the same mischievous look in her eyes that he had seen earlier in the day during Mr. Rosten's class right before the book hit him on the shoulder and broke Leif's mental bond. "I want you to teach me how you do mind magic without maintaining a direct sight line," she said. "If I can learn how you do that then I can translate it into my own gravitational manipulation and be able to move something even if I can't see it."

Leif stared at her. "That's easier said than done. No Witch Warrior can understand the specialties of others. Besides, my specialty is different. I… I just don't know if it'll work," he said, raising his hands in a gesture of helplessness.

Mara shrugged. "Okay," she said and turned away, starting to leave the room.

"But I could try!" Leif said, a desperate look on his face. "I'm sure it'll work if we spend enough time on it!" Mara could hear the desperation in his voice and the tone of uncertainty, but still she turned back towards him.

"You're on," she said simply. "Come here every Friday after school. There's a sewer line entrance underneath one of the picnic tables in the school courtyard. If you get in there and take two rights and then a left, you'll come up right over… there," she finished, pointing out the window at a manhole cover underneath a tall birch tree.

"Two rights and a left," Leif repeated. "Got it. So this is a secret operation?"

"Look, I'm not weirdly happy all the time like most girls are, but I don't *enjoy* torturing people who don't deserve it. I wouldn't make you come through the sewer if it weren't necessary. My parents may have all the money they need, but that doesn't mean they're willing to give it away," Mara explained. "Now I've got to get going. Kat and I have a sparring session starting at 6:15 and then a tambo vs tongfa session, and I'll have to get all the extra sparring mats from our cobweb-filled basement if I'm late. See you Friday, nerd."

Leif stared after her and shook his head, smiling. *This is gonna be fun.*

CHAPTER 7

"*I* see *someone* has gotten up the nerve to talk to a boy," Kat teased. She and Mara were in full sparring gear and standing on the mats that had been dragged from the basement by Mamba.

"Shut up," Mara said. "You're one to talk. Eighty-five percent of your words are wasted on boys." Kat laughed, throwing a jab that Mara easily blocked. Twisting her base foot she threw a side kick at Kat who stepped into the liveside and blocked it, but then caught Mara's roundhouse elbow to the head. She jumped back, shook her head, and circled Mara. She edged slowly closer until she was close enough to deliver a left uppercut to the chin. Mara's right arm shot out and knocked the uppercut out of the way while Kat brought up her free foot into a right crescent kick. It connected with the side of Mara's body, but when Mara stumbled off to the side she grabbed Kat's arm and dragged her into the fall, too. Mara landed on top of Kat. Kat hooked her leg around Mara's and swung to the left, flipping Mara over so that she was under Kat.

"You like him, you really really like him," Kat teased. Mara kicked both feet up into Kat's stomach and flipped backwards up onto her feet.

"I made a deal with him. Besides, you're the one who beat him up. I'm just trying to smooth over what *you* did." Kat swung her foot around and connected with Mara's left ankle. Falling hard on her right side, Mara pushed herself back up just in time for her face to catch Kat's back hook kick.

"I'm not blaming you," Kat said. "He's cute, good at fighting, and he *clearly* likes you. Why else would he come here in the middle of the night to ask for the assistance of a brave maiden?" Kat mocked the last few words. Mara stuck her tongue out at Kat and twisted her leg around, flipping Kat head over heels and slamming her down onto the mat. Kat grabbed for Mara's ankle but missed, so she jumped back upright and remained light on her toes. She and Mara exchanged a few more punches, all blocked or dodged, before Kat spoke again.

"I really think you should take this opportunity and run with it, Mara. You know, because you don't even *try* to attract boys' attention, another boy may never have a crush on you." Kat laughed out loud and made a face.

"Because of your *constant* attempts to attract attention you may never be able to *keep* a boy for more than a few weeks," Mara shot back. Kat lunged at her and was blocked, but got in a good blow to Mara's momentarily unguarded rib cage. Kat, sensing she had the advantage, came in for a left hook to the jaw but Mara, moving in a blur, grabbed her hand and twisted it back, sliding in for a side elbow and stepping behind Kat's left leg. Mara swung her left leg up and then let it drop, crashing into the back of Kat's knee. Continuing through the sweep Mara kept her leg from being trapped and let Kat fall flat on her back, chocolate brown hair spreading around her. Standing over her sister, Mara looked down at her with fake pity.

"That's what you get for being obsessed with useless boys," Mara said. Kat laughed sarcastically and lay on the ground for a second, panting. Then she reached out in a flash and inserted her arm between Mara's legs. Grabbing one she used her leverage to collapse both. Mara flopped to the ground beside Kat.

"So, it's a tie then?" Kat asked. Mara looked at her like she would bury herself alive before agreeing to that, but then nodded and laughed.

"Just as well. I'm gonna crush you in tambo vs tongfa," she taunted.

"Oh no you're not," Kat said. They both flipped up to their feet at exactly the same time and took off sprinting towards the weapons shed, throwing their sparring gear off behind them while they ran. Their laughter filled the air with the sound of sibling rivalry.

It was another Friday at the Academy. During seventh hour defense Professor Erros drew Mara aside to talk to her. The class had been working on the art of Aikido, applying it while working with your specialty. Students had to learn to split their brain in half, with one half focused on the martial arts skills being performed and the other half on magic. This was an especially difficult technique for most students and Mara was surprised that he'd pull her away from practicing.

"Mara, I need to talk to you about your specialty. I think... well, I think you can be much more powerful than you are right now. I've been watching you and there's promise in you for so much more than simply fighting Gone," he said, staring at her with those captivating brown eyes. His specialty was persuasion. He could bend anyone to his will if their mental barriers were down, and because everyone loved him a lot of people let their barriers down when they were around him. Mara didn't; she even strengthened them a bit because she had seen his power in action. She was not about to become this man's puppet.

"What do you mean? My specialty is powerful, but I've pushed it to its limits time and time again and I'm pretty sure I've found the full extent of it," Mara said confidently. She had taken all the specialty enhancement classes and she had discovered the precise limits to her powers, both fog and gravitational manipulation.

"Well, yes," Erros admitted, slightly annoyed that she had disagreed with him, "but I believe that I have found a way to, how do you say, extend your powers even more. If you'll just follow me I'll show you what I mean." He offered her his hand but she ignored it. Offended that she had brushed him off he contained himself and quickly walked off down a corridor.

"The thing I'm about to show you hasn't been unveiled to anyone yet so I need you to keep this a complete secret. I believe I have found a way to amplify specialty magic and the user's ability to harness it!" He sounded so excited that Mara couldn't help anticipating, at least a little bit, what he had created. Reaching up he drew back a cloth covering a very small, circular object sitting on his desk. What he revealed was a dish holding about fifteen small, white pills.

Holding his hands up proudly he announced, "I call them... The Extenders!" Mara stared at him in disbelief.

"No offense, Professor, but you come up with an amazing piece of technology and you call it 'The Extenders'?" she sneered, looking at him with her arms crossed. His expression fell into one of annoyance and he quickly turned on his heel. *Something is really bothering him.* Mara walked in a circle around the dish. The pills were small and ordinary looking, just white capsules.

"So... what do you do?" she asked, picking up a pill and examining it. Erros immediately snatched it from her fingers.

"No, no! No touching," he said, shaking his finger at her as if she were a toddler. Glaring at him, she snapped, "So I'm, what, supposed to take one every three hours and they'll eliminate all common cough and cold symptoms?"

"No, you take one a day and over the course of about a week it will amplify your specialty to the point where no one will be able to beat you," he said, his eyes lighting up. "I can't wait to see if it works on an actual Witch Warrior!"

Mara stood for a few more seconds looking at the pills, then reached down and scooped up a handful. "Okay, fine. I'll try your weird pills. But on one condition. If it doesn't work you give Chase some one-on-one private lessons, and if that doesn't improve his skill set, talk to the leadership at this school and get him off my team."

Professor Erros smiled at her. "Done," he said, and rubbed his hands together in gleeful anticipation.

Mara pushed open the door to her and Kat's house in the back yard and plunked down on the sofa. It had been a truly exhausting day despite the fact that it was Friday and school had let out early. Leif was due any minute for their weekly training session and to pick up the sum of money they had agreed upon – 500 dollars per week. It wasn't super generous but it wasn't measly either, and Leif said his dad was getting better with the new prescription medicine he had bought.

"I can't thank you enough, Mara. Without this my dad probably would have died," he said after coming up through the manhole cover. The sewer line Mara had instructed him to use had been out of use for years, so all he brought up with him was a few dried-out leaves and the occasional dead rodent. There was never enough time in their training session to cover everything so they always had to cut it short but Mara enjoyed it, nonetheless. She was getting better at moving things without looking at them; she was more of a physical learner so Leif didn't have to talk all that much.

"You can thank me by teaching me how to better use my talent. Hey, what's your talent, by the way?" Mara had never thought to ask Leif this until now, but his answer was not what she expected.

"I don't have one," he said simply. "I just never developed anything except for basic magic and my specialty. I don't really care; it doesn't hinder me, but it's kind of embarrassing to admit."

Thinking for a second about her answer to this, all Mara could come up with was, "Oh." Leif looked at her as if he was accustomed to people not understanding his lack of talent.

A great clang echoed throughout the house. The precariously tall stack of books that Mara had been moving across the room fell into a disorganized heap as her concentration broke. Mara moved forward with quick but silent steps towards the door. Leif followed her, placing his hand on the door frame near Mara's bent head. Mara disappeared into smoke and Leif leaped back, shocked until he realized what had happened. Mara seeped under the crack in the door and, still in fog form, looked around. There was no one there, but their largest crockpot had been tipped off its shelf and now lay on its side on the cream tiles. Mara materialized and absentmindedly back-kicked the door open behind her. Leif jumped out of the way, then walked in when he saw it was only her.

"So, nothing?" he asked. Mara jerked her heel backwards, kicking his shin. The message was clear – *be quiet*. For a second Mara held her fighting stance; then she relaxed and stood normally, her arms crossed as if waiting for something she knew would happen. Raising her hand so Leif could see she held up three fingers. Dropping them individually she counted down without saying anything. Three… two… one…

"Aaaahh… !" the scream was cut short. Mara took off, jogging out of the room and into the backyard. Leif followed her and found her standing over the still form of a boy, somebody he didn't recognize.

"No one gets past our home security system," Mara said sounding very pleased with herself. "Kat and I designed it ourselves." Leif stared at her, thinking the worst, until he saw a tiny green-tufted object sticking out of the boy's left shoulder – a tranq dart.

"He'll be out for about an hour," Mara added. "Come on, let's go back inside. It was just some stupid prank." She motioned for him to follow her back through the kitchen into her training room. On her way she reached down to lift the crock-pot off the floor. Floating it up back to its shelf she set it down gently, all without even casting a glance at it. Leif looked at her proudly.

"You're moving along way faster than I thought," he said, expressing mock worry. "I may have to find a different source of income in a few more weeks." Mara reached over and shoved him playfully on the shoulder. He shoved her back, not even thinking that she might take it the wrong way, but she didn't and threw her head back to laugh.

CHAPTER 8

Mara and Leif were standing in the kitchen, Leif leaning against the fridge door and Mara standing over the sink. She filled a glass with water. Reaching into one of the many pockets in her black sleeveless gear shirt she drew out one of Professor Erros's pills. She held it up to the light, examining it. It still looked like something you could buy over the counter in an ordinary drug store. Shrugging, she placed it on her tongue.

In the split second before the pill touched her tongue Leif stared at it. *I didn't know Mara was on medication. Maybe she's sick?* It didn't seem likely – she was the liveliest person he had ever met – but it was always a possibility. Still, something seemed weird about the pill, almost as if it was giving off an aura.

"Aura," he whispered, and then it came to him. *Aura!* Auras meant magic, and the dusty, muddy-colored aura coming off this pill meant black magic. All of this raced through his brain before the pill had made it into Mara's mouth. Instantly Leif launched himself upward. WW are born with heightened reflexes and naturally well-developed muscles, which allowed Leif to easily clear six feet in a single jump. Flipping over in midair so his feet were toward the ceiling, Leif reached down and swatted Mara's hand with the pill in it a micrometer from landing on her tongue. With bad magic the slightest touch could have catastrophic consequences. Mara only swayed to one side slightly before regaining her balance. The pill had flown out of her hand and landed a few feet away on the floor. Leif flipped back over and landed hard, his left foot squashing the pill. Straightening himself, he looked over at Mara, fearing the worst.

"What the hell, Leif?" she asked, turning to face him. She didn't sound angry, only confused. Her boots clacked on the tile floor as she took a few steps towards him. "I... I read about the pill in the library and it says it's supposed to 'amplify your specialty'. It's impossible, of course, they're probably just cheap over-the-counter pills." It wasn't the truth, but until she knew what was going on here she wasn't telling Leif where the pill actually came from. She looked expectantly at him, clearly waiting for an explanation.

"Uh, well, it had an aura," Leif said, knowing he sounded stupid. Mara looked at him like he was a patient who *really* needed a doctor.

"Aura!?" she said disbelievingly. There were a lot of strange things that went on in Atherian and the Academy, but auras were truly things of myth.

Leif looked slightly ashamed. "It's the other thing I can do. I can see them, the auras. They signify when something has powerful magic in it. A soft, orangey sunset glow signifies beneficial magic, and a sort of muddy gray signifies black magic. That pill had the muddy gray aura." Looking back up at her he said, "I just didn't want you to get hurt. Whatever was in that pill, it's not Tylenol." He shifted his left foot slightly, unwittingly moving it off the crushed pill. Mara, who had been looking at him suspiciously, dropped her half smile and stared at something next to Leif's left shoulder. He glanced over, not really registering anything, and looked back at her for a split second before doing a double-take and staring. He had seen something. A large... well, he didn't really know what to call it, was swirling up next to him. *An apparition, I guess*, he thought. The muddy gray smoke was exactly the same color as the aura surrounding the pill he had seen just minutes earlier but, unlike that one, Mara could clearly see this... thing. It didn't have a face, only two misshapen and glowing off-white spots that Leif supposed were eyes. As he recoiled from it the small of his back hit hard against the granite countertop. He ignored the pain; the thing before him was capturing all of his and Mara's focus.

Mara, typically undaunted by danger, had taken several steps closer to the apparition. Leif slid over and reached across the island, grabbing her upper bicep and pushing her back. She looked over at him, startled, but quickly turned her attention back to the thing that was moving, however slowly, around the island, focusing intently on Mara. She held her ground, clearly not afraid of it, but when two tendrils of its smoke wafted toward her she nimbly jumped back.

"Not so fast, cowboy," she said. With a lightning fast turn she spun around and swung her leg through the midst of the fog. If passed right through, not appearing to hurt the thing but clearly annoying it. It shook itself, if that was even possible for something made out of vapor, then turned its creepy glowing eyes back to Mara. Advancing again, faster this time, it chased Mara around the island. Now standing right beside Leif, she leaned over and whispered, "Okay, now I believe you." Nodding slightly, Leif thought, *if this is what it's going to take every time I need to convince her of something, we'll both be dead in less than a week.*

"Okay, I'm gonna try and get into its mind," he whispered to her. "Maybe I can change its thoughts so it'll want to attack the snack cupboard instead of us."

Mara looked at him, stricken. "Not the *snack* cupboard!" she pleaded. Snorting slightly, Leif couldn't help but smile; somehow Mara was never too scared to make a joke. How she did it baffled him.

Focusing on the waves that emanate from the mind of every living thing, Leif stretched out his own awareness and connected to the thing's. Suddenly he jerked. As if from another world he felt Mara's hand on his arm and heard her voice, murky and diluted.

"Leif?! Leif? What's happening?" She slapped his arm hard, evidently trying to wake him up from the stupor he must have fallen into, but he hardly felt it.

Mara looked at Leif desperately. The second he had tried to get inside the creature's mind he had shuddered and then become as still as if frozen in a glacier. Bending to look at his face, she gasped at what she saw. His eyes, still open, were liquid black as if filled with tar. She could just make out that the inky black substance was moving slightly like small whitecap waves on a calm day. Looking around at the smoky creature she saw that it had stopped moving too, frozen in the same way Leif was. Even the spindly arms of smoke that extended from its 'body' were hanging in suspended animation in midair.

Stepping back from Leif and the creature, Mara pressed her back against the wall and disappeared into fog. You could just barely make her out against the off-white wallpaper. She had never tried this but she had been told that her fog, if inserted into the human heart correctly, could jar someone out of a suspended state. Gathering her fog into a ball, Mara shot herself forward as a long stream of wet particles. At almost her top speed she careened straight towards Leif, entering his body just left of the centerline, right where his heart was, and in a split second she was out again. As she condensed back into human form, Mara bent over slightly and held a hand tightly against her left arm. Leif stayed put. *Darn it! Why didn't it work?* She stood there in a vulnerable position for a second, hand still clamped tight to her upper left arm. Suddenly Leif shuddered violently, as if having a seizure, then stopped abruptly and collapsed, unmoving. The smoke creature let out a horrendous yell and dissipated into the air. Mara dropped to her knees beside Leif. Pressing her fingers to his neck she felt a strong pulse. *Just passed out.* She leaned down and slid her arms under him. Lifting him easily but wincing and favoring her left side, she walked out of the room and down the hall to her in-house hospital.

It had been almost six hours since the showdown with the smoke beast and Leif had gotten significantly better. When Mara pulled back his eyelids his eyes were their normal deep green with no black except for the pupil. He had regained some of his color and, thanks to the IV drip Mara had started, was looking almost normal. Except for the fact that he wasn't waking up. Mara had gotten increasingly bored after having watched him for a few hours so she brought in her punching bag and trained, checking on him every twenty minutes. No change.

She was in the middle of practicing her back hook kicks when a faint sound came from the makeshift hospital bed.

"Why am I on an IV?" Leif asked, scanning the sterile-looking white room and spotting the needle sticking out of his right wrist. Reaching down he yanked it out and sat up. "Mara? A little explanation?" he said, sounding weak and *very* confused.

Mara stopped her kicking immediately and plunked down on the end of his bed. "Question number one: How much do you remember?" she asked.

He shook his head slightly. "Not much. I was reaching out my mind to that thing and then it was like I was on a roller coaster that was going at the speed of sound and I was surrounded by these dark shapes crashing into one another and disappearing, replaced by something worse. I was being tossed around and thrown into things. It was chaos. Dark chaos. Then I felt a pulling in my chest, as if my heart had stopped for a second, and then complete darkness. Silent darkness." He looked at her as if for confirmation of the events he had just described. She nodded slightly.

"That's pretty much it," she said, then continued. "But your eyes, they..." she trailed off and stopped.

"They what?" Leif asked.

Mara shook her head. "They... nothing. They were just blank, I guess." It wasn't the truth, but it was much better than what had actually happened. In the myths, black eyes were a symbol of demons or of something affected by demons. The symbol for demons in the WW world was always associated with black eyes.

"That thing... you saved me from that thing," Leif said, slowly remembering. Mara shrugged.

"You saved *me* from taking the pill in the first place. Now we're even," she said flatly.

"Well, where did you get it? The pill?" Leif asked, suddenly remembering and grasping the whole situation again.

"I told you, I read about it in the library and wanted to see what it was all about, so I fogged up and flew to get one from a specialized store up in very northern Atherian," she said. Even though the pill had proved to be awful, Professor Erros had seemed so excited about it and, besides, he was the country's most loved WW. She *had* to give him the benefit of the doubt.

Leif's gaze moved down and landed on the gauzy white bandage that was wrapped tightly around her upper left arm. "What happened. Did the thing hurt you?" he asked. The amount of bandage on the arm suggested that it had been a serious cut. Mara quickly slapped her hand over it, looking slightly guilty. "Mara, what is it?" Leif said, his voice dropping a few notes and his deep green eyes leveling to look straight into hers.

She removed her hand and pulled a small tab. The whole bandage fell off, revealing a chunk about the size of a half softball missing from her arm. The bone was almost showing through the thin layer of muscle that remained. She looked at him, hoping he would understand without her having to tell him. Of course, he didn't. He had no idea how her specialty worked. Mara chided herself for being disappointed in him. *To him, we must seem like the weirdest family ever. I need to cut him some slack.*

She looked directly at him as she spoke. "You were in a trance, another world, and I couldn't just let you stay there, so I tried something that someone once told me about my specialty. If I implant some of my fog into someone's heart in just the right way it can jolt them out of anything, even wake people up from comas." She paused for a second. "So I turned into fog and flew through you. I gave you a bit of my fog and it woke you up." She finished quickly. It was a relief to get it off her chest but she looked at him cautiously, afraid of how it would affect him. "It'll grow back soon. I went to see a healer when you were all settled in. She said it'd be about two more hours and it would be back to normal."

At first he just stared at her. Then he said slowly, "So when you gave up part of your fog, you gave up part of yourself." She nodded.

"Well, is it still inside me?" he asked, glancing down curiously at his chest. Mara shrugged, a look of helplessness on her face.

"I don't know. I've never done this before," she said quietly. "And... I don't know how it will affect you." She looked very ashamed of herself.

Leif sat up and reached forward to put a hand on her good shoulder. "You saved my life. Why? You could have been rid of me forever. I mean, I'm just the guy who's asking you to give him money. Why in the world would you want me alive?" It was a rush of words that came pouring out of Leif's mouth before he really had a chance to think about them. She looked up at him suddenly. Of all the things she had been prepared for him to say, this was *not* one of them. She answered quickly.

"You're teaching me stuff, and it's working. And besides, I don't hate you. Just because you're *friends* with Chase doesn't mean you're like him," she said, scoffing slightly at the last sentence. She still couldn't believe that Chase had chosen to include *Leif* in the popular group. Of all the boys in the school who would kill to be friends with Chase, he had chosen the most introverted, bookish, and powerful one of them all – just another example of his timeless ignorance. She stood up suddenly and walked around to the IV holder. Picking up the needle she quickly slipped it back into his arm. "You should keep this in. You're still pretty dehydrated," she said flatly. "Don't get up or take this out until I come back and say you can," she instructed. Leif nodded.

He had almost gotten through to her. He knew he was close. But her mental barriers were strong as ever. Walls of titanium and steel and concrete blocked off all her thoughts from him. She strode quickly out the room, braided hair swishing out behind her.

CHAPTER 9

K at hadn't seen Mara all day and was beginning to get worried. They always had training sessions in the magic practice room after school on Saturday. She was thirty minutes late and she hadn't been in school all day, either. For once Mr. Rosten had had to mark someone as absent on his record sheet – the first mark it had ever received. Over the loudspeaker the principal instructed that if anyone had seen Mara they should report to the main office immediately. No one did. Leif was also out of school, but for someone just coming from the Human world that was to be expected. There was no loudspeaker summons for him.

Kat looked around one last time trying to feel the presence of her sister but, getting nothing, she morphed into her tiger and took off running, heading home to search there.

As a tiger Kat got home in under thirty seconds and smoothly transformed back into a human a few steps away from the door. Using her remaining velocity she glided gracefully through the front doors, letting them slam automatically behind her. Walking down the corridor to her left and through the painting of the seven-legged gazelle that served as the secret entrance to her and Mara's home, she entered the sitting room. Looking around she saw nothing out of the ordinary. There was a small mouse scurrying along the floor board. Swift as a falcon Kat swooped down and caught it between her hands. Venus would have liked this mouse as a special treat, but Kat had put her on a diet a few years back. Cupping the mouse in her hands, she cracked open the front door and let it scurry out into a shadow. Kat had sympathy for few things, but one of them was mice. Mice had always been hated over the years, mistaken for rats, and killed. *They have never done anything to us*, Kat thought. Whenever she could she saved a mouse's life but, as Mara had the opposite opinion on "vermin", that was sometimes hard.

"Mara?!" Kat called out. Almost immediately the door to their in-house hospital opened and Mara poked her head out. Smiling, she opened the door the rest of the way and went to give her sister their team handshake. Kat smiled back but almost immediately dropped her expression into one of worry.

"Is someone hurt?" she asked, trying to peek around Mara and into the hospital.

"It's a long story, but Leif passed out and got really dehydrated. He's on an IV and sleeping now. Please don't disturb him," Mara half-pleaded.

Kat turned, a dangerous look in her eyes. "Did he hurt you?" she asked, looking very much like she would rip his vocal cords out if he had.

Mara shook her head. "No, Kat," she said, exasperated. "You know, there is such a thing as being overprotective, right? And anyway, if he had really tried to hurt me he wouldn't be on an IV right now. He'd be in a coffin." Kat made a face at her even though she knew what Mara had said was true, and then she demanded the whole story.

Three hours later Mara was just finishing the story. Leif had insisted that he felt back to normal and had been allowed out of bed. He now sat next to them, adding details that Mara missed.

"... and then I started his IV and waited for him to wake up," Mara finished, exhausted from recounting every little detail for her sister. Kat nodded, satisfied with the story. They all sat in awkward silence for a few more seconds, then Leif stood up and brushed off his black gear pants.

"Well, I should probably get going," he said. "I've got a lot of work to do to explain to my dad where I've been this whole time." He grimaced, clearly not looking forward to the experience. "Then again, he might be too drunk to remember who I am." Mara got up too, pulling a wad of money from her pocket and extending it towards him.

"Even though the session today was kind of botched, I still owe you," she said. He looked at her gratefully and took the money, slipping it into one of his many pockets. Giving her a slight smile he turned and walked quickly out the door, making his way to the fence and easily scaling it. Because it was now the weekend he didn't have to use the sewer to get to and from her house.

Mara collapsed on the couch, dead on her feet. Kat immediately poked her. Opening her eyes again with a groan, Mara said, "Okay, I've heard of short naps but that was ridiculous."

"Ha. Ha," Kat mocked. "So… is he coming back?" she asked. Mara looked at her.

"Um… I assume," she said. "I mean, what?"

Kat stared at her like it was the most obvious thing in the world. "Leif! Have you completely scared him off?" She scanned Mara's face, trying to read her emotions but finding nothing. *Ugh! How can she be so unemotional?* Kat poked and prodded with a few more questions and again Mara gave ambiguous answers. Groaning and tilting her head back in exasperation Kat looked over at Mara and saw something in her face change. It was probably just amusement at Kat's disappointment, but Kat saw it as something else entirely.

She gasped. "Did something happen?" she asked, elbowing her sister hard for not telling her. Mara looked at her, trying to keep her face emotionless but letting something slip through. It was not the something Kat had been hoping for, however. It was mild horror.

"Kat, you are the most messed up person I have ever met. And that includes Chase!" Mara said. "Leif got paralyzed and then knocked out by a demon spirit from an evil pill and had to spend seven hours in hospital. Yes, something happened, but not *that!*" It was her turn to give Kat the 'that's so obvious' look. Kat, dismayed, slumped down into the overstuffed cracked leather couch.

"I thought this was finally it! Your moment!" she said, raising her hands and then letting them fall again. "Ugh. I *hate* it when I'm wrong. And I've *never* been wrong about a boy before this." Kat looked at Mara pleadingly. "Don't make me wrong," she said, her tone filled with unhappiness.

Mara shrugged and held her hands up. "Sorry, but some things just aren't meant to happen. Besides, it's not like he's gone forever. He's still coming over next Friday, and he *does* go to our school." She pushed her chin forward slightly, something she often did when trying to make a point.

Kat nodded. "Oh, I know, but it has to happen at the right moment and that right moment just passed." She looked grumpily down at her hands and pouted. Desperately trying to come up with a way to cheer her up, Mara unthinkingly asked "So, how are things with Chase?" She regretted the words as soon as they came out of her mouth, expecting Kat to snap at her about Chase's disloyalty and his complete obliviousness to her flirting. Instead, however, she turned to her with an expression of giddy happiness on her face. For a second it was like she couldn't talk but could only smile dumbly.

"Ookee," Mara said, keeping her gaze on Kat. "Not really the reaction I was going for, but okay." Waiting patiently for Kat to regain the power of speech, Mara folded her hands in her lap, ready again to be the less dramatic sister and just listen.

In a rush of words and gestures and smiles and giddy laughs, Kat began to unload on Mara every single detail about her meeting with Chase right after fifth hour. Apparently Chase had come to talk to her looking "more serious than ever." Mara had absolutely no idea what that meant, but figured it wasn't hard to look more serious than Chase. He had begun with "Hey, Kat, what's up?" Kat flushed when she told Mara this. Without thinking Mara asked, "That's good?" Kat dropped her happy expression into one of pity and total misunderstanding. Holding her hands up and shaking them slowly in front of Mara's face, she enunciated as she spoke very slowly. "Y-e-s."

Mara looked innocent and held up her hands. She could imagine what was going through Kat's head: "Why am I even trying, she knows *nothing* about boys."

Why am I even trying, she knows nothing *about boys*, Kat thought. Dropping her hands back to her lap she continued. Chase had gone on to ask her what day it was, and she had answered. It was the most romantic moment of her life.

"Well then you have a seriously sad life," Mara declared with her classic judgy expression. Sticking out her tongue, Kat continued, this time cutting to the 'chase'.

"He asked me out!" she shrieked, her words carrying for a mile in every direction. "We're meeting at the Human café a week from Sunday! I. Can't. Believe. IT!" Again with that ear-splitting shriek.

"*I* can't believe you said yes," Mara commented sarcastically. "And if you're both so eager, why wait so long? A week from Sunday is, like, nine days.

Kat smiled as if this was the best part. "A week from Sunday is the only day he has off from football practice." Grinning with glee she clapped her hands together like a little girl.

"Haven't you guys been kind of going out for months now?" Mara asked. It wasn't that she wasn't happy for Kat, she just loved finding loopholes, or in this case a reason Kat shouldn't be so ridiculously happy.

Kat stared at her with her patented 'are you stupid' face. "Uh, no, everyone just loves us so much that they believe we *should* date. But we've never actually gone somewhere, just the two of us."

Mara could easily think of one place. "You've gone to Detention," she said brightly. Kat looked even more stricken at this comment.

"I know, I know, but the teacher always makes us sit across the room from each other and since Hazen won't let me borrow Kaeli I can't talk to him." Again she made a pouty face worthy of someone half her age. Glancing over Kat's shoulder Mara saw Venus twisted around the resting stick that Kat had installed on the wall at a ninety degree angle next to the kitchen door when she was only six.

"Get over here and comfort her, jerk," Mara told the shiny red snake. Venus, despite being a snake, managed to look sufficiently guilty and slithered down, appearing a second later over the armrest of the couch. Moving smoothly into Kat's open lap, Venus curled into a ball and stretched her neck up, nuzzling her shiny red head against Kat's cheek. Kat stroked her gently, looking at Mara. Suddenly a smile stretched across her face.

"*There's* your unattractive I-have-a-really-stupid-idea face," Mara teased her. Ignoring her, Kat told Venus to curl around her arm and she obeyed. Jumping up off the couch, Kat flew into action. Mara watched dumbstruck as she worked, not offering to help mostly because she had no idea what Kat was doing. In less than five minutes Kat was done. She jumped up and ran over to Mara in excitement.

"Mini-golf!" she yelled. It took a moment for Mara to realize that Kat was serious. Looking around in astonishment, Mara slowly stood up and turned around. Random household objects were tied together and fastened onto walls, light fixtures, you name it. In one of the corners of the room there was a small strip of fake grass with a revoltingly bright orange tee and golf ball on it.

"Um…" Mara said.

"Playing mini-golf always cheered me up," Kat explained. "So, we're playing mini-golf!" Nodding slightly, Mara accepted the challenge with a loud "You're on!" and the team handshake. Picking up a club leaning against the wall, Kat proceeded to explain the course to Mara with many fine points and high sweeping gestures. When she was done, Mara nodded again and promptly said, "Well, now we're all saved. I've found someone out there crazier than that weirdo guy who volunteered to be bait for Gone and ended up being sent to the infirmary in a matchbox." Kat punched her on the arm, and they both laughed. They were sisters – deadly competitive.

They had been playing for over an hour – neither had made the shot. "We just need to hit it into that inverted lamp shade taped to the door," Kat explained for the thousandth time, trying hard to make it sound simple.

"I KNOW!" Mara said loudly, barely resisting the urge to punch her in the nose. She swung again, directing all of her energy into it. On one part of the course the ball had to go uphill through an old drain pipe and then fall into the bathtub that Kat had yanked out of one of their many spare bathrooms. The ball flew off the tee at nearly fifteen miles per hour, clanging loudly into the many objects that had become part of the course. Mara stood back up, crossing her arms and looking extremely pleased with herself.

"That's gonna make it pretty far," she said, pointing to it as it flew past, nearly crashing into their mom's oriental dinnerware cabinet that she had given them to 'spruce the place up a bit.' Neither of them had understood *that* comment.

Mara laughed as the ball flew closer to its target. "It's gonna make it!" she squealed excitedly. She didn't really care about mini-golf but she wasn't about to pass up a chance to beat Kat. Kat, surprisingly, seemed equally excited. After about the fiftieth hit they stopped trying to beat each other and just focused on making the shot. Watching with bated breath as the ball got closer and closer to the finish, they went up on their toes to get a better look as it flew across the old Welcome mat attached to the ceiling. The ball avoided the knives Kat had embedded in the mat. It fell off the mat and hit the collider, a device invented a few years back that threw off any object that touched it, rather like a very powerful trampoline. Adjusted by Kat multiple times so it was at the perfect angle, the collider threw the ball straight towards the inverted lampshade that served as the end of the course.

Just then the door opened and a handsome ageless face with deep brown eyes and short black hair appeared in the doorway. Bam! The golf ball, going at full speed from its recent encounter with the collider, smacked dead center into the man's forehead where the lampshade was supposed to be. The impact threw him back out of sight, and they heard a thump as he landed on the hard ground outside the door.

"Oh yeah, it made it," Kat said, an expression of pure horror on her face.

"Didn't really think *that* one through, did ya?" Mara asked angrily, turning towards Kat. Kat opened her mouth to respond but abandoned the argument and ran towards the door. Mara took off after her. They both stopped dead in front of the figure of the man whose head had just eaten their golf ball.

"Someone's been having some fun," he said. They both rushed forward and tried to explain but he held his hands up. "I understand. You're teenagers." He held out his arms to give them a hug.

"We're *so* sorry, Uncle Niko. We were playing mini-golf and *Kat* put the hole on the door..." Mara started to explain but decided to just stop talking and get him an ice pack. Turning to walk back into the house, Mara's foot crunched on something. Looking down she saw the shards of the horrible orange golf ball. It was completely shattered. "Well, at least we know you're stronger than that ball," she said.

Niko just said, "Yeah, sorry about that," looking ashamed. Mara waved her hand, indicating that it didn't matter at all.

"Trust me, we're all better off without *that* colored golf ball in the world," she said. Niko snorted. One of their father's two adopted brothers, Niko was a vampire. Immortal, ever young and ageless, graced with super senses, speed, and strength, vampires were by far the most beautiful of the magical creatures. All vamps were in hiding because of Human persecution, but Aerick had taken Niko in before Mara and Kat had come into the family and had treated him like a brother.

Niko was a fairly unusual vampire due to his black hair. Most vamps were either blond or brunette, but Niko's black hair was short and spiky which set off his deep brown eyes and gleaming white teeth. Vampires were predators and they had evolved to look perfect because that tended to attract Humans, or as vamps liked to call them, food. With his super strength and rock hard skin it was no surprise that the golf ball had lost. It hadn't even stood a chance.

"Tom's here too, but he and Etta got into a major dispute about his new beard so he might be a while," Niko said, gesturing back up the hallway to where their uncle Tom and mom were undoubtedly having a heated argument. Tom, whose full name was Thomas, was their other uncle, the other man their father had taken in with Niko. Tom was a werewolf, the most unkempt of the magical creatures and the exact opposite of the vamps. Wolves were not immortal and Tom was almost the same age as Aerick, around forty. They definitely weren't ageless or otherworldly like the vamps, but they did have their strong points. They had super strength and could run extremely fast when in wolf form. Probably the most amusing talent they had was the strongest sense of smell either Mara or Kat had ever encountered. He could tell what either of them had had for lunch three days after they had eaten it.

Kat sidled past Niko and yelled up the hallway, "Tom! None of us cares about your beard. Just come down here so we can hug you."

Mara patted Kat on the back. "Tactful way to put it, sweetie," she said. Kat made a humble gesture of acknowledgement. Mara turned and followed Niko back inside their house.

"So, what brings you here?" asked Mara "I thought you were on a camping trip up in one of the northern glaciers."

"Yeah, I was, but conditions got bad and I had to eat my trail buddy. Figured I might as well come back here and say hi to the family." Niko said, turning his oh-so-perfect head around and admiring the golf course. "So, Kat, you made all this?" he asked, admiringly.

Kat stared at him. "How do you know it was *me*? Mara's the one who always makes messes," she joked. Niko walked over and patted her on the shoulder. Looking her directly in the eyes he said simply, "It was you." Mara nodded and strode into the kitchen.

"You want anything, Niko?" she asked.

"Nah, I'm good. As I said, I had to eat my trail buddy," he replied, making a disgusted face and shuddering.

"Druggie?" Kat asked. Niko nodded. Vamps weren't very picky about what type of blood they got, but drugs *really* put them off. Mara emerged from the kitchen carrying a small syringe filled with light green liquid. Niko stared at it.

"You keep that in your *kitchen*?" he asked, not disgusted but merely surprised.

Mara nodded grimly. "You have no idea how many 'accidents' happen around this place. Your forehead may have been the end for that golf ball but you're still bleeding underneath. I can see it. Take this, it's for vamps only. Should restock your blood in about thirty seconds." She gave him the vial and he stuck the needle into the inside of his elbow, expertly finding the vein. Looking up at his forehead Kat realized Mara was right. You really could see the blood. A stain of dark brown was spreading out underneath his skin. *Boy, that golf ball hit* really *hard.* The vamp color of blood was mahogany[2], their international identifier. Almost immediately, though, the stain of mahogany was disappearing as the supplemental blood worked its miracles.

"Thanks," Niko said, tossing the syringe over to the kitchen counter where it rolled directly into the trash bucket. Mara nodded and then looked at Kat conspiratorially.

"Should we?" she asked. Her sister nodded and they both dashed off into the other room. Kat came back triumphant, holding the golf club high. She tossed it at Niko who caught it gracefully, and motioned for him to step into place behind the tee. Mara bent down and placed a golf ball, this time a traditional white one, on the tee.

"You want *me* to try?" Niko asked, unsure. They both nodded simultaneously, grins spreading across their faces like it was Christmas.

"If you make the shot we'll tell our parents. If you don't no one ever speaks of this outside this room. Deal?" Kat said. Niko nodded and readied himself in an overdramatic and frankly hilarious routine. Neither Mara nor Kat could help bursting into laughter. Even though he was over two hundred years old Niko looked twenty-three, and eventually you forgot that he was any

---

[2]The one way you can tell a WW from a Human is by their blood color, which is a deep lavender with strands of white. Each species of magical people has a different blood color. It's like an ID card. Quirks, mentally disabled WW or WW with a change in their DNA strand all have different colors of blood, too.

different from you. Mara and Kat loved him like the older brother they never had. Tom was more the homely, welcoming uncle that you would expect, but Niko was their resident playmate. Swinging the club back and aiming his shot perfectly he swung and smacked the ball into the first obstacle. Through the course it went, just barely making it past some of the obstacles, and rolled off the welcome mat onto the collider. Mara and Kat both slumped, aware that they were going to have to tell their parents about the whole debacle.

"Hey, guys!" Tom called as he opened the door. Wham! The golf ball slammed into his forehead and sent him tumbling backwards. Kat and Niko both covered their mouths with their hands. Mara jumped the couch and ran out the door to help.

"That doesn't count," Kat whispered to Niko. Breaking out of their trance they followed Mara out to help Tom back to his feet.

CHAPTER 10

*A*nother Friday had arrived, time for Leif to sneak into Mara's back yard for their weekly training session. Picking up the manhole cover with one hand, Leif sat down and slid into the sewer pipe, replacing the cover over his head as he did so. He had to kneel in order to continue moving into the cylinder of old, rusty copper. A truly ancient pipe, it was only about four feet in diameter which meant Leif, who was six foot six, had to abandon what was left of his dignity and crawl the entire way. When he came up on the other end Mara was waiting for him and held the manhole cover, also with one hand, while he climbed out. Setting it back down in its place she straightened up and looked him over. He felt her hand on his shoulder, and then a serious yank. He stumbled back a few feet and looked at her, annoyed. She held up a large water rat by the tail, soaked but still living and squirming violently, as explanation. She picked up the manhole cover again and dropped the rat back down to its dark, dingy home. She looked disgusted when she turned back around, but then her expression brightened. Lunging forward, fast as her sister's tiger, she wiped her dripping hand all over Leif's shirt. He jumped back, but not before his shirt had been slathered with essence of sewer rat. Holding it out from his body he looked down at it disgustedly. Mara laughed, a charming but somewhat dangerous sound, and walked triumphantly off towards the house. "Come on, you can borrow one of my uncle's shirts," she called out. Leif considered his actions, but just for an instant. Using his WW enhanced speed he shot up behind Mara and jumped, aiming for her back, ready to tackle her like the jocks did in that strange game called football. At the last second Mara sidestepped, her waist-length braid whirling out behind her, and Leif, not having enough time to reorient himself for landing, fell flat on his face. There was grass in his eyes and something he didn't like moving around in his mouth. He heard Mara's voice above him. "You'll never outwit the master."

Getting stiffly to his feet, Leif stumbled over to the house and draped his jacket on the post outside the door. To Mara and Kat, this was rustic living, but having indoor plumbing was luxury to Leif. They lived not fifty miles from each other, his father's tiny house just outside the borders of Atherian, and yet their living styles were so different. The money that Mara had been giving him each week was helping greatly, but most of it was being used for his father's treatment. He had a rare kind of cancer and went in once a week for chemotherapy. They could barely afford it, and the only food they ever got was what the hospital gave them and what Leif could smuggle out of the school cafeteria. Mara, despite Leif's best attempts to lie, had found out about the whole thing and offered to give him a raise, but Leif had turned it down. She was already paying well over what his lessons were worth, and he wasn't about to accept more. Mara was learning surprisingly fast, especially considering that gravitational manipulation wasn't her specialty. Everyone was good in their talent, but Mara was unusually strong. Last Friday she had succeeded in moving Kat's large vanity from her bathroom into the entryway without even casting it a glance. Frankly, it freaked Leif out a bit.

"Okay, lazy, are we gonna get started or not?" she asked, pulling off her jacket and rolling her neck around. Snap! Crack! Mara's neck cracked easily and she often used that to intimidate fighting partners. She had tried to teach Leif how to crack his neck, too, but with no success. Eventually, concluding that his bones weren't quite in the right spot for cracking, they had abandoned the effort.

Leif laced his fingers and stretched out his shoulders as he said, "Okay, you can start by shifting the table around a bit while doing something in the kitchen. I'm going to change my shirt. Where's your uncle's closet?"

"Oh, right, the shirt," Mara said, remembering. "Follow me, I'll get one for you. That one doesn't match your outfit at *all*." *How is it that boys have no sense of color?!*

As if he had heard her thoughts, which was a real possibility since Mara hadn't strengthened her barriers for several days, Leif replied, "I'm color-blind."

Mara turned her head while walking and smiled at him. "That's the *only* good excuse for not having good taste," she said. Looking rather pleased with himself that he'd finally passed one of Mara's tests, Leif followed the sound of her clacking boots out of the kitchen and down a long flight of stairs that he hadn't known existed.

"Most of the house is underground," Mara explained as they walked down a long corridor with doors of all different styles branching out on the left and right. "We have eight floors underneath the big house and four underneath this one." She gestured to a set of elevator doors on their left. "That one takes you to the fifth underground floor of the big house."

Mentally reminding himself to get to know this house better, he asked, "Did you dig all these yourself? You and Kat?" Mara shook her head and laughed.

"No, I'm flattered that you think Kat and I could have done all this, but even now we can't dig the depth of four fully developed floors. Bedrock is all around us right here. No, my parents bought some construction equipment and an AI to control it," she said as a strange expression came over her face that Leif couldn't identify. The second she felt him prodding her mind the expression disappeared and she scolded him. "No poking! If I wanted to let you into my mind I would have let you in. You can't dig through this much bedrock either, even if it's just the walls around my mind." Holding up his hands in surrender, he laughed softly.

"I bet I could," he whispered, barely loud enough for Mara to hear but a challenge just the same. Whipping around to face him and walking backwards, Mara smiled and shook her head.

"You are making a *big* mistake," she teased, her dark brown high braid swinging as her head moved. Despite being six foot three and having over six feet of hair it looked terrific and seemed as light as a feather. Of course, Leif had never dared touch it for fear of losing a hand, but the glossy shine always amazed him, especially when Mara was in the sun. Correction… *girls* always amazed him. Amazed and baffled.

Focusing his mind back onto the task at hand he couldn't help but smile. They both knew they were just playing a game with each other, but the challenge was real enough and Mara was ready to crush the life and soul out of him. Figuratively, of course.

After she and Leif had descended two flights of stairs underground, Mara led him off into a corridor with stained hardwood flooring and the kind of walls that made echoing easy; call out a single sound and you can hear it reverberate several times. Mara liked to practice her falcon call for Mamba down here, and she did so now. As she cried out the harsh screeching sound with no warning she sensed Leif's slight jump behind her. He immediately realized it was only Mara and continued on, giving her an amused glance. Mara listened for her echo and it came, the reflection of her call. A second later Mamba came swooping in and landed on Mara's right arm. Leif, noticing for the first time that she didn't wear a glove, winced and said, "Doesn't that hurt your arm?"

She replied nonchalantly, "It did until Mamba learned how to land softly and I learned how to catch her." Letting Mamba fly above their heads, she turned her right arm over and spat on her hand. Rubbing it against her arm she removed her makeup, revealing something Leif had thought he had seen many times before, but Mara always moved so quickly that he was never sure and had always attributed it to shadow. Lined across her arm were deep scars covering almost all of the skin. They weren't obvious, just a few shades darker than her natural skin tone, but when you looked at the arm you could definitely tell that there were deep dents in the skin.

"Why do you cover them up?" Leif asked. "It's normal for WW to let their scars show." Mara shrugged quickly, as if caught off guard by this question, and then answered, "I guess I just don't like people looking at me like I'm a walking freak show. I already have more scars showing than anyone else at the Academy, maybe as many as Kat, and I don't need any more." Nodding his head to show he understood, Leif let his mind wander slightly. His thoughts, as they always did, went right back to the pill. He had the sense that Mara was hiding something from him about the origins of the pill, but he had seen her in action. She was a very practiced and *very* good liar, so it was possible he was imagining it all. While he was lost in his mind, the sanctuary Leif always retreated to when people were picking on him or he was unsure of what to say, a hand grabbed his arm and yanked him playfully off to the right, catching him completely by surprise. Pulling himself back to the real world he saw that Mara had drawn him through one of the doors; they were now standing in a large sitting room with several open doorways going off of it.

"This is Niko's room. Since he's a vampire, be warned. His clothes might smell a little weird," Mara said. She had told Leif about Niko and Tom, and he had met both of them about two months ago. Tom had seemed very nice, and Leif had had a nice long discussion with him about the pros and cons of being a werewolf, but it was Niko who really fascinated him. He had never met a vampire before, never even seen one, and Niko had been very happy to talk. When he first saw Leif he had called him "the boyfriend." Further interrogation had revealed that Kat had told him Mara was seeing the new guy in school. At this Mara had punched him lightly in the gut and teasingly scolded him for believing a single word that came out of Kat's mouth.

"Come on," Mara said. "His closet's this way, I'll help you pick out a shirt." Looking him over head to toe, she considered. "Maybe a nice pale blue," she thought out loud. Whenever someone looked at him closely Leif always felt supremely awkward and on-the-spot, but for some reason when Mara did it all he felt was embarrassed and slightly pleased that she cared enough about him to work on his outfit. She finished pondering the color of Leif's shirt and turned to walk through the door on the far left of the sitting room.

"Oh!" Leif heard her exclaim. He poked his head around the door and saw Niko pulling his earbuds out, shirtless, having sprung up from the couch.

"Mara," he said, looking *very* embarrassed to be caught in a half-dressed state. "And Leif too. How nice to see you." He was trying to be polite, talking and looking at them while searching earnestly for a shirt. Leif couldn't help himself and stared. Niko had scars too, covering his back in irregular lines. For a vampire, he was very tan. *How in the world…* Leif thought. Mara elbowed Leif, breaking his stare, and he quickly stepped back. Mara did too, waiting patiently outside the door until Niko emerged several seconds later, fully clad in jeans and a t-shirt.

"Well, I guess your vampire senses don't save you from everything," Mara said, making light of the situation as she usually did. Niko laughed, smiling widely. He didn't seem too concerned by what had happened now that it was over. Leif knew that Mara and Niko were practically siblings, but he still couldn't help but feel suspicious that something might have happened between them. Being a vampire Niko was aesthetically perfect, and he had been around Mara her whole life. Quickly banishing this thought from his head Leif got straight to the point.

"Mara wiped sewer rat grime all over my shirt and she said I could borrow a clean one from you. Plus, apparently, this shirt doesn't match the rest of my outfit," Leif said, faking exasperation although he knew Mara was probably right.

Niko laughed again and rolled his eyes. "Come on in. Thanks to Mara and Kat I have a walk-in closet bigger than any of my previous houses," he said, gesturing that Leif and Mara should follow him across the room which seemed to be just a TV and exercise room. Turning the handle of a door next to the couch, Niko revealed a walk-in closet that, just as he had said, was three times bigger than Leif's father's house.

"Wow," was all Leif was able to say, as quietly as he could.

"Right," Niko said, his tone indicating disbelief that he had stumbled upon such a generous family to take him in. "The casual t-shirts are over there. Take your pick." Mara walked over to one side of the room-closet and began rifling through the shirts, rejecting one after another. Niko sidled over to Leif and whispered in his ear, "Who knew I had such bad taste." They both laughed silently, sharing the common ground of not understanding girls' innate sense of what goes with what.

Mara turned around, holding up a washed-out sky blue shirt triumphantly. "Success!" Leif said, waving his hands in the air in mock exaltation. Mara couldn't help herself. She smiled and laughed at Leif's goofiness. *For someone in his situation he's remarkably hilarious.* Composing herself, she handed the shirt to Leif.

"Here, go put this on. The bathroom's…" she trailed off and looked to Niko for help.

"The door on the left side of the TV room," he supplied, pointing in its general direction. Leif thanked him and exited the closet, followed closely by Mara and then Niko.

It had only been about thirty minutes into their training session before Leif was sure beyond doubt that something was bothering Mara. He held up his hand, signaling for her to stop, and just stared into her eyes for a moment. They were green with tiny flecks of ocean green-blue, not washed-out but dark and intense like the color of new growth on a very old tree. She broke the gaze first, looking away slightly and focusing on something behind him. He tried to catch her eyes again but she wouldn't let him. Finally he spoke.

"Something's wrong, I can see it," he said softly, trying to be gentle but knowing that however he put it Mara would deny it at first. She did, saying that nothing was wrong and they should get back to work. Leif just shook his head and persisted. "Mara, I know that look. Besides, you've crashed three things just in the past half hour. That's not like you."

Mara looked down at the couch, her right pinky finger turning into fog and then back into a pinky over and over. Leif had seen her do this before and had come to associate the small movement as a sign of stress or worry.

"I didn't buy the pill in northern Atherian," she said suddenly, turning to face him, dead serious. "Professor Erros gave it to me. *He* was the one who said it would amplify my specialty and that he thought I could do great things if I took it." All the words came rushing out in a torrent of guilt. Leif stared at her. He had been right, she *had* been hiding something. He was about to say something when she continued. "I'm sorry for not telling you but I've known Professor Erros since I was three and he's been teaching me for just as long. He's the golden boy, one of the most respected young Witch Warriors of our time, and it just didn't make sense for him to do something like that. I gave him the benefit of the doubt – perhaps he just picked up the pills somewhere random – and I started investigating him. Anyway, a few days ago I walked into his office and I caught him going over some schematics. He yelled at me for sneaking up on him and when I tried to look at the schematics he armbarred me from behind and threw me out of the room." She paused. "That's when I knew the pill was no mistake. I've been sneaking into his office after school every day and destroying all the pills I can find, but his machine makes them so fast that I'm sure he's given them to other students by now." She shook her head.

"Don't say it," Leif said. "This isn't your fault."

Mara shook her head vigorously. She wasn't crying, wasn't showing any outward signs of emotion, but even through the barriers Leif could feel the turmoil in her mind. "You must be furious that I lied about something this important," she said, purposely avoiding his eyes.

"No, I understand why you lied to me in the first place. What I *am* mad about is that you didn't tell me when you found out he was responsible. I could have helped you destroy those pills," he said, forcing her to meet his eyes. He had said mad, but that wasn't the right word for it. Mostly he was scared, and not for himself and, horribly, not for anyone else who might have taken the pill. For Mara. He had seen Professor Erros in action and, though he respected Mara and knew she was deadly, he wasn't sure of what the outcome of a fight between the two of them would be.

Mara looked straight at him, still no emotion showing on her face, but she briefly let a few pieces of her mental wall down and sent two words into Leif's mind. *I'm sorry*. He nodded and Mara's expression softened slightly for just a second before hardening back into an unbreakable wall, not just the emotionless mask she often wore. This was her "you messed with me and my friends and you're going to pay for it" face.

Rushing into action they grabbed their spring/summer battle gear and went into different rooms to change. Full battle gear designed for warmer weather consisted of a sleeveless, collared black leather vest, tight fitting black jean-like pants, and high-heeled sleek black fighting boots for girls, and a short-sleeve black shirt, tight fitting black jean-like pants, and heavy duty fighting boots for boys, all made of material that was thin, light, and strong. They came with several weapon holders built in but you could add more if you needed them. Both Mara and Leif had customized their gear to accommodate many more weapons. Pressing her thumb against the thumbprint reader and leaning down so the iris scan could complete, Mara unlocked their cache of weapons hidden behind a large painting of a ridiculous sleeping ginger cat. They each pulled out several throwing knives, two of which Mara stuck crisscross through the top of her braid. Two more went into her boots and one each on the insides of her lower arms. Around her wrists she strapped her black leather dart cuffs that held six darts each. Her left wrist held poison, her right hand tranq-darts. Taking two automatic double swords, her specialty weapon, she stuck them into the small pouches on either hip, easily accessible. Finally, taking several hunting knives, she put them in the remaining pockets on the insides and outsides of her legs.

"Hey, you forgot your blowers," Leif said, handing two small unassuming devices to her. Differentiating them by the color icons on the top, she put the red one (fire) on her left hip and the blue one (ice) on her right hip. Even though she wasn't a big fan of blowers they were made by her parents' company and she was required to take them with her.

"You want some, too?" she asked, pointing to a large bucket of them in the corner of the weapons cache. He grabbed two at random, slipping them into small snap pouches on the inside of his arms. He nodded his thanks, but was clearly more focused on getting his specialty weapon out of the back of the cache and into his jacket. Leif had been taken with boomerangs ever since he was young. At the age of five he had bought his first sharp one at a shady shop just down the street from where his father lived. He had begun practicing with them, buying more and more of better and better quality until he could throw one down a line of men, slitting all their throats, and then have it fly back to him down another line of men, slitting all their throats, too. Catching it wasn't too hard; you just had to wear the right kind of gloves so it wouldn't cut your hand off. He slipped his gloves on now, grabbing the last of the boomerangs and putting them anywhere he could find room. It had taken him a while to devise the perfect system for carrying them. Eventually he came up with a very strong type of leather to hold the boomerangs in place without getting slit. He had cut this leather into strips and attached them to the outside of his jacket, lower legs, and upper arms. The boomerangs would simply hang from him on each strip of leather positioned for easy removal. He could fit three on a side on his jacket, one per leg, and one per arm. Because they always came back to him (unless they were blown up or stuck in someone's chest) he didn't need that many, but he always liked to have backups.

"You ready?" he asked, looking over to where Mara had been a few seconds earlier. She was gone. He ran out into the front hallway just in time to see her motioning to him from the yard before flipping over the fence. Running out the door he sprinted after her, leaping over the fence and almost colliding with her on the other side. Quickly jumping out of the way, Mara offered him her hand.

"Come on," she said, gesturing that he should take her hand. "You saw how fast the pill turned into that demon-thing. We're never going to get there before something happens to someone who's already taken it if we don't go as fog." Leif took her hand without hesitation and suddenly felt something inside him light up. A wonderful feeling spread through him as he and Mara vaporized into fog and began traveling at the speed of sound. He didn't know what it was, and even though he had never been fog before it felt right and natural to him. Weaving around tree trunks and animals and houses he felt as if he, not Mara, was in control. Thinking rationally he knew that wasn't possible, and he could feel Mara's hand on his, guiding him, but the feeling just wouldn't go away. In less than twenty seconds Mara was depositing them on the grass in the school courtyard. She let go of Leif. He swayed slightly, the sensation of ground under his feet returning to him, and the wonderful feeling in his chest leaving as suddenly as it had come. He placed his hand over his heart for a second, trying desperately to remember what it felt like, but it was gone. He saw Mara looking at him strangely so he dropped his hand self-consciously.

"I'm good," he reassured her. Mara nodded and clicked her tongue twice. Leif looked at her, puzzled.

"Oh, sorry," Mara apologized. "That's the signal in my team for 'move in'." Leif nodded, remembering that she had once told him that. They ran, using their enhanced speed but keeping their weapons out and at the ready. Reaching Professor Erros's hallway they slowed to a walk. Leif looked for auras but saw none except for Mara's and his own. They turned the corner and Leif scanned again, this time seeing muddy gray radiating from a door to their left. He pointing at it with the tip of his boomerang. Mara nodded and they flattened themselves against the wall. Booby traps were most often hidden in the middle of hallways because it took a lot of equipment to set one up and you couldn't fit it all in a corner or right up next to a wall. Sure enough large metal jaws suddenly emerged from the ceiling and the floor, soundlessly slamming together several times but not quite reaching to the edge of the hallway where their feet were. For a device of this magnitude you needed a lot of wiring and someplace to put it all.

"Turn around," a voice said from behind them. Mara knew that voice. Turning around slowly, knowing that the person would be armed, Mara saw the familiar face.

"Mara!" Hazen said. Her long blonde hair was pulled back in a high ponytail but it still managed to look electrified, sticking out in all directions. She smiled at Mara and slid her butterfly knives back into their pockets before reaching out to hug her friend. Still holding the handle of her double sword but taking her fingers off the buttons, Mara hugged her back. They had gone on an assignment a couple of days ago, routine Gone battle, and Chase had again asked what the assignment was about. Mara and Hazen had just taken off after that and Kat, unable to share her power of turning into a tiger, was forced to leave Chase behind. Lo and behold, the assignment went three times faster than expected.

Hazen pressed herself up against the wall, too, and looked over at Leif, smiling warmly. He smiled back. When he first met Hazen he had shaken her hand which had caused all of his arm hairs to become singed because he accidentally squeezed too hard and her power had sizzled up his arm. He liked Hazen, though. She was welcoming and fairly easy-going, the opposite of Mara, and they had worked well together. Besides being witty and fun to hang out with, Hazen had kicked butt on a number of occasions in their class both in magic and in fighting. Leif knew better than to mess with her.

"What are you doing here?" Mara asked, looking Hazen over for any injuries. Finding none, she looked back at Hazen's face, her eyebrows raised in question. Hazen's expression darkened. "Probably the same thing you're doing. The demon-pills?" she asked. Mara nodded in confirmation before saying in outrage, "He gave them to you, too?" Not waiting for an answer she looked around Hazen and saw Kaeli. Pressing her fingers to Kaeli's temple Mara imparted a message to her. Kaeli looked into Mara's eyes for a second, then took off running down the hall.

"Where did you send her?" Hazen asked.

"Message to Kat," Mara explained. "She has to know what we're doing."

Leif made a shushing noise from behind them and they lowered their voices.

Mara repeated her question to Hazen. "He gave them to you, too?" Hazen nodded grimly.

"Son of a…" Mara said. Hazen put her hand on Mara's arm, calming her, and quietly said, "I've been hearing talk about them all over school. No one's figured out what they do yet, but a lot of people from our class have been taking them. Apparently Erros has only given them to people sixteen or older."

As Mara listened to the information she got that faraway look in her eyes that meant she was thinking hard. After only a few seconds her expression took on a dangerous light.

"Before you rush into anything…" Leif began, but Mara was already moving. Sliding along the wall with Hazen right behind her Mara grabbed her hand. As Hazen grabbed Leif's hand he felt the mysterious floating sensation again. Mara guided them as fog through the crack under the door. Leif felt just as he had on the trip here, except this time it felt like something was pulling at his heart trying desperately to escape. Suddenly it hit him, like a stone thrown between your eyes. *The fog! The fog Mara had used to save him from the demon inside her pill.* She said she didn't know if it was still inside him, but clearly it was, trying to get out and reconnect with the source. That was why he had felt in control on the flight over. Because he *was* controlling the fog, if only the small part that was inside of him. He was so deep in thought that he didn't realize Mara had condensed them back into people, and that the two girls were staring around the room they were in.

"I've never seen this place before," Hazen said. "And I've been *everywhere*." Mara shook her head in agreement. Looking behind her Mara saw Leif gazing around in wonder.

"Me neither," he said. All around them were high, beautifully painted walls that reached up into a sort of multi-sided dome. The name came to Mara from her structural engineering class of many years ago. "Domed octagonal tower," she said to herself. All eight sides came together at the top, where there was a small hole that couldn't have been more than five feet in diameter letting in a few rays of light. Most daylight was artificially created by man-made suns that had been shot up on spaceships into the atmosphere around CSO-244 to provide light for the planet. Because they were inside a black hole they had no natural sun.

At first glance the enormous room was beautiful and somehow ethereal, but upon closer inspection they began to see traces of things that defined what the room was used for. Leif tapped Mara on the shoulder and pointed over to a large worktable that was sitting in one corner. There was something next to it, something huge and dark and covered by a sheet.

"There. There's aura everywhere, but it's all coming from there," he whispered. Mara nodded her thanks and signaled for them to move towards it. Hazen sidestepped to the right and came at it from a different angle. Leif copied her on the left.

Shli-i-ck! Mara pushed the button on the top of her handle and out came the shining blade. Hazen pulled a long, deadly looking hunting knife from a pocket on her right thigh, holding the blade at the ready. Leif slipped his boomerang back into its slot – he doubted it would be of much use if the machine started to act up – and pulled out a curved, double-edged knife. All the while he was searching the room and the surrounding area with his consciousness, feeling for any other minds out there. Even if they had barriers he couldn't penetrate there was no way of concealing a mind's presence. There were none.

"We're alone," he said quietly. "At least for now."

CHAPTER 11

A clang echoed violently in the great room. All three
of them spun around, weapons raised and ready,
dropping into fighting stance. They had been in the
room for over an hour, Leif doing periodic scans of the
area, never finding anything. Uncovering the machine
had turned out to be a bust. There were no pills in the
little dish that collected them, and the machine was
silent and dark. Lifeless. Splitting up, they covered the
entire room, searching every nook and cranny, finding
lots of stuff but nothing important.

Leif did a quick scan and this time felt the presence
of another mind. Flicking the tip of his knife in the
direction of the person, he put it away and pulled out
two boomerangs, one in each hand. He was good with
knives, but boomerangs were his specialty weapon.
Mara couldn't see the person's features but the
silhouette was clear enough. It was a man, and Mara
was willing to bet anything that it was Professor Erros.
He was holding something shiny, metallic, most likely a

weapon of some sort, and was hitting it repeatedly on the floor as he walked.

"Well, well, well," the voice said. Mara's suspicion was confirmed. Professor Erros walked almost lazily into a shaft of light coming from the hole in the roof. "Trespassers," he said in a teasing voice. Mara growled, a low and dangerous sound. "I see you've found my room," he said matter-of-factly, as if he were talking about the new shrimp special at the café. Moving fast as a shark he shot out his hand and let loose his specialty weapon – the kama. The short blades attached at ninety degree angles to a stick that was also connected to a string, which was looped many times around Professor Erros's wrist. Twirling in and out in front of him the sharp weapon whirled straight through the place that Mara and Hazen's heads used to be. At the last second they had used their enhanced reflexes and ducked as the kama came whistling through. Releasing his other kama from his other wrist he had them both zigzagging back and forth unpredictably around Mara, Hazen, and Leif. Grabbing her ice blower with her right hand Mara pressed down the button on the top and shielded her face. A stream of synthetic ice flew out of the blower. For at least a few seconds the kamas were trapped in the ice, unmoving, but soon Professor Erros yanked them free and twirled them back into his wrists.

Only a few feet in front of them now, he swung one out at Hazen. Mara grabbed her shoulder and turned them both to fog. The kama passed right through them. Materializing again she blocked the flying kama coming at her and grabbed it, pulling Professor Erros in. His foot flew up in a side kick and Mara's hand flew down to block it. With both Mara's hands occupied Professor Erros swung his free kama at her head. She tried to move out of the way but it caught her on the cheek. Blood welled up. It wasn't a deep cut but it did force her to let go of the kama she had been holding.

Mara looked around, spotting Hazen who had launched herself into the air behind Professor Erros for a spinning back crescent kick, but she couldn't find Leif. The kick slammed into Professor Erros's head and Hazen landed safely at Mara's side. Mara took the opportunity to come in with a stamp kick on the inside of his knee, forcing him down. He unleashed one kama and it collided with Mara's ankle, knocking her off balance for just a second. He sprang back to his feet and brought the kama down on Mara's side. She rolled out of the way and the blade struck the hard floor. Twirling her legs out and up she grabbed Professor Erros's head and, while pushing herself up from the ground, held on tight and whipped her feet down, slamming his body into the ground. He reached above his head and grabbed her arm, swinging her around until she was lying on the ground, too. Lightning fast she spun her hand around and thrust the handle of her double sword onto his leg. Pressing the button she felt the blade slip out directly into his leg and heard Professor Erros's cry. She pulled the sword out of his leg; it was dripping with lavender and white blood. She pushed off with her hands and arched her back, flipping up onto her feet and spinning to face Erros. Hazen had found a long, heavy piece of metal in one of Erros's piles of junk and had hooked it over his head, choking him. He did what any experienced fighter would do – grabbed her and flung her over his head. She was prepared for this, though, knowing he would do it, and while in the air she reoriented her body so that when she landed she would be on her side in perfect position to lift her leg and drive it hard into his gut. Purple and white blood was dripping out of his leg and onto the floor. He stumbled back several feet but regained his bearings almost instantly. Whirling out his kamas again he kept them spinning in front of him, an impenetrable shield because they were moving too fast. Mara and Hazen both sprang to their feet and pulled out weapons. Hazen reached up and tried to pull lightning from the sky, then looked desperately at Mara, her electric blue-green eyes saying, "I can't." Erros laughed from behind his kamas.

"I built this roof especially to block you, Hazen," he said. "You can't access your power while under it." He laughed again.

"There's gotta be a compliment in there somewhere," Hazen sneered.

Erros looked at her murderously and charged forward with his kamas whirling faster than ever. This time Hazen grabbed Mara and the meaning was clear. Turning into fog Mara darted behind him and materialized again, Hazen with her. Jumping and spinning around, Mara delivered a hard thrust kick to the small of Erros's back. He flew forward several yards, his feet actually leaving the ground, and fell onto his hands and knees. Mara landed gracefully and ran back to Hazen.

"Where's Leif?" she asked.

Hazen pointed to the other side of the room which was hidden in darkness. "Destroying the machine," she said. Mara nodded and took hold of Hazen's arm, vaporizing and flying over to the machine. She could feel Erros on her tail but she didn't care anymore. Condensing into her human form Mara saw Leif crouched by the machines, boomerang out, cutting wire after wire.

"Ahhh!" Hazen cried out from beside Mara. She spun to see Erros standing there, bloody and scratched but with a maniacal look in his eyes. One of his kamas had caught Hazen across the arm and had dug deep. She was holding her hand along the cut but the deep ocean blue blood specific to Glukons was leaking out between her fingers. Even though she was just half Glukon, her dad being a full WW, she shared their blood color. Looking at Mara for a split second and somehow conveying what she was going to do, Hazen took off, leaping into the air and activating her sticky coating. Colliding with the wall Hazen didn't fall off, just remained there. Despite the fact that the wall was straight up she began climbing like a gecko, her hands and feet sticking to the wall every time she touched it, and soon she was nearly fifty feet above the ground. A few drops of blood splattered onto the floor next to Mara. Turning to Erros, she lashed out and he ducked from her blow. Blocking his kamas left and right Mara stayed in the clear, but didn't have a free hand to strike Erros with. Instead of using her hands she used her mind, just as Leif had taught her to, and picked up the piece of metal that Hazen had used to choke Erros earlier. Picking it up, she brought it painstakingly towards her. It was heavier than anything she had ever moved before, but it was moving just the same. Turning it so the flat side was facing Erros she slammed it into his back, slowly but powerfully. Letting it drop to the ground Mara looked back at Leif. He was staring at her with a proud expression on his face.

"Is it disabled?" she asked.

"I've cut every wire and destroyed every power source in here," he replied. "There's no way this thing is making any more pills." Mara nodded, satisfied.

Crack! A blinding flash of white light lit up the whole room for a split second, leaving the outline of the lightning bolt burned into Mara's retinas. Erros lay, twitching slightly, on the ground. Mara looked up and there was Hazen, stuck to the ceiling with one hand reaching up through the hole. Scampering back down the wall and landing solidly on her feet, Hazen turned off her sticky coating and hugged Mara. They had learned the hard way to do this gingerly. Sometimes a bit of the residue stayed on Hazen after she used her Glukon ability. Once when they were nine they had gotten stuck together and had to be pried apart with a crowbar.

"He said I couldn't use my power while under the roof, so I just moved out from under it," Hazen said, laughing a bit. "Boy, for a professor, this guy isn't very smart."

"Come on!" Leif said urgently. "Let's get out of here before he can get up again." Mara and Hazen nodded in agreement. They were both bleeding, Mara's dark lavender and white blood running down her cheek and Hazen's ocean blue draining fast from her arm.

"We need to get you to the infirmary," Mara said to Hazen. She took both of their hands and turned into fog, taking them with her. Erros, who had somehow already regained the power of speech, yelled after them as they shot out through the hole in the roof.

"I'll kill you! I'll kill you and everyone you care about!"

CHAPTER 12

*K*at had gotten Mara's message through Kaeli. *Stay away from Professor Erros. We don't know what he's up to but it's dangerous.* The message was short and clipped, Mara's usual tone, but Kat heard something in it, that inner instinct that triggered fear which Mara had trained to push down and ignore. This was serious.

She had left the second she got it, not really caring what Mara wanted her to do but determined to find her. Slipping on her spring-and-summer battle gear as she ran, she stopped by the weapons cache and loaded up on everything. Putting on her black and silver claw-gloves and clawed fivefingers boots, she flexed her fingers to put enough pressure on the trigger button and the claws shot out, gleaming silver, lethal. She could do the same flexing trick with her toes and the claws would shoot out, but she never did this until they were on site because of the horrible clicking sound they made when she ran.

Jumping over the dropped clothes and dressers that lay between her and the door, she threw it open and morphed into a tiger, taking off down her street and into the patch of wilderness that her parents had bought years ago and never had the time to develop. She loved being a tiger; she loved the feel of the muscles rippling beneath her skin and the looks everyone gave her. Her tiger was tall, almost five feet, taller than a normal tiger and with glorious striped fur. She had large, deep brown eyes with a curious pattern of small black stripes and dots around them. Crashing through the trees and bushes she made good time towards the Academy. She could have flown using her pressure to push her off from the ground, but that was much slower and required a lot of her energy. Using her talent was quicker and easier, the obvious way to go.

She emerged from the undeveloped land still at full sprint, legs pumping and body rocking, taking the impact from her huge paws hitting the ground. Running through the yards of people's houses she may have knocked over a tree or two, but she didn't care. She was almost there, almost at the Academy, when she heard a whoosh and stopped abruptly. Looking behind her she could just make out a stream of fog disappearing into the treetops, moving at the speed of sound. She turned back into a human and sighed, looking mournfully after it. Getting back down on all fours she took off again, paws pounding the ground, and re-entered the forest.

"Where the hell were you?" Kat demanded, not even casting a glance at Leif but looking straight at Mara and Hazen. She had gotten to the house about two minutes after Mara, and had found her and Leif tossing their unused weapons back into the cache and Hazen standing over the sink washing the distinctive lavender and white WW blood off several blades.

"I took off for the Academy the second I got your message, but you passed me when I was almost there," she said, her voice raised to a dangerous level.

"What is going *on* in here, anyway?" a sleepy voice said from the hallway. "Did someone die?"

Kat recognized the voice. "Mara, Hazen, and Leif snuck out to do *something* with Professor Erros without me," Kat complained as Niko came around the corner, looking like he woke up about three seconds ago, hair sticking up every which way and wearing a creased shirt and mismatched pants with no socks or shoes. Bleary eyes instantly alert, he looked over at Mara and Leif, the former wearing no expression at all and the latter looking slightly guilty. Hazen was standing behind them, trying to pay attention while using a small abrasive cloth to scrub with all her might, her mission to get the dried blood off the blade of Mara's double sword.

"I told you in the message, Kat, you have to stay away from that man. He just tried to kill all of us!" Mara explained, emotion entering her face now. Leif nodded in agreement.

"Yeah? Well you're damn well lucky to be alive," Kat retorted. She looked at them with eyes saying, "this excuses *nothing*" but reached over and took the double sword from Hazen and began cleaning. "Explain," she said flatly. "Explain why the most loved young WW in the country would try to kill *you*."

Mara took a deep breath and began to talk extremely fast, knowing that Kat would understand from their years of rapid-fire banter. When she finished the story her double sword was sparkling clean and the cloth reduced to a small, smoking piece of ash. That was because as Kat listened and heard the part about Erros trying to turn students into the demon-like thing Mara and Leif had seen earlier in the year, then almost killing them for their successful attempt to destroy the machine, her hand had sped up faster and faster, scrubbing with pure anger and betrayal, until smoke had started to rise from the cloth and it had burst into orangey yellow flames. Hazen turned the faucet on and doused the thing in water, but the cloth was a goner.

"Sorry," Kat said quietly. Mara gently eased the sword out of her white-knuckled grip, knowing that Kat could sometimes take her anger out on totally inanimate objects. Just a few weeks ago when she had caught Chase making gooey-eyes at another girl she had come home and completely destroyed her favorite overstuffed comfy chair with a short sword before she calmed down enough that Mara could get near her and take the sword away. This time, though, Kat relinquished the sword easily and turned to look at Niko, who was staring at them all with a shocked and angry expression.

"And you went after him?!" he asked, incredulous. *"On your own?"* Now he was just angry, but the kind of angry that came from being very worried about someone. Mara nodded, looking guilty, an expression that rarely crossed her face.

"Look, we're sorry, but Erros is turning kids into *demons*. Demons!" Hazen said defiantly. "We're not going to just sit around and wait for them to come after us, we're Witch Warriors. And we'd be pretty crappy Witch Warriors if we let that happen." With that she turned on her heel and left the room, followed by Mara and, a few moments later, Leif. Kat started after them, too, but Niko hooked her arm and pulled her back.

"Let them go," he said. "They're just going to blow off some steam."

Mara led the three of them down two stories underground and into a room with a high ceiling and sparring mats on the floor. She pointed to a door on the other side.

"That leads into a tunnel that comes out in one of my favorite places in the forest," she explained. "We need to leave now."

Leif looked confused but then the memory came back to him and he nodded. She was right, of course.

"He threatened to kill us. If he thinks we're here then he'll come and probably kill Niko and Tom and your parents," Hazen reasoned. "If we find a way to get his attention away from here, send up a signal or something from where we are, then he'll come after us and leave everyone here alone."

Mara nodded. "Hazen, you could draw an especially large bolt of lightning. That'd show him where we are." Hazen nodded.

"Won't that set the forest on fire?" Leif asked, feeling as if he was missing something.

"I can contain it in my hand," Hazen explained. She had a wonderful way of never sounding superior, even when spelling out the most basic thing. "If I make the bolt run between my hand and the sky and hold it there, it'll never touch the forest floor." Nodding, Leif motioned that they should probably take off now. They had restocked at the weapons cache on the way down with everything they could fit without weighing them down, and they were already in their battle gear. Mara started to follow him towards the door but Hazen stopped her.

"Shouldn't we bring Kat? Or at least tell her?" she asked.

Mara shook her head slightly. "Kat never did anything. For some reason, Erros hasn't approached her with the pill yet, and I'm not about to drag her into a dangerous situation. Besides, if Erros knew that she knew where we are he'd come after her first."

Knowing that Mara was right but still feeling horrible about leaving her friend behind, Hazen took off towards the door, followed closely by Mara.

$$\Large\diamondsuit$$

They made their way into the forest. Leaves were rustling in the warm wind. The school year was over, so they were spared from classes for two weeks; the time usually spent at the Academy was now free.

"Hazen," Mara said. Activating her sticky coating, Hazen climbed gracefully up a tall, sturdy tree and perched on a high branch about fifteen feet off the needle-strewn ground. Reaching up into the sky she felt the pull of the lightning that was always there inside her. She left the stickiness on both of her feet so that she couldn't fall off but removed it from the rest of her body. Sending the energy inside her up into the sky above, she formed a great lightning bolt. Drawn down towards her in a swift, cracking motion the light lit up the forest. Mara and Leif both shielded their eyes, but Hazen looked right at it, unaffected by the blinding light. The lightning formed a crackling and constantly moving rod between her raised hand and the sky. Holding it there for almost ten more seconds before letting it down Hazen was sure that Erros would have seen it. He was no doubt looking for any signs of the only three people who knew his secret. Drawing the energy back into her body the lightning disappeared as quickly as it had appeared. Turning off the sticky coating on her feet Hazen dropped to the ground and landed in a front roll back onto her feet. Then she brushed the leaves out of her hair, straightened up, and wiped her hands on her pants. Bringing lightning down from the sky always made her hands sweat. Light didn't affect her but heat definitely did.

"He's gonna be here really soon," Hazen said. "We need to move." Mara nodded and, maintaining her role as team leader, signaled for them to move out. Hazen would have preferred to travel as her lightning bolt but that was rather obvious and Erros would find them much faster with such a bright light guiding him. Both Hazen and Leif took Mara's hands and vaporized into fog. The stream of light gray droplets took off through the forest, dodging everything that came its way. In a few seconds they were far away from the spot where Hazen had launched her bolt, and Mara stopped them. Landing with her knees slightly bent to soften the impact Mara dropped briefly into fighting stance before returning to a normal position.

"This distance should buy us another few days while Erros searches everywhere around the lightning bolt," she said. "He'll be moving fast, and the kids that have taken the pills have definitely turned into those demon-things by now. He's probably controlling them through some remote neural chip and has brought them together as an army."

"Let's set up some sort of camp," Hazen said. "Leif, can you go somewhere fairly far away and pull up a tree for us to use? With a few nails and any luck we should be able to build some kind of lean-to by sundown."

Leif set off to find an appropriate tree, his feet crunching pine needles every step. Mara made her falcon call, as softly as she could, and Mamba came swooping down from somewhere up in the canopy. Mara twisted as she caught the bird, taking the impact of the landing and moving with it. Mamba folded her wings and looked intelligently at Mara.

"You brought her with you?" Hazen asked. She hadn't seen the bird anywhere, but pets and owners often bonded in ways that people without magically-enhanced animals would never understand.

Mara smiled, a genuine smile that came from her love of Mamba. "She follows me everywhere, even to school," she said, stroking Mamba's sleek blue-grey wings lovingly.

Hazen looked slightly amused. "Well, I'm one to talk," she said, and turned towards the forest behind her. Making a low clicking noise in her throat she held out her arm and a small black hand grabbed it, followed by the swinging body of Kaeli. The black Lar gibbon had been swinging from tree to tree all the way with them and was now hanging by one hand from Hazen's arm, dangling like a marionette, the white fur surrounding her eyes making her look like a raccoon that had reversed its colors. Looking adorably innocent she switched her gaze from Hazen to Mara and back again.

Dropping to the ground she sat obediently, waiting for instructions.

"Go find food," Hazen told her. "If you see anyone out there other than Leif or us, you hide." Her tone remained gentle but had an edge that meant she was dead serious. Mara looked at her with a knowing expression, a smile slowly spreading across her face. Without saying anything she and Hazen burst into laughter simultaneously. Mara whispered something to Mamba and the bird took off from her arm and flew off in the direction of the nearest town, staying below the canopy

"I sent her to get nails," Mara explained, still laughing. Having been best friends since their second year in the Academy Hazen was one of the two people on CSO-244 that could get Mara to laugh. Not a sarcastic laugh – anyone could get that from her – but a true laugh of happiness. For a long time Hazen and Kat had been the only members of that club, but now she was starting to wonder if Leif had joined it, too.

Leif came crashing back into the clearing holding under his arm a large, sturdy light brown tree with smooth bark. Mara pulled out one of her double swords and opened a blade. She set to work slicing the top of the tree, the leafy part, off of the trunk. Hazen reached down and grabbed all the small branches and leaves and held them away from Mara's hair as she worked.

A small scuffle next to her on the ground alerted Mara that Mamba had returned.

"Take the nails from her and start cutting the trunk into beams," she yelled to Leif, and soon heard an exclamation from behind her.

"She bit me!" Leif yelped.

Hazen responded. "It's probably just a play bite. You're a Witch Warrior so it shouldn't even break the skin." Leif admitted that it hadn't but that he had expected Mamba to be nicer to him because he had known her for almost nine months now.

Mara called a soft bird call from inside the mess of leaves and Mamba took off to find a place to roost, the wind from her wings blowing through Leif's hair.

"We should move camp in the morning," Mara said. "We can't stay in one place long."

Hazen nodded. "I'll get Kaeli back here. She can go out scouting for someplace else to sleep tomorrow night." She turned to the forest behind her and made the low, throaty clicking noise again. Emerging from the mass of leaves and twigs Mara shook out her braid and got up, bending over to grip the trunk of the tree. She separated the leafy top of the tree from the useful wood and tossed it to the side of the clearing. Leif had cut many good boards from the trunk already and was beginning to construct a rough lean-to using the nails that Mamba had brought and using his fist as a hammer. A small red circle was developing on his fist where it had been hitting the head of the nails; it was getting more painful-looking by the second.

"Here, let me do that," Mara said, grabbing Leif's wrist as he swung down for another hit. Looking grateful, he stepped aside. Mara slammed her own fist onto the nail, driving it into the board. *Ow. Ow. Ow,* she thought to herself at each impact. It wasn't the kind of hurt of serious injury, just the annoying repetitive pain that you wished would go away.

CHAPTER 13

"*I*f she were here, she would have responded to the *eight* urgent assignment notices we sent her!" Kat shouted at Niko. Holding his hands up and backing away a few steps Niko waited to speak until her breathing had slowed and her expression was slightly less murderous.

"Why don't you and I gear up so we're ready for anything that might come here, and then we can think about our options. If Mara's taken off then she doesn't want to be found. Searching for her will only lead to more dead ends," he said, trying to keep a reasonable tone and the note of worry out of his voice. Kat nodded, clearly still seething, and walked briskly out to unlock the weapons cache. When she touched her thumb to the reader it beeped once and turned green. The iris scan blinked on and off, signaling that it was ready. Bending down from her full height of six feet, Kat brought her right eye level with the scanner. A small beam of light passed over her eye once, then again. The scanning device also beeped and flashed green before multiple locks popped open in sequence and the thick door to the cache swung open. Stepping inside Kat looked along the many shelves that extended nearly fifteen feet to the back wall, which was covered in cubbies for the smaller, less often used weapons and extra holders. Her gloves were already on – she hadn't taken them off since she heard the news about Erros – and her fangs were literally built into her mouth. She grabbed hunting knives, fire and ice blowers, throwing knives, darts, and anything else she could reach and fit into her gear. Niko had utilized his vampire super-speed and rushed down to his room, returning seconds later in full gear. Technically, he wasn't allowed to wear WW gear, but then again he wasn't supposed to be in contact of any kind with WW so following the rules was kind of out the window. With no warning Niko slipped his arm around Kat's waist, lifting her over her vigorous protests, and super-sped them both up and out into the back yard. Setting her back down Niko stood up only to buckle over again as Kat instinctively drove her elbow into his gut, stepping into a low side stance to put all her power behind it. Vampires were tough but WW were just as strong and could hurt them when not many other species could.

Kat's mind wandered off, remembering the awfully boring day in History class when Mr. Rosten had lectured them on the characteristics of Quirks. The only other magical people strong enough to harm vampires, other than demons, were Quirks. Quirks were usually autistic or mentally disabled WW who didn't have the cognitive power to control their magic and who ended up in hospitals or containment facilities, but some Quirks were perfectly normal WW with altered DNA who simply didn't have a talent or basic magic and who had a specialty that wasn't normal for a WW. Quirks came in all different kinds, grouped by their unusual specialty. There were the Fear Quirks, identified by their shiny bronze blood, capable of manipulating someone's fear to their will. There were also Water Quirks, Sun Quirks, Greenie Quirks, Steel Quirks, Kinetic Quirks, Volt Quirks, and many more. According to legend Quirks were formed when some of the people who were first brought to CSO-244 had brains that reacted with the chemistry of the black hole in a similar way to WW, but the chemistry also messed up their neurological functions.

Kat shook her head, drawing her thoughts away from what happened thousands of years ago and returning to the present. When she saw the manhole cover, her eyes lit up. Niko held his hand out and started to say something, but she had already grabbed him and was moving towards the large circular disk of metal. Lifting it she looked down into the dark, dusty, horrible smelling tube below her. Dropping the cover on the ground with a resounding thump she turned to Niko.

"This'll take us to the Academy," she said. "If we can't go above ground, then we'll go below." Niko shook his head vigorously. Ignoring him, Kat dropped down onto the hard, copper surface of the sewer. She began to crawl down into the darkness, desperately trying to keep her newly washed hair from touching the grime coating the walls. Systematically exploding small chunks of air in front of her for light she had made it almost ten feet before she heard Niko drop in behind her.

"Not exactly what I had in mind when I said consider our options," she heard him mutter. Waiting a bit for him to catch up, Kat continued, remembering the directions Mara had told her all those years ago. *Two rights, then a left.* Kat couldn't tell how much time had passed, but it felt like forever and her knees were seriously starting to smart. *Boy, Leif must really love her to come all this way every Friday,* she thought. Taking the left into a much smaller pipe Kat heard Niko curse quietly behind her. He wasn't heavy but he was tall and muscular, and the smaller pipe meant he had to double over into a ball and shimmy forward.

"It's only, like, fifteen more feet," Kat called out behind her in a comforting tone. Pushing the palm of her hand upward Kat lifted the anticipated manhole cover off and deposited it on the grass next to the opening. Kat swung her legs over the edge and stood up, not even bothering to reach a hand down and help Niko. She knew what vampires could do, and one of those things was to jump unusually far and high. Just as she suspected, he appeared a few seconds later, shaking himself out and cracking every joint in his body.

"I am *never* traveling by sewer again," he said disgustedly as he rubbed a painfully tender shoulder. Kat laughed, a sound that drew people in and almost *made* them like her. It was one of the many reasons she was popular. Combing her fingers through her high ponytail, she drew a strand of her light brown hair before her eyes and inspected it. She didn't approve of having hair as long as Mara's, but her own hair reached her waist when let free. Deeming the strand worthy to remain on her head she let it fall back to join the rest of the ponytail, swishing it around slightly as she liked to do. Niko had already taken off towards the school and Kat followed, heading for the seldom used side door near the Defensive Magic wing of the school. Pushing it open Niko flattened himself along the wall, as did Kat, and he heard the distinctive shli-i-ck of her claws and fangs coming out. They walked past several booby traps that were easy to avoid, appearing to have been almost half-heartedly set up.

"Erros isn't trying to keep us out," Kat whispered. To prove her point she reached her hand out the next time they passed a trap – a large rolling spike wheel.

"Kat, no!" Niko said in a whisper-shout, his hand flashing out to grab hers but knowing he'd be too late. She stuck it straight into the spike wheel… and nothing happened. Her hand passed through it as if it weren't even there. The spike wheel kept on rolling. "It's a hologram," Niko declared. "It's obvious. Erros would have access to all this Academy technology and he would know how to use it to scare people off." Nodding her head grimly Kat nudged Niko to move faster.

"She said the door was large and had a really weird looking handle," she explained repeating what Mara had told her. Niko looked across the hall.

"Like *that* one?" he asked, pointing past a pair of crushing jaws to the high door opposite them. Kat stared at the handle. It was a beautiful twisted ball of tiny metal strands, each individual but intertwined in a way that just *looked* evil.

"Yeah," was all that Kat said. Walking straight through the hologram of the metal jaws Kat turned the knob and flung the door open. The room looked exactly as Mara had described it – eight tall walls that rose up several floors, and many machines and other items stacked around the room haphazardly. The only thing that was different was that there was no hole in the ceiling like Mara had said, but Kat assumed that Erros had simply closed it since Hazen had used it to lightning-bolt him. In the very center of the room several consoles were set up with at least two glowing computers each. Kat walked over and looked at the many screens all lined up in a semicircle around the desk and chair.

"It's security camera feed," Kat said, pointing to the many views the screens showed, some of random sections of forest, some of the town around the Academy, and one of their house. "He's searching for them but he's not getting anything." Every ten seconds or so the view on each of the screens changed to a different camera, usually in some part of the forest.

"He knows they're in the forest," Niko said, his eyes scanning everywhere the camera feed showed, trying to notice some kind of landmark that he remembered. "I have no idea where any of these places are," he sighed. "Everywhere in the forest looks the same." Kat turned her attention away from the computer screens and looked around the rest of the room, awed at how much stuff Erros had.

"This guy is serious," she said to herself.

"Kat!" Niko said urgently. Kat spun around and ran back to where he was bending over the screens. On one small corner of one there was an image and a beeping red alert that flashed "CALLING" over and over again. In the camera feed there was a small clearing. The drone that Erros was using to hold the camera flew in closer and they could see the faces of the people on the screen clearly.

"Mara!" Kat said, instantly recognizing the proud face of her sister framed by strands of dark brown hair pulled up into her signature high braid. "Hazen and Leif too." Niko pointed to the "CALLING" alert.

"He's coming," he said. "Erros. He programmed the system to call him if it detects anything suspicious.

We've got to get out of here." Running towards the door they paid no heed to the hologram dangers along the hallway but ran through them, knowing that even if they were real they weren't nearly as deadly as Erros himself would be if he found them here. Turning the handle on the side door and sprinting across the grass, Kat felt something squish against her boot. For the first time she didn't care. Niko wrenched the manhole cover off and jumped into the sewer. Kat stopped for just a second to reach up and pull the cover back over the hole before Niko grabbed her hand and yanked her down into the system.

"He can't be far away if the computer system was able to send a direct signal to his brain," Niko explained as they crawled as fast as they could. "He'll know we were there. I don't know how but he's got to have some sort of sensors around to detect personal heat signatures, and even if those can't tell him if it was us he'll be suspicious and come to our house and search. If we're not there he'll know we saw his lab and come after us."

Kat kept on crawling but replied, "You don't have a heat signature. You're a vampire." Niko made a grunting noise that Kat suspected meant "yeah" and answered more completely once they had made the final right turn and were on the home stretch.

"Exactly. The sensors will pick up my *lack* of heat signature," he said. Punching the cover off the hole Niko jumped up out of the sewer, followed by Kat, and they both started to super-speed the annoyingly long distance from the tree to the tall door. Sliding the cover back on with her foot as she started to run Kat saw that the metal had been dented and almost broken through by Niko's fist. Sometimes when vampires, or any magical species for that matter, got stressed or threatened they lost control of their powers. This had clearly happened to Niko. Kat sped up and passed him to open the door, afraid that he might rip that off its hinges. Casting a glance at her gratefully Niko flew downstairs to change back into regular clothes. Kat did the same. A couple seconds later they were both up and in the kitchen, dressed rather sloppily but at least not in battle gear, and Kat began dumping a random mix of ingredients into a bowl and splattering some on her face. She saw Niko's fist, the one he had used to punch the manhole cover. It had turned a dark mahogany, the color of vampire blood. *Punching the cover that hard must have broken even vampire skin.* Gesturing for him to hide himself in the very likely event that Erros could identify vampires and would rat him out to the Council as a vampire illegally living with WW, Kat watched as he dove around the corner and out of sight. She had never actually cooked anything before, mainly because no one ever really needed to cook due to the marvelous invention of food pellets. All your nutritional needs for a whole day were covered by one tiny pellet! Some WW still cooked, of course, but most didn't waste their time and consequently didn't know how. Kat was of the latter category. Dusting some flour on her face and hastily tying an apron around her waist, she set to work mixing the random ingredients that she had thrown into a stainless steel mixing bowl she had grabbed from the dusty storage space downstairs.

Less than three seconds later a knock came on the door and then, without waiting for a response, it was pushed open revealing the smiling face of Professor Erros. He was really quite handsome, with silky black hair and black stubble covering his chin. He had the look of the bachelor that won the girl's heart in every romantic film ever made – a strong face with pronounced cheekbones and chin, deep set eyes, and lustrous hair. He had on the winning smile that he wore whenever he was using his specialty, the ability to persuade people to do whatever he wants as long as their mental barriers are down and he can access their minds. Since everyone in the country loved him, most people let their barriers down when around him, either because they were female and had a crush on him or because they were male and wanted to *be* him. Kat used to do this too, as smitten with him as anyone else, but now she was making no mistakes.

Giving him exactly the reaction he was used to from girls, she said "Oh, Professor Erros," easily putting surprise and giddy happiness into her voice as she smiled widely. Years of practice with Mara and her parents had made Kat an expert liar; she could fake almost any emotion at will. Widening her smile she set down her whisk and pushed the bowl of inedible mush she had been working on off to the side of the counter. "What brings you here?" she asked, keeping her tone airy and hopeful as if she was *so* surprised and delighted that he'd deigned to come to her house. Slipping her apron off over her head and smoothing her hair, she looked at him questioningly, widening her eyes and adopting her innocent expression perfected from years of practice. Erros waved his hand dismissively.

"Oh, nothing much, just checking on my favorite student," he said, smiling down at her as an owner would smile at a dog. Seeing clearly what he was doing, Kat smiled and forced herself to blush slightly, careful not to let a single stone of her mental barriers crumble. Most people would be so flattered by something like this they'd melt like butter, and Erros could simply look in their eyes, smile, and tell them to do something. They'd obey like a marionette who had just handed over its strings to a puppeteer. His flattering expression faltered just slightly when he sensed her barriers were just as strong as ever. *He's not used to encountering obstacles. He doesn't know how to deal with it,* she thought, determined to use this to her advantage. Moving a bit closer to him, knowing that the distance would make it no easier for him to get into her mind, she said coyly, "Why, thank you, but are you worried about my progress? I believe that I have never gotten less than one hundred percent in your class. Is there something I'm doing wrong?" She managed to maintain the tone of a lovesick girl who would do anything to impress him, but just barely. Just thinking about what he did to Mara, what he threatened to do to her, made her blood boil. Pushing down her emotions as she had been taught to do during battle she offered Erros a drink and, without thinking, asked if he would be staying for dinner or if this was just a drop-by. Immediately realizing her mistake Kat turned away to hide her expression and pretended to get him something. If Erros did stay for dinner he would have enough time to set up thermal scanners and try to match her heat scan to the one he had found in his lab. He would inevitably see that it was the same heat signature; he would know that she knew what he was doing, and would of course question her about everything to do with the situation. When she couldn't answer his questions because she honestly didn't know Mara, Hazen, and Leif's plan of action, he would become infuriated and it might come down to a fight.

"Oh, no, I should be on my way soon," he said, ending her whole mental breakdown with a few simple words. Turning around quickly, shocked and relieved, all Kat could say was, "Oh, okay." Then plastering on an expression of disappointment and poutiness that was just enough to convince Erros she was unhappy about his leaving but not enough to make him stay, she pulled the bowl back towards her and picked up the whisk. Erros was looking around the room as if hoping Mara's plan was written in blood on the ceiling or something. He ran his hand over the back of their couch and then began to walk around the sitting room, scrutinizing every piece of furniture with narrowed eyes.

"So, Professor Erros, would you..." Kat began, trying to distract him, but he quickly strode back around the couch into the entryway and waved his hand. Turning to leave Kat saw something near her catch his eye. *Oh no. Busted*, she thought, looking around desperately for something to spill on something or someone else. Walking back towards her Erros reached his finger down and scooped out a lump of whatever it was that Kat was mixing. Putting his finger in his mouth he grimaced and swallowed, clearly with difficulty.

"I don't know what you're making, Katalina, but you might want to consult a book," he said, looking at her one last time before he turned on his heel and headed for the door, waving his hand behind him to slam the door shut. Kat caught his expression as he turned away from her; it changed to one of anger and darkness just a split second too soon. His eyes had darkened, turning into something almost not human; his eyebrows furrowed, and his face collapsed into rage and disappointment. *He thought he could break me, get inside me. Now he has to go out and find Mara and the others without an inkling of what they have against him.* Kat, too lazy to separate them, dumped the goopy slop and the bowl into the large trash container mounted on the wall.

She wiped her face, removing the traces of flour. Typing code into a computer disguised as a microwave, she used their home security system to scan the yard and surrounding area. Erros was walking down the lawn and onto the neighboring yard. In case he decided to come back she punched in another code that would set off an alarm if anything came within twenty feet of the front door. Then she walked through the door out of the kitchen and descended the stairs two at a time. At the bottom a super-speeding hand in a backfist whizzed out from around the corner of the wall, nearly connecting with her face. She whipped her hand up just in time, catching the fist millimeters from her nose.

"Easy, cowboy," she teased. "It's not proper to attack your niece." Dropping his arm Niko slapped her on the shoulder and laughed.

"I heard what you said up there," he said, still chuckling. "That accent, that innocent girl accent, was *hilarious*. Doesn't sound at all like the Kat I know." She smiled and then began to laugh, too. His mocking happiness was contagious.

"It *does* sound like me," she protested. "I sound like that all the time when evil teachers trying to take over the world with an army of demons come over for a chat." The sentence jolted her out of her celebration. Her smile faded and she held Niko's arm tighter. "The demons," she said. "Even if Erros doesn't know that *we* know, he's still going to go after Mara. *With demons!*" Niko's smile disappeared, too, and they both started running up the stairs, grabbing gear and weapons as they did.

"And we're off running… again," Kat said angrily, her expression changing into one of annoyance.

They had just made it up into the kitchen and were heading for the side door when a booming voice from their large television screen filled the room. "Attention all Witch Warriors," the voice said. "Until further notice the Academy that trains our young has been shut down. Everyone is to evacuate immediately. Once outside no one is allowed on the premises of the Academy. Effective until specific orders to resume classes have been issued." Now a face, and a name, were being connected with the words. There on the screen, on live broadcast over the entire nation, was the leader of the WW Council and, by extension, of all WW on the planet. High Chairman Kurthian, more commonly called Kurth, was a proud WW with many credits to his name and many lines on his face testifying to his years in government. He had straight, short black hair, eyes so dark brown they were almost black, and very tan skin. Despite being only forty-eight he looked at least sixty. He had been High Chairman for over twenty-two years, voted into office at the record-breaking young age of twenty-six. Generally everyone liked him, or at least tolerated him, and nothing had gone horribly wrong during his tenure. According to the people he worked with he was a strict and rather harsh man who did not enjoy socializing. Unmarried and with no children, he usually preferred to stay at home and work on his 'inventions', devices he believed would stop Gone forever. He had never revealed anything, however, and after the first few years everyone had just summed him up as a solitary man alone in his big house all day needing something to do.

His face disappeared from the television screen and it went to the WW symbol accented in white on a blue background, reminding everyone to always put their role as WW first, and then the screen went to black.

"Great," Kat said.

"You haven't been going to classes for the last few days anyway. What do you care if the Academy's shut down?" Niko asked. It was true, Kat hadn't been to the Academy during school hours since the beginning of the week and she was starting to feel guilty about it, but she still needed access to the storerooms.

"The Academy was our source, our way of getting all the tech we need to help Mara, Hazen, and Leif. Those storage spaces under the weapons wing are *full* of cool toys," Kat said, sighing. Shrugging it off, Niko opened the door and walked over to the tree.

"We don't have to travel by sewer again, do we?" he asked hopefully. Kat shook her head.

"That sewer only goes to the Academy and the water treatment plant. We're going to the woods."

CHAPTER 14

Mara and Hazen were sleeping, pressed up against each other on one side of the lean-to, legs curled up under them for warmth. Leif, on the other side, was crunched into a little ball and was still taking up more than half of the space. He wasn't heavy, but he was six foot six, slim, and long. They weren't comfortable but at least they were far away from where Erros was no doubt searching for them in earnest. Mara stretched her neck up and peeked out of one of the cracks between the boards of the lean-to. It wasn't quite light yet. She poked Hazen in the ribs. Hazen's messy blonde head rose up as she pushed herself off of Mara, still favoring the arm that had been sliced by Erros's kama. It appeared to be healed now, of course, but sometimes wounds run a little deeper. They both got up, keeping a bent posture because of the low, rough roof. Hazen wasn't quite the exceptionally tall girl Mara was, but she was still five foot eleven and a half, about average for a WW. Mara nudged Leif with her boot. When that didn't wake him she pressed her heel into his ribcage.

"Ow!" he awoke with a howl. Then he immediately changed his response to, "Oh, morning, Mara," and smiled at her. Hazen watched the two conspiratorially as Mara leaned down to offer her hand to Leif. There was something going on there and, even if she didn't know what it was now, she was determined to find out.

"Come on, guys, we need to move camp," she said, motioning for them to get out of the lean-to so she could destroy it.

"Or…" Leif said, an idea occurring to him. "Or Mara could take it with us. As fog. Then we wouldn't need to build a new one each time we moved."

"Good idea!" Hazen said, realizing the sense Leif's plan made. After packing up their things Mara placed one hand on the lean-to structure. Holding out her other hand Hazen and Leif both grabbed it. This time they moved in a zigzag pattern, Mara searching for places to land. She would have liked Hazen and Leif's help, but to them traveling as fog was like being in a black vortex; they couldn't see, smell, hear, or feel a thing. It took a long time to find a space that was inhabitable. The things she gradually began to see were sinkholes, trees packed so tightly you couldn't fit a hand between them, vicious animals, and a number of other devastations of the forest. It used to be that places like these were well taken care of, but as the numbers of Gone increased and the battles became bloodier the environment was completely abandoned. No one was allowed to be anything other than a Warrior, teacher, medic, or manufacturer of weapons, and those last three had limited availability. If all the necessary teaching, medic, or businessmen spots were filled, you had no choice but to become a Warrior.

Dropping Hazen, Leif, and the lean-to off in a small clearing littered with branches, Mara remained as fog and flew around to check the general area. About forty feet to the east a large sinkhole would need to be avoided. Other than that this area of the forest seemed fairly peaceful.

Mara landed and condensed back into human form, jogging over to help Hazen find their possessions in and around the clearing; Mara could transport loose stuff just fine as fog, but once she let them go she had no control over where they landed. Their bag of food pellets was in the crook of a tree several feet off the ground, and a few of Leif's boomerangs were stuck into random trees around the clearing. Leif was circling the treeline and retrieving them, sticking them into their slots on his gear. Mara did a quick check over her body, feeling for all of the weapons that should be there. Nothing was missing.

"You people from around here?" a voice asked, cracking in the middle of the sentence. All three of them whirled around, hands on their weapons. The source of the voice was a middle-aged woman with sunken eyes and a drooping face. She looked and smelled as if she hadn't had a bath in a month, and her stringy brown hair told the same story. She smiled at them weakly, then pointed over her shoulder. "I came from that way," she said simply, as if that would clear up the whole issue of what she was doing there.

"Umm… okay," Mara said warily. Moving forward, staying light on her feet and never taking her hand away from her double sword, she approached the woman and held her other hand out as if wanting to shake hands. "Hello, it's a pleasure to meet you," she said, smiling. The woman seemed relieved that Mara had accepted her and she offered her hand. Quick as a panther Mara grabbed the hand and pulled it towards her as she drew out a hunting knife and sliced the upturned palm. Mara only had to glance at it to see the blood color that was welling up from the cut – murky brown.

"Gone!" Mara called out to Hazen and Leif. The woman snarled at her and kicked out at her stomach. Mara was faster. She looped her opposite leg around the woman's kicking leg, trapping it. Sweeping backwards she brought the Gone's legs out from under it and, using the grip she still had on its hand, threw it across the clearing to where Hazen stood at the ready. Hazen brought her foot down on the Gone's chest, making it convulse, but it grabbed onto her leg and used the momentum of the kick to bring itself upright. Hazen spun off the ground, disengaging the Gone from her leg, and came down.

From the other side of the clearing Leif came at it with a running start, pushing off with his front leg and bringing his back leg around lightning fast in a flying sweep kick. It connected with the Gone's head and snapped its neck to one side, throwing the entire body several feet away. He landed in a low fighting stance, knowing that even after all this the Gone would still be ready to fight. Rising from the ground it ran at them with demonic speed. Mara sidestepped and grabbed its outstretched punching arm, crouching down to get more power and flipping it over her head. It landed hard on its back but almost immediately brought its feet up to kick Mara in the gut. Mara instantly turned into fog and the Gone's feet passed right through her.

A blood-curdling yell echoed from above them. Mara snapped her head around and saw Hazen jumping down from a high branch with a sword aimed directly at the Gone's chest. Gone were very hard to kill, but if the demon soul that powered them could be destroyed then they really were gone. The sword plunged into the Gone's chest. Mara held its arm down to make sure it didn't move, but Hazen's aim had been true. The Gone had no light in its eyes, nothing to show the life leaving it but something changed about it. Shaking her hair out of her face Hazen pulled out the sword, now covered with muddy gray-brown Gone blood. Small trickles of brown blood were leaking out of the corners of its mouth. Mara stepped away from it quickly, careful not to get any of the fluid on her hands. It wasn't poisonous or anything; Mara just didn't like the feel of it. It was somehow different from all the other types of blood.

"What was with that battle cry, anyway?" she asked Hazen. She was smiling despite the grotesque sight before them.

"I don't know. I guess I was just angry because of everything that's been happening. But, I know, it was weird," she said.

Mara nodded. "No kidding," she added. She turned to Leif to give him a quick once over for injuries, and then to pick several pine needles out of his hair, explaining, "If we're going to live out here we're not going to turn into savages."

"Savages are defined by the number of pine needles in their hair?" Leif teased her. Mara just rolled her eyes sarcastically.

"I should do some scanning," she said. "Gone travel in herds. There's probably a nest of them somewhere around here." She started to turn into fog but Leif grabbed her arm before she could complete the transformation. Condensing again she said, "Or not?"

Leif shook his head and explained. "I looked inside its mind right before it died. It's alone." Mara tilted her head to the side, her way of saying that she has something to say but she isn't because she's worried it might sound superior. Leif gestured. "Go ahead."

"You once told me you can't look into Gone's minds. You said it was just a mass of whirling blackness and shapes, like a storm," she said.

Leif nodded to confirm the truth of this statement, then said, "It's true, I've tried to look into their minds before and saw nothing, but it's like this one was different. Like it was only half demon. It had coherent thoughts. I've never seen anything like it."

Mara and Hazen exchanged glances. "We all saw the blood color, Leif," Hazen said. "It was Gone."

He nodded. "I know. Maybe there are just different stages of Gone. Something the history textbooks don't talk about." Mara knew there was truth in his statement. The Academy was the best school in Atherian but tended to leave out the blurry or the not so pretty elements of their history. She had found at least ten instances where the book didn't tell the whole story, and she knew there were more.

"Yeah, it happens more than we like to admit," she said, casting her eyes down for a second. "It's possible."

"It doesn't matter whether it was alone or not," Hazen said. "We should get out of here, find somewhere far away to set up camp."

Mara sighed. It had taken her so long to find this clearing. "How 'bout I take us out of the forest and we set up camp where no Gone can be?" she asked, looking at both of them for the stamp of approval. "We can go to the nearest underground shelter facility. They have wards up that should prevent against any Gone entering."

"They're tiny," Hazen said. "The wards can only cover a very small area."

Mara shrugged. "So? We're only three people and a few belongings. We'll fit just fine."

"Let's go," Leif said, reaching out for Mara's hand. "Leave the lean-to, we don't really need it anymore." Mara nodded and took Hazen's hand, too. Vaporizing, they took off, careful to stay under the treetops. They headed towards the shelters that were built in case the Gone ever won the war and took over the planet, just as they had so many years ago on CSO-97, the oldest of the CSO chain and now a dead, desolate planet.

Dropping onto the hard, concrete floor of the warded shelter Mara and Leif set about collecting the things strewn across the tiny area. The wards were created generations ago by Quirks working with WW, but they weren't very advanced. Able to keep out any demon-souled creatures, they covered only about a six by six by five foot space. Once the roof was closed over the shelter everyone had to bend down and drop the weapons they couldn't sleep with in piles on the floor. Only knives and Mara's double swords could remain on their bodies – most weapons stuck out in ways that could impale a restless sleeper.

A high-pitched beeping came from a small device in Mara's pocket. She pulled it out and looked at the glowing screen. WW didn't have phones but they did have Devices which were basically the way that WW communicated with each other over long distances.

"Kat just sent a voice memo," Mara said, clearly confused. "But we agreed to use these only in emergencies." Worry and fear laced her tone. She pressed the play button and Kat's voice floated out of the device, airy and light despite the words she was saying.

"Oh, my God!" Mara said, pure horror on her face. "Kat."

CHAPTER 15

*T*rees flashed by as Kat ran through the forest, Niko on her tail. Her soft orange and black fur was ruffled by the wind, and the many sharp things on the forest floor poked her footpads but she didn't care. Out of the corner of her eye she saw a streak of something flit past her on a nearby tree branch. It was Venus, traveling through the trees to avoid the dangers of the forest floor. Kat didn't know where Mara was; the clearing she had seen on the security feed was totally unremarkable but she knew that Mara would have traveled as fog which meant she had to be in a general area about fifteen miles from where Kat was now. Mara could only hold the fog form for five minutes max, and she wouldn't have exhausted herself just traveling. She probably traveled for close to two minutes at the speed of sound, the time limit for which she could remain as fog but not tire herself out, which would have taken her out about... Kat did a few mental calculations and came up with 25.576 miles in two minutes. She was now at least five miles, probably more, into the forest. *This is plenty close* *enough,*she thought, and stopped running. Morphing back into human form Niko skidded to a stop next to her, sending up a flurry of leaves as he abruptly stopped super-speeding. Kat made a scary hissing sound and Venus came down from the trees and wrapped around her arm. The shiny red snake had always fascinated Niko even though she had squirted him many times with her burning venom. On vampire skin all it did was itch and form a small rash, but despite this Niko still liked her. Kat rubbed the snake's head as Venus slit her eyes in pleasure.

"Niko, I need you to leave," Kat said suddenly. "Go home, protect my parents, tell Tom what's happening. You just can't stay here."

Niko responded immediately. "No way am I leaving you alone in a forest of demons." His voice was deep with warning and fear. "I'm barely okay with letting you come in here with me!" He shook his head, planting his feet defiantly. Kat shook her head right back at him and insisted.

"If you don't leave now I'm just going to find another way to get rid of you," she said, apologetic but also firm and decisive. Niko still shook his head. *Nothing is making me leave her alone.*

She whispered down to Venus. "Go." The snake flashed off Kat's arm in the blink of an eye and wrapped tightly around Niko in the same second. Using her tail she drew him against a tree, stretching her magically-elongated body to wrap several times around both Niko and the tree. With her small, determined yellow eyes she looked at Kat for approval. Kat nodded and said, "Good girl!" in a low voice. Niko struggled against his bonds but Venus held strong, hissing loudly at him and fanning out her hood, a darker scarlet color that

146

contrasted nicely with her bright red body. Niko looked desperately at Kat.

"Don't do this," he pleaded. Kat shook her head apologetically and looked down at the ground, unable to meet his eyes.

"I'm sorry," she whispered, gazing at him one last time with sadness and determination in her sparkling grass-green eyes before transforming back into a tiger and taking off, heading west.

Kat had been traveling for a while now, wanting to put a fair amount of distance between her and Niko. She had hated leaving him like that, but she knew he would just try to stop her. The best thing for him was to be away from the action, from the danger. Besides, she knew if he was in any real danger that Venus would unwrap and let him defend himself. Stopping for a moment Kat twisted her head around to lick a spot on her back where a bit of sap had fallen. Even though trivial stuff like this wouldn't transfer back to her human form she still cared about how she looked both as a person and a tiger. Rubbing her rough tongue across the horribly sticky drop of sap she slowly dissolved it. Satisfied with her hygiene she stood up, human again, and readied herself for what she knew was coming. She had sent Mara a voice memo that told what was happening and urged her to stay away. She hoped Mara would heed the warning but she honestly didn't know what would be going through her sister's mind. She clenched her hands, summoning the deep anger that lived inside her, built up from all the times unfair or unjust things had been done to her or whenever someone had dismissed her skills because she was just a pretty girl. She opened her mouth and let the words pour out.

"Professor Erros!" she shouted at the top of her lungs. "I know you can hear me. I know what you're doing. I'm offering a trade. Take me and stop looking for my sister and Hazen and Leif." She paused for a second to regain her breath before continuing. She didn't know how, but she could feel his eyes on her. "Meet me at the huge birch tree at the south end of the forest in ten minutes. If you can prove to me the search is off I won't fight." She finished her proclamation. Even though she was far away from Niko she knew he probably heard what she said and would be fighting even stronger now. Banishing the thought she dropped to all fours and began to run, feeling the wind blow past her, trying to lose her problems and worries by simply running. It didn't work, of course, but still she headed south for the birch tree, having already calculated that she was fast enough to reach it in just under ten minutes.

She was sure thorns had punctured her paws and that several more drops of sap had fallen on her coat, but her legs kept pumping away, the muscles burning from the prolonged running and her lack of sleep and nourishment. Ever since she found out her teacher was an evil supervillain with plans to exterminate all WW and replace them with teenagers-turned-demons she hadn't had time for such trivial things as eating. She could see the birch tree now, the stark white bark standing out against the mass of gray-brown trees that surrounded it. Stopping, she turned back into a girl with light brown hair swept up into a high ponytail with small braids adorning it. Walking slowly towards the tree she swung her head around, searching for somewhere to hide. Her eyes landed on a large fallen tree, fungus and ivy growing over so much of it that you could hardly distinguish it from the general greenery. It must have been at least ten feet in diameter, and it was extremely long. Kat assumed a hunched down position behind it, glancing at the small implant in her arm that served as a watch and a television screen. Touching it lightly caused a seemingly normal section of her arm to light up, displaying the time in glowing white numbers. 9:11.01, the watch read. *AM*! She stared at it for a second, not believing her eyes. She had been sure it was at least afternoon, if not evening. Shaking her head, she attempted to think clearly. *9:11,* she thought. She was pretty sure that she had left at 9:02, but "pretty sure" meant only about fifty-five percent. Lifting her gaze she scanned the area around the birch tree again. Still nothing.

"Well, Katalina, I have to say your acting has improved *greatly*," a deep, male voice rumbled from her left. Jumping to her feet Kat dropped into a fighting stance, claws and fangs popping out. She hissed at him, baring her teeth and exposing her fangs fully. With one hand she reached out, threatening to fill the ground underneath him with her deadly pressure. Erros held up his hands and took several steps forward, carrying with him that arrogant confidence that Kat used to think was so appealing but now just seemed like another reason to hate him.

"You think you're the best at *everything*, that it's going to be *easy* for you to win this, but in truth you're just an insecure little boy who wants attention and power," she shot at him, not lowering her hand.

He smiled indulgently at her. "You know, I really did believe that you were innocent, Kat," he said. "You had me fooled. And now you're giving up everything to save your brat of a sister."

Kat snarled at him. "*Don't* call me Kat. And don't call Mara a brat!"

"Now, now, Katalina, you said you wouldn't put up a fight," he reminded her using a chiding tone as if she were six and shaking his finger at her.

"And you said you cared about every one of your students, but that hasn't really worked out either, now has it?" she taunted. "You know, 'cause you just *happen* to be turning them into *demons*."

This got under Erros's skin. His expression changed from playful to dark anger, the maniacal side that Kat had seen only once before. "I *will* ensure the survival of our kind. The Witch Warriors now are weak underprepared beings that will stand no chance against the growing population of Gone. Once my demons have wiped the Witch Warriors from existence they will start a new and better race that will destroy Gone *forever*!" His voice had risen to a mad chant. *He really is crazy*, she thought, feeling for a second just a spark of pity for this ruin of a man that stood before her.

"*You're* a Witch Warrior," she said. "Didn't really think *that* one through, did you?" She was purposefully trying to get him angry; even if the power of anger made someone more dangerous it also degraded their common sense and quick thinking. His years of experience would evaporate in the face of his pure rage, and he'd fight like a beginner. "How do you know your demons won't be able to resist the pull of your Witch Warrior blood?" He looked uncertain for a split second. *It's working*, Kat thought. *He would have thought of this; he has an answer, but his brain isn't pulling it up because he's so angry.* A second later Kat was proved right. Erros's expression cleared up and he answered easily.

"I control them, of course. I *created* them," he said, doing his best to keep the expression of confidence on his face but failing, letting some doubt creep into his eyes.

Suddenly it hit her. She knew how to take him down, using only words. "You've never been challenged before," Kat whispered, softly enough that he didn't even realize she'd spoken. Kat quickly transferred her line of thought inside her head.

He's so used to getting his way, either through his specialty or his reputation, that he has no idea how to deal with someone who knows he's evil and who isn't coming over to his side. Kat smiled dangerously, a small movement but one that conveyed a lot. Erros was going down.

"So, while you're *failing* at your job and betraying anyone who ever loved you, you don't think there might be some reason to stop pursuing Mara?" she asked, adding verbal jabs whenever she could. If there was one thing she'd learned about unstable maniacs it was that even if they had the upper hand they were easily manipulated. She walked closer to Erros, confidently adding a swagger to her step and never dropping her attacking hand.

His face was turning red, his eyes near black with rage and his eyebrows lowering.

"Wow, I never thought that after all the makeup you use to look good, your face could still turn that red," Kat laughed, taking the opportunity to show off her fangs again.

Erros looked alarmingly similar to a dangerous explosive from World War VI, but honestly, Kat didn't really care. If he was going to explode, this was a very good time and place for that to happen.

"Your sister and her *companions* are the most powerful students in the school. I *will* have them, and once I do I will be unstoppable," he said, his voice losing volume but becoming more deadly. He narrowed his eyes as he spoke, and Kat was surprised to notice he was wearing guyliner. *Eugh. Gross. Now* that, *that is overkill.* Blowing off this annoying detail, she shifted on her feet, ready to spring forward or back at a moment's notice.

"I'm just as powerful as they are, but I notice you aren't snatching me up, even after I offered myself to you as a trade," she said, this time genuinely confused.

Erros shook his head slightly, as if having to explain something to an ignorant child. "I really do care about you, Kat, and I wasn't going to drag you into this whole thing. I had plans to save you from the destruction of your kind, but if you don't want salvation…" he trailed off, raising his hands to signify that he tried. Kat scoffed.

"You *care* about me? *Please.* You care about your hair dye more than me," she said, snorting. He drew his head back sharply, surprised at the harshness of her remark.

"I know you may not see it now, but what I'm doing will save this planet. When I'm through I'll be worshipped as a hero. And you could be at my side!" He seemed excited by the idea, a demented smile forming on his face. Suddenly he didn't seem as handsome and perfect as Kat had remembered him. Something about him was dead. Kat guessed it was his soul.

"If you go through with this there will be no one left to worship you," she said.

He looked completely unconcerned by this. "Oh, but see, my demons aren't just mindless killing machines. Because of my genius, they have retained every aspect that they had when they were Witch Warrior students. Magic, fighting skills, memories. *Everything*," he explained, looking very pleased with himself.

"Well, if they retain their memories, won't they remember *me*? It'll be pretty hard to kill the person who taught you most of what you know." Kat asked, poking as many holes as possible in his grand scheme.

He shook his head. "No, no, silly Kat. I would never let something as petty as that get in my way. As I said, I control them. They may remember, but they won't have free will," he said.

"You're vile!" she said, letting all her anger and hate pour into her voice. His head snapped around to stare at her, a deranged look entering his eyes. There was something else there, something you wouldn't expect to see in the eyes of a homicidal maniac. Pain. Pain and loss and disbelief. "You really thought I'd join you?" Kat persisted, sensing she had the advantage. "I would dig my own grave and bury myself alive before I *ever* sided with you." The small amount of sanity left in him disappeared as soon as the words left her mouth. He snarled and grabbed her arm.

"That's it. I accept your deal. I will call off my search of Mara, Hazen, and the boy if you agree to come with me willingly and without a fight," he said, trying to pull her away from the birch tree and off to wherever he would force feed her the demon pill. Kat dug her heels in, pulling back against Erros.

"First, you have to give me proof that your search parties are disabled," she reminded him, her tone hard as rock. He sighed, annoyed, but pushed a button on his wrist implant. It beeped twice.

"There," he said, turning the screen to her and showing her the wording authorizing the search parties to return along with a live feed that showed the weird, smoky black demon creatures all flooding in one direction. "They're all coming back to our base camp. Happy?" he asked.

Kat scoffed. "Far from it," she answered dryly. "But fine. Take me to this *base camp* of yours."

CHAPTER 16

R ecently extinguished fires peppered the large clearing. Some fires were still burning, giving off light and heat and sending pungent smoke up into the trees. Small stumps were everywhere, a clear sign that the area had been clear-cut by Erros and his minions for the construction of their 'base camp'.

"You're not really trying to hide, are you?" Kat half-asked, half-observed. "You know, sending up smoke signals is a way to *draw* things here, not repel them." He looked at her with those eyes, the same ones that used to melt the hearts of hundreds every day but which now seemed dark, maniacal,… dead. The outer charm and charisma that Erros once had was gone, as if all the shiny paint had been stripped off a piece of furniture, leaving plain wood with knots and splinters and cracks down the middle. Kat couldn't see the man she used to be so enamored with. He just wasn't there anymore.

"Let them come. My demons will kill them all. No one, not one measly little Witch Warrior can stop me now," he smiled. Of all the things about him that had deteriorated, his smile was the one thing left unchanged. It was still irresistibly handsome, the kind of bad-boy lopsided grin that every girl found appealing.

Kat felt something in her hair. Her hands were securely tied behind her back but she ducked away, running backwards several steps. Immediately three demon guards were all around her, arms circling but not quite touching her. She could feel a strange aura of heat radiating off of them. She looked back to see Erros with his hand raised, staring at her forlornly.

"You always had such pretty hair," he commented as if they were on a talk show and someone had asked him what he thought of her physical appearance. He got a distant look in his eyes, as if he was remembering the good ol' times. Kat had a hunch about what he might be remembering but she wasn't about to ask.

"Get away from me, you filthy scum-suckers!" Kat hissed, glaring at one of the demons. She thought it visibly recoiled. Erros waved his hand dismissively, muttering something to them in a strange, garbled tongue that Kat instantly recognized. *Yyuligian*, she thought. *The ancient language of the Witch Warriors derived from Arabic roots, almost never used nowadays.* She carefully kept her face totally blank so as not to give away her only advantage. Though she doubted it would work, both she and Mara had taught themselves Yyuligian outside of school and were fluent. If it was what Erros used to communicate with the demons then she had a chance to try and control them herself.

"Interesting that you would call them scum-suckers," Erros observed, strolling around the large camp lazily but always keeping his eyes on her, checking for a reaction. "They are, of course, your classmates. Your friends." It was meant to be a jab, a reminder of what he had taken from her, but Kat kept her face impassive while internally filing this latest offense into her folder titled "Reasons I Will Destroy Professor Erros." The folder was getting *really* thick.

"Those aren't my classmates. My classmates are dead, killed by you," she said, not letting her voice rise but putting as much venom as possible into it. Erros was unperturbed.

"If I turned your beloved sister or her annoying Glukon friend into one of my demons, I wonder if you'd be saying the same thing," he said, not really asking but acting like they were participating in a philosophical discussion. Kat made a face at him and slid her fangs out. Erros raised his hand and several demons came rushing in, surrounding Kat. She would have loved to kill them all but she could count and the odds weren't in her favor. Letting her fangs retract she calmed herself.

"I don't want to hurt you, Katalina, but you make it so hard," he said, wincing at his own words. Sucking on his teeth he shook his head. "I'll let that one pass, but don't try anything else. You're mine now, Katalina."

He muttered something else in Yyuligian and this time Kat caught the words. Now she knew what to say to call the demons off. Even if they wouldn't listen to her, at least it was something. She scanned her surroundings for anything she could possibly use. There had been simulators back at the Academy that would create a dangerous situation that you had to deal with by using only the things around you. Kat loved those simulators. Then she remembered that Erros had been the one who ran them and that memory was forever blackened.

The next moment she was startled by something she saw across the clearing; some*one*, actually. It was a girl putting out a fire, watching as the smoke trails drifted up and disappeared. Kat was reminded of Mara and Mara's fog. A great sadness and regret flowed through her, regret that she'd never done things with Mara that she wished she had done. Shaking the feeling off, Kat focused again on the girl she had seen. *Girl*. Not black smoky thing, *girl*. Kat knew her. Her name was Ashley. She was a small girl with straight black hair, upturned brown eyes, and caramel skin in Kat's class back at the Academy.

"Ashley?" Kat murmured. The girl's head snapped up. Kat gasped. It was Ashley, but not Ashley. She looked completely normal except for her eyes. They were total, liquid black. No pupils, no irises, no whites. Just an endless black void, a soulless, deadened color that was remarkably similar to what Lucifer, the King of Hell and ruler of all demons, looked like in the ancient illustrations that were in all the records WW had of him. Upon closer inspection the thing began to look less and less like Ashley. It had dark circles under its eyes and its makeup was really weird; it looked as if it had been applied by a blind Sunday School teacher. Kat cringed, but not about the makeup. Ashley's expression was blank, a stone mask of nothingness.

From a few feet away Erros laughed. "She can't respond. None of them can talk," he explained, sweeping his hand out to indicate all the smoky black forms that were now condensing into people that Kat recognized.

"But… how…" Kat trailed off, waiting for an answer. A smart person would never have told her such a thing, and the words that Erros said next proved what Kat had been thinking the whole time.

"See, they might be demons but, as I told you, they retained everything from their former lives through the transfer, even their physical appearance. The only thing I couldn't figure out was how to fix their eyes. Maddening." He spoke in a very superior tone, schooling Kat on what she didn't yet know, just like always. "If I weren't controlling them they'd probably be able to respond, but I would never let them do that."

Kat pretended to look interested but inside she was laughing. *He is* so *dumb.* A group of 'students' were gathering at one end of the clearing. Huddled together, kind of like players do in that strange game, football, they spoke in soft voices. A Human wouldn't have been able to hear them, but Kat was a Witch Warrior and with that came enhanced senses. She kicked in her super-hearing and listened closely. Yyuligian sounded somewhat close to Arabic and was written with very similar characters, but consisted of a flowing set of sounds combined in different ways on different pitches to make words and phrases. The same sound said in a low pitch could mean something entirely different when said in a medium or high pitch.

Listening to what they were whispering Kat translated in her head to the current, much simpler language. "Boss said to move out after he brought the girl. Let's go. Can't waste any more time not looking for the girls and the boy," one of the boys, a short compact person and seemingly the leader, said in a disturbingly low, deadened monotone. They all nodded their head in creepy unison and began to walk out of the clearing in unison. *Yep. They are definitely being controlled.* Kat pulled her gaze away from them, focusing on something else, anything else. Erros turned around to look at her, a guilty expression on his face, making sure she hadn't seen anything. Kat kept her head turned away from him and the departing demons, clenching her jaw as she did so. *How dare he?!* she thought. This too went in her "Reasons I Will Destroy Professor Erros" folder. She heard his footsteps coming up behind her, crunching on the pine needles and dead leaves that covered the ground. Turning to face him with an expression of cool questioning she wanted to make it abundantly clear that she didn't want to be here but that she also wasn't going to put up a fight. With people as deranged as Erros sometimes the tiniest thing could set them off. Kat wasn't about to lose her upper hand and send Erros off into a destructive rage. Erros gazed into her eyes for a few more seconds, blocking her view of the departing search team. Convinced that she had seen nothing he moved aside and walked over to one of the few demons who had remained in their smoke form.

"Shy?" he whispered to it in Yyuligian, taking on the expression and tone of a caring, worried father. "You are deadly, you are not afraid of anything." When he spoke his voice had changed; it deepened and took on a tantalizing tone. Yyuligian was a naturally beautiful language with just a hint of danger, so when he used persuasion on the demon the language ascended to a whole new level of beauty and captivity. The demon, of course, wouldn't have mental barriers up. That would allow Erros to bend the demon's will to his. The black smoke shape moved a bit, as if nodding its head, and its glowing red-white eyes lit up a little brighter.

Kat shook her head, very confused. Until now she had thought that Erros had put something in the pill, some kind of neurotransmitter that allowed him to directly control their brains with his, but now she saw that she was wrong. He was using his specialty individually on every one of them, keeping them all under his control. It didn't make sense. *Using his specialty on that many things at the same time should be completely sapping him of energy. Depending on how many demons he actually has, he should be either passed out or dead by now.* Kat thought hard, running through a list of possibilities, slowly discarding one after the other as each one made less sense than the last. *How is he using so much magic without it affecting him?* She had never seen anything like this continued use of magic on so many minds. She was confident that he had at least forty demons, if not more, under his control. That was unprecedented. There had been plenty of promising students sixteen or older at the Academy, and she was sure that Erros wouldn't have missed a single opportunity. He was now strolling around camp, absentmindedly raising his hands every so often to move something using magic. Kat sat down on the hard ground, dried out from months without precipitation. In a black hole there is no natural rain, so scientists had sent devices into orbit that would periodically spray parts of the planet with synthetic rain so it wouldn't use up the planet's water resources. The rain device that serviced the section of ground that the Academy was on had been damaged. The Council had people up there fixing it, but it had been months since the last shower and plants were starting to die. Kat desperately wanted to find a blanket to sit on, but she knew that even if she *was* the last thing Erros cared about he wouldn't get her a blanket. He probably didn't *have* a blanket. *Those demons produce enough heat, they probably just surround him while he's sleeping and keep him warm*, Kat thought. A sharp thing poked her thigh and she lifted her leg, twisting around awkwardly to try and push it out of the way. Failing at that she simply scooted over several feet and rested her legs there.

Kat tried to look nonchalant while pulling at something that was stuck in the waistband of her pants. She honestly couldn't believe that Erros had forgot to check her for it, but he was older than she was, if only by a few years. Her Device, a small thin piece of technology with a glowing screen that lit up when you touched it, was her main way of communicating with people far away. She had been using one since she was just a little girl, and she could easily type a message without looking at her hands. Shaking it slightly and pressing her thumb to the screen she unlocked it, and then pressed where she knew the message button was. Scrolling down exactly three swipes she found Mara's name at the top of the screen and pressed it. Typing quickly, with the speed and accuracy of a true virtuoso, she slammed out a hastily worded message that basically said "Hey, Erros is coming after you with a bunch of demons that look just like our classmates. Hide really well." She pressed the send button near the bottom of the Device and heard the soft whoosh sound that signaled that it had been successfully transferred to Mara's Device. Slowly slipping it back in her waistband she pulled her gear shirt down and tucked it in well. If Erros ever found out what she had done he would explode, and Kat did *not* want to see what was inside of him, figuratively or literally. She settled herself back down into the needles. Right now, warning Mara with a message was about all that she could do without escaping from Erros, and she was saving that for later. For now she contented herself with looking all the way around her and memorizing every detail in the camp if she ever had to fight in it which, considering her situation, was likely. Knowing where a tree was or wasn't was sometimes the determining factor between life and death, or at least life and serious injury.

Several demons in their student forms were entering the clearing about five feet away from Kat. She looked straight at them, daring them to stare back at her, but they continued to face forward and their eyes remained blank. Somehow, and Kat still didn't have the answer for this, Erros was completely controlling all of them. The group of demons made their way over to Erros, who smiled broadly and turned as if expecting them. He reached out toward the demons with both hands. They grabbed onto him, one on each of his hands and the rest spaced evenly along his arms. A strange, orange-red light began glowing at each point of contact between Erros and the demons. From each point the light began to split off into tiny tendrils that laced their way along his arms and up his neck to his head. Erros tilted his head back, his smile growing larger. The orange-red light disappeared once it reached his chin, but instead of just popping out of existence it seemed to fade into him as if it was being absorbed. *Absorbed!* Kat suddenly had the answer. She was certain that Erros didn't want her to see this but she had, and now she knew. *He's getting the extra energy from the demons. It's like a power circle, neither element starting until the other one has already begun. When Erros controls the demons he must give them enough energy for them to become very powerful, sapping himself in the process, and when they are done at the end of the day they give him back the energy that they've collected throughout the day. He then takes that energy and rebuilds his specialty so that he can keep controlling them and giving them back the energy that makes them more powerful.*

So his only weaknesses are the times of transfer, when he has the energy and not the demons, or if all the demons are killed. He must have become dependent on their power by now, so if Mara can take his source away he'll be weakened enough that we could easily defeat him. Power circles were very complicated and almost none existed in the world; Kat had to think through the whole thing several times and fact-check it to make sure her assumption was right. She glanced up just in time to see that the light pulsing through Erros had diminished. The demons were withdrawing their hands from him, moving robotically as always. Erros had dropped his head back down. She quickly checked the implant on her wrist. She had done this at the beginning of the ritual, too, purely by chance. 7:17 the implant read. *Three minutes,* she thought. *We would have three minutes to take the demons out while they're giving their energy to Erros.* Kat immediately looked away and pretended to be interested in examining a mark on a tree.

"Looking for ways to escape?" Erros's voice said from high above her. Like most WW Erros was tall and well-muscled, nearly as tall as Leif. "Don't worry your pretty little head about it. There aren't any." He reassured her as if she were a small, worried child.

Kat kept a blank expression and raged inside. "*No one* calls me a pretty little head and lives to tell the tale," she whispered, speaking down at the ground so Erros wouldn't hear. Tilting her head back up she snapped in a normal voice. "I know. If there was one I would have been gone hours ago." Erros recoiled.

"Katalina, I truly care for you," he said, crouching down so he could stare into her eyes. Determined not to act like a petulant child Kat held his gaze. "After everyone else has become my soldiers and the world has fallen before me I will need someone to stand by my side and always be there, still a Witch Warrior but one of the most powerful."

Kat couldn't help herself. She dropped her uninterested expression and sneered at him. "So you want a pretty face for the camera? I honestly don't think I'm up to the task." She promptly turned her head away from him, looking in the opposite direction. She felt a hand on her shoulder. *Ugh! Doesn't he know that girls don't like overly persistent guys?* Kat turned exasperatedly. Glancing down at his hand on her shoulder she twisted around to bite it. Knowing how much damage a bite of hers could do Erros quickly withdrew his hand, sliding it awkwardly back down to his side.

"You are the most beautiful girl I have ever laid eyes on. I'm sure you'd be perfect for the job, and I have *no* interest in turning you into a demon," Erros said, looking rather desperate as he spoke soothingly. "Why would I turn the last person who cares about me and who I care about into something that is pure evil?" He asked this question as if it were a normal thing that someone would say around the dinner table after work. Kat looked at him, this time not with pure anger but with a mix of hate, disbelief, and pity.

"You have created a fantasy world that revolves around you, and you have rested all your hopes on it. But it's *fantasy*. It won't happen; that's just not how life works," Kat explained to him, still in a hard voice but this time heavily laced with pity. "I don't care about you," she added. Erros growled slightly.

"I know that's a lie. And I think you know it too," he said, looking straight into her eyes, daring her to deny it.

Kat snapped. "You know that meant nothing. That happened before I found out you were planning to kill everyone I love," she said. This time it was her voice that was darkening.

"My plan is perfect. I am so powerful now that no one can take me down. Not even you and your sister and all your worthless little friends combined," he said in a low, inhuman voice, coming threateningly close to her face, "and when they try and stop me I will wipe them from the face of this planet." Evaluating her options for a split second Kat decided that it was best to back down now and then drop a mountain on him once she was free and back with Mara, Hazen, and Leif. Leaning back from him she smiled, not even bothering to try to hide the fact that it was forced.

"Of course, of course. I'll have to think about your offer. It may take a while," she said in the most pleasant tone she could muster, which under the current circumstances wasn't very pleasant. Erros's eyes returned to their normal chocolate brown as the dark light diminished, and he grunted. He stood up and strode quickly away from Kat without glancing back at her. *Disgruntled*, Kat thought. *He told me I'm the last thing he cares about, and he knows I can use it against him.* Even though the first part of her reasoning made sense, Erros's reaction hadn't. Why would he just keep her around to see if she chose his side. If she didn't she'd be unbelievably dangerous, knowing all or most of his secrets. *He must be so deranged that he thinks I'll actually chose him over my own family just because he's the handsome golden-boy.* Kat shook her head slightly. Any sympathy that she might once have felt for Erros had evaporated when he stated that he would obliterate Mara, Hazen, and Leif. Any threat to her family and friends was a threat to her.

"The last thing you see in this world will be my eyes, and *not* like in romantic movies," Kat promised herself. This promise was all that kept her going as she waited for news of either Mara's capture or her escape.

CHAPTER 17

*K*at's message had disturbed them all, but Leif had been the only one clear-headed enough to realize that they should just trace the signal of her Device back to its location instead of searching the whole forest until they found her. Hazen, the resident computer genius, set to work backtracking the signal through her Device.

"She tried to save us because she *knew* that Erros cared about her, and now she's trapped. This is *all* my fault," Mara said, looking completely miserable. Grabbing weapons off the floor of the shelter she started sticking them back in her gear. Leif did the same. She sat down on the cold, hard concrete, and waited while Hazen was sitting in the opposite corner, hands flying around her Device, transferring coding and the message from Mara's to hers.

"Got her," she said, holding up her Device to show a glowing red dot in the middle of the blackness that represented the forest. "That's where the message came from, at least. I can't tell if she's still there."

Mara shook her head. "I don't care if she's still there or not, if we can find traces of her we can track her. Good work, Hazen," she said, nodding to her best friend and giving her a small smile. She lifted off the trapdoor-like roof of the shelter and stuck her head out. Finally able to stand up straight for the first time in days she stretched her arms backwards and all the vertebrae in her back popped at once, relieving the pain from having been so cramped. She did a quick scan of the area but didn't focus too hard. There wasn't time for stuff like that. Pushing off with her hands and jumping up and out of the shelter, Mara landed on her feet in a crouch. Straightening up she began shaking her head in an attempt to loosen the leaves that had gotten stuck in the razor blades that lined the sides of her long high braid. Whenever she prepared for a *big* battle (defined as fighting forty or more Gone) she embedded small razor blades along each side of her braid. She had killed before just using her hair, turning around suddenly and whipping it behind her. Since all the gear shirts had high collars made of nearly indestructible material her neck never got hurt by the razors. She heard a soft thump behind her. Hazen had jumped out, too, and Leif's hands were on the edge of the shelter. He raised himself up a second later and picked up the shelter's roof and set it back down, perfectly covering the hole in the ground. The three of them set off towards the forest, knowing that if they traveled using magic Erros would most likely spot them. The Academy had lots of technology that could be used to scan the area and detect any WW who were using magic. Erros surely would have stolen some and would be scanning the area at that very moment. Walking was a pain, but at least enhanced speed didn't count as magic and wouldn't be picked up by the scanners. Entering the treeline they moved through the forest quickly, their enhanced speed letting them almost glide across the forest floor, bypassing obstacles easily.

"How close are we?" Mara asked, looking over at Hazen who glanced down at her Device and pointed off to the right.

"We need to turn that way," she said, pointing her feet in that direction and taking off, followed closely by Mara and Leif. What seemed like years but was really only about fifteen minutes later Hazen signaled for them to stop. "It should be about twenty feet in front of us and a little to the left," she said, gesturing in its general direction. "He's so arrogant that he probably doesn't even have guards, but in case he does someone needs to stay back here as emergency backup." She looked at Mara. "I'm assuming you're going in?" Mara nodded grimly.

"That vain little imp is going to pay if he hurt Kat," she growled. There was light coming from the clearing in front of them, but it was flickering and wavering. "Fire," Mara said.

"I can stay behind," Hazen volunteered. "I'm the tech person so if anything goes wrong I can block the signal from all his computers and whatever else he has in there. He'll be in the dark, not able to monitor anything or communicate with anyone." Mara nodded.

"Fine, but keep your weapons at the ready. This part of the forest is crawling with demons, and Kat said they look just like our classmates," she warned Hazen. "Leif, come on. Time to kick some demon butt." She held her arm up and flicked her fingers forward twice then started moving. She circled the clearing so she would be opposite Hazen in case they had to make a full on attack. Pulling back some of the thick foliage that hung off the trees like Spanish moss, Mara stared into a surprisingly large clear space. No natural clearing in a forest this thick would be this big, and Mara's suspicions were confirmed when she saw what appeared to be hundreds of stumps. A large campfire in the middle of the clearing burned bright and crackled loudly, casting light and warmth into the cold night air. Around it were the seated forms of many people, all working on something that Mara couldn't make out in the darkness. *Not people*, Mara reminded herself. *Demons.*

"Can you hold this back?" Mara whispered to Leif, pointing to the many leaves that blocked her view. His tanned hand reached around her face and grabbed the leaves, pulling them off to the side. Mara spotted a slightly larger form in the circle around the fire.

"That's him," Leif whispered in her ear. "He's not giving off as much of an evil aura as the rest of them." Mara nodded slightly. She couldn't see Kat anywhere, but it was the middle of the night and the only source of light was the fire. Kat could be in any of the shadows that ringed the area.

"Ok, get ready," Mara whispered. Holding the leaves back with one hand Leif pulled a boomerang out of his gear with the other. "The second I make my move they'll know we're here. We have only one chance to plow through them, find Kat, and send a signal to Hazen to interrupt his tech." Even though she couldn't see him Mara felt Leif nod behind her. *Please don't die*, she thought, before reaching both her hands out and pulling at the air. She could control fog in every way, which meant she could also condense it into water. Pulling all the water particles from the air around her she formed a very large ball of fog. Pressing her hands in on it made it slowly shrink and condense into a swirling sphere of clear water. A whole lot of fog made only a little water, but it was enough. Pulling her hands and the water back as if aiming a slingshot she pushed her hands out in front of her and sent the sphere of water flying straight towards the large fire. It splashed into it, putting the fire out completely and plunging the clearing into a dusky darkness illuminated only by the weakly glowing strips of black hole particulate strewn across the sky. The demons and Erros all looked up from their tasks with matching expressions of shock on their faces. Literally *matching*. Mara looked over at Erros and saw that he wasn't looking at her but at the demons. Leif had already slipped into the clearing and was sneaking around the campfire away from Mara, his shiny silver boomerang out and ready.

"Get her," Erros said, now looking straight at Mara with a deranged look of triumph. Several demons were already on their feet, moving quickly towards Mara. She turned into fog and shot around the circle, landing as a human behind a seated demon. Double sword already in hand she put her free hand on his cheek and pulled away while slitting his throat with her sword. He fell to the side, dead as a doornail. Mara felt a hot hand close around her ankle, trying to pull her down. She swung her sword and felt the hand detach from its arm. An inhuman scream of pain came from behind her. Four or five demons were now facing her, and for the first time Mara noticed their eyes. Pure black. That must have been what Kat meant when she said they looked like our classmates but not. She saw Leif fighting several more demons behind Erros. He was throwing boomerangs behind them and waiting the split second before they returned and stuck into the demons' backs, probably

severing their spines. Knives flashed and Leif parried all
the thrusts, occasionally just kicking a knife out of the
way. Mara ducked and dodged, bobbed and weaved,
avoiding the blows of the infuriated demons. They came
at her with small, flimsy knives that she knocked out of
their hands with her sword. She pressed the other
button at the bottom of the handle with her pinky and
another sword shot out the hilt. Now with double-edged
sharp blades on both ends of her weapon she had to be
more careful, but she was quite practiced at using it with
both blades out. Twirling it above her head she sliced
and chopped at the incoming demons, cutting them in
half or dismembering them. Stepping to the side to
avoid the blow of one particularly strong demon she
drove her sword deep into his side. He choked, black
blood dripping out of his mouth. Legend had always
said that the demonic color of blood was black, but Mara
had never seen it before with her own eyes. She felt a
sting on the back of her arm and turned to see a small,
timid looking girl behind her with the universal black
eyes of a demon holding a knife to her upper arm. It had
cut the skin but it wasn't deep. Feeling only mild pity
Mara lifted her leg and did a back kick, knocking the girl
several meters into the air. She landed in a crumpled
heap off to the side of the clearing. Mara turned back to
see one demon still in front of her, a blade in each hand,
snarling at her. He came low and high at the same time.
Mara did a side drop so he only cut through air. Pushing
off and doing a kip up she landed on her feet. There was
no easy way to get at him with her sword, but while he
was off balance from swinging with all his might and
missing she turned on her heel quickly and whipped her
braid out behind her head, yelling as she did so to add
some extra power. The familiar sli-i-ck of razor blades

connecting with skin was followed by a scream cut short. She finished her 360-degree spin and felt her braid circle around her neck, blocked by the collar. Looking at it with disgust she saw that it was covered in black demon blood. *The one disadvantage of killing with your hair.* The demon boy was on the ground, head completely severed from his body. As black blood pooled around Mara's feet she quickly jumped away to a drier patch of ground. There were bodies around Leif, too, about ten, all leaking the sticky black fluid. Mara retracted both sides of her automatic double sword and made a mental note to clean it thoroughly once they found water. Walking over to Leif Mara was relieved to see that he had only a few minor scratches.

"You're okay," she said, slightly out of breath. She had learned that killing demons was definitely harder than killing Gone. Leif wasn't paying attention; he was looking frantically around the clearing.

"Where is he?!" he cried. Mara realized suddenly that the one person she hadn't fought was Erros. Seeing his computer equipment near the remains of an old fire she called out "Now!" in a loud voice and abruptly the computer screens shut down and turned black, one of them sending off a few sparks as it did so. Hazen crashed into the clearing several seconds later, skidding to a stop to prevent from tripping over the decapitated body of a female demon. Picking her way through the rivers of viscous black blood Hazen made her way over to them.

"There. Done. He's not seeing anything," she said, looking around in confusion when she saw neither Kat nor Erros.

"He's gone," Mara said. "He expected us to travel using magic and that he would get advanced warning that we were coming. We caught him unawares, so he ran and probably took Kat with him." She sounded broken. Despite the thrill of killing demons for the first time, her expression was morbid, a mask of stone cold hatred for the person who had taken so much from her.

"No," Hazen whispered, shaking her head slowly. "No, she has to be around here somewhere. Unless Erros took her and not her Device." Her voice was growing in confidence as she spoke. "I have mine on instant update using the excellent signal strength from Erros's tech. Her dot is still right here in this clearing." Mara looked like she could kiss Hazen, but decided not to and turned to Leif. He was one step ahead of her and already scanning the area for any minds.

"Got her!" he said, smiling, showing off his perfect white teeth. He pointed at a slightly deeper patch of darkness. Hazen summoned up a small ball of lightning in her hand and held it out in front of them. At first they just saw a tree trunk, but Hazen lowered her hands and there was Kat, knocked out, gagged, and tied hands and feet to the tree.

"Erros must have done this while we were fighting. He wanted us to think she wasn't here so we'd just leave without her and start searching again," Mara said. Hazen kept her lightning in her palm. The electric currents flickering and brightening felt pleasant, like a fire in Mara's fireplace back at home. She and Mara immediately set to work undoing to the ties around Kat's hands. Strong rope bound her and the knots had been tied many times over by a very capable person.

"Leif, keep a look out for minds," Mara called around the tree. She heard nothing in response but that was probably because Leif was already scanning and couldn't talk while he was doing it. Mara quickly gave up on trying to untie the knots with her bare hands and pulled out a lethal looking hunting knife with a beautiful handle engraved with a goddess holding a knife in her tiny carved hand. The blade, like most well-maintained WW blades, was extremely sharp, and after just a few slicing motions the rope was shredded enough for the knife to cut through it like butter. She used this technique on the rest of the ropes, trying her best not to nick Kat but worrying that she might have to because of how tightly the ropes were tied. Hazen moved around to Kat's front once Mara was done with Kat's hands, and Mara copied her. With one hand Hazen held the light up and with the other began to untie the brown gag that was sloppily tied in Kat's unbrushed hair. Beginning to cut through the ropes tying Kat's feet together, Mara noticed something. "Erros spent a lot of time on her hands and feet and not much time at all on her gag," she said. "Hazen's almost got it undone using only one hand." Hazen nodded to the truth of this statement.

"It's tied super loosely. If she weren't passed out she could probably talk right through it," Hazen said, looking just as confused as Mara felt. Mara shook her head. This she really couldn't make sense of. Slicing through the last of the ropes that bound Kat's feet Mara got up again and walked over to Kat's side. Hazen mimicked her and reached under one of Kat's arms, sliding her arm up and over the opposite shoulder. They lifted together, Hazen keeping her light shining out in front of them and Leif serving as their escort, continuing to scan 360 degrees to make sure no one was anywhere near them. Kat's feet were dragging on the ground, her left a little more than her right because of the height difference between Mara and Hazen, but despite that they moved quickly.

"We've got to get her back home. We have no idea what Erros did to her while she was here," Hazen said. "The tech we have can make her good as new in a few hours." Mara nodded.

"Leif, which direction is home?" she asked. After so many days in the forest and in that tiny godforsaken shelter she had no idea where they were. Leif stopped scanning for just a second and actually looked around him.

"Umm… maybe that way?" he said, sounding very unsure of himself and pointing off to their left. Mara smiled at him encouragingly. It was good to be cautious but sometimes Leif was a little bit too cautious, probably because he hadn't been in Atherian a whole year yet. Turning in unison, Hazen and Mara lifted Kat a little higher and started trudging the way Leif told them to.

"Oh, forget this; we're traveling as fog," Mara said after about a minute of very slow walking. As she was about to vaporize Hazen put her hand on Mara's arm.

"No!" she said urgently. "When I examined Erros's tech area his device that scans for magical behavior was gone. I don't know if I sent out the debilitating signal soon enough to catch him and disable that, too, but I'm not taking any chances. He could have already been too far away for my code to work." Mara tilted her head back and groaned.

"I know Kat's, like, the skinniest girl in our class but she really needs to lose some weight if she wants to be carried everywhere," Mara said, only half-joking. Hazen and Leif both laughed for the first time in days, the sound refreshing to their ears and hearts. After a few seconds Mara laughed, too, a rarity but a welcome one. Leif, returning to his scanning, stopped laughing but kept on smiling. Mara noticed that whenever he smiled the whiteness of his teeth really set off his deep green eyes. She had always hated her own smile but as she had gotten older people began telling her that it was improving greatly. OK, well, *Hazen* told her it was really good. Hoisting Kat up again Mara signaled that they should keep moving so they could reach home by mid-afternoon. It was still night and Hazen's lightning was necessary for them to see, but by Mara's calculations there should be the first light from the artificial sun in about an hour. She had no idea how far into the forest they were but she knew how long she had traveled as fog so it was at least twenty or twenty-five miles, if not more. Normally that would have been nothing, but with Kat as deadweight and no magic usage allowed it was really going to be a pain.

Hazen had extinguished her lightning hours ago when the artificial sun first showed its face over the horizon, but still the trees were as thick as ever. Mara's wrist implant said that it was only 7:30 in the morning, but Mara thought that Hazen's destructive wave had fried its inner workings. Heading home wasn't what they had originally planned when they found Kat but, given her state and the fact that they needed more warriors if they were going to take on Erros and his demonic army, heading back to the Academy was an unpleasant necessity.

"I'm picking up someone . . . or some*thing*," Leif said suddenly. "They have barriers but it's something I haven't felt before. Not a Witch Warrior, not a demon, not Gone. It's moving fast." He stopped scanning and looked confused. "I have no idea what it is."

Mara and Hazen deposited Kat near a tree and stalked forward. "It's over there," Leif said from behind them, pointing off to their right. "It's stopped moving, probably heard us." Mara and Hazen pulled out weapons and took up positions behind two trees. Mara felt a presence several feet away from her. Using only her eyes she motioned to Hazen where the thing was. Lightning fast she spun around her tree trunk, grabbed the person's arm, and twisted it around. It was a man, taller than Mara, with black hair. He pulled back, demonstrating great strength, and with his face still turned away he wrenched himself out of her grip. Hazen was on his other side and was about to grab his arm with electrically charged hands when she stopped and smiled, taken aback.

"Oh, sorry," she said. The man spun around and faced Mara.

"Niko!" Mara sighed in relief, pocketing her hunting knife and hugging him. He was wearing full WW battle gear and was perspiring, a rare thing for a vampire because it takes nearly four days of twenty-four/seven hard physical activity for their pores to open up at all, let alone start producing sweat. Their rock hard skin and enhanced physical strength are a defense against sweating, but everything has a breaking point. "Why are you all the way out here? What have you been *doing?*" She looked him over for injuries, finding only purple bruises in a striped pattern as if something had been wrapped around him very tightly, tight enough to bruise a vampire. "Were you tied up?" she asked, concerned. Niko laughed and shook his head.

"Kat ordered Venus to hold me to a tree so I wouldn't follow her and try to stop her from giving herself up to Erros," he explained. "I escaped a few days after she tied me up by convincing Venus that she was in serious trouble, and I've been using my super-speed to run around here ever since, trying to find Kat." He sighed, looking forlorn and very worried.

"We got her," Mara said. "She's unconscious and it looks like she has some internal bleeding, but nothing our tech back home can't fix." Niko's eyes brightened as he focused on something behind her. She turned around to see Leif holding Kat's limp body in his arms. Without thinking Mara smiled at him, and a few seconds later he smiled back, pleasantly surprised. Niko walked past her and sniffed Kat, a seemingly weird thing to do but when you're a vampire it can be quite helpful.

"Yeah, she's bleeding pretty badly inside," he said, pointing to her lower abdomen. "I can smell the blood." He turned back around to Mara. Coming closer he sniffed a little bit and recoiled several feet. "There's blood on you, too, but not your own. It smells *horrible*," he said with a look of disgust. Mara looked down and saw that there was a large smear of demon blood on the side of her arm. Instinctively wiping it with her fingers she was surprised to find that it was ice cold. Blood doesn't stay warm for long but it usually doesn't get ice cold, either. Bringing her fingers towards her nose Mara sniffed the stuff and recoiled just as Niko had.

"Ugh, that's *gross!*" she exclaimed, wrinkling her nose and dropping her hand back down to her side. "It's demon blood."

"*Ohhhh*," Niko said. "It was always rumored to smell as evil as demons do." Shaking his head in disgust he walked back over to where Leif had gently set Kat down on the ground. Niko hefted her onto his shoulder. "We're actually not very far from the edge of the forest. It should only be about thirty minutes more." Mara and Hazen smiled at each other, both tired from carrying Kat for hours on end. They started towards Niko to help him with Kat, but he held up his hand.

"I only need Hazen. No offense, Mara, but you and Leif both smell like demonic marathon runners," he said, chuckling and looking as innocent as he could. Hazen continued towards him and Niko dropped one of Kat's limp arms onto her. Mara and Leif looked at each other and then back at Niko, mouths open in mock horror.

"*Excuse* me?" Mara scoffed, overly dramatic but putting on a good show. "Bet Leif and I can get home three times faster than you without that deadweight. Are we on?" She was purposefully teasing them and Leif was glad she did. He liked races, liked the exhilaration of participating followed by the disappointment or the joy of the end result.

"Oh, you're on," Hazen said, pointing a finger at Mara's chest and making a ridiculous face. They all started laughing, and in the middle of the happy confusion Leif grabbed Mara's arm and sped away, going slowly until Mara realized what was happening and gained her footing.

"Hey, no fair!" she heard Niko's voice shout out distantly and trail off. Mara laughed, a full, genuine laugh. Smiling uncontrollably she and Leif both laughed, shaking their heads while running. Elongated steps and the ability to glide over the forest floor made them much faster than the best human, but that caused the wind to whip by them much faster, too, destroying Mara's braid and making her hair fly around wildly.

Dodging trees they bobbed and weaved, sometimes squeezing through the same gap together and sometimes running almost ten feet apart to find big enough spaces between trees to fit through. Behind them they could hear the distant pounding of feet. That head start really helped because Niko and Hazen were quite far behind them by now.

They began to see light through the trees, a sure sign that they'd be seeing the artificial sun soon. After several more steps and a few more branches whipping them in the face Mara and Leif broke out of the tree line and stopped for just a moment to reorient themselves before continuing. Mara pointed in the general direction of the center of town, identified by the tall, sleek skyscrapers visible in the distance. She then pointed slightly left of it. Her house was not in the city because her parents had enough money to afford to live in a quieter, suburban neighborhood in a huge house that would never have fit in the tiny, crowded streets of the city. Leif nodded. He was fairly directionally-challenged, and even after almost ten months of coming to Mara's house to teach her magic and collect his money he couldn't find his way to her house from the Academy above ground. Then again he had never been brave enough to show her his father's house; embarrassment had stopped him, so he doubted she could get there, either.

They took off again, both keeping the same pace as the other, listening carefully for the footsteps behind them. In the forest groundcover of various plant-like materials had softened their footsteps enough so they couldn't be distinguished from other natural sounds, but the second they hit the hard, dry ground where the forest ended Mara and Leif's enhanced hearing picked them up as loud, rhythmic thuds. One set of footsteps was heavier than the other, probably Niko's. Mara tried to step more heavily so as to send small shock waves back at him just for fun. The ground flashed by under their feet, trees and rocks and landmarks just different colored flashes that they barely noticed before they were gone. Mara's heart beat steadily, her breathing keeping time with it. Sounds were blurry but still there; enhanced speed didn't allow them to go anywhere near the speed of sound. Mara and Leif looked at each other, smiled, and sped up. Behind them they heard the other feet speed up, too. No doubt Niko and Hazen could hear them running ahead of them. The house was in sight now, only about a mile away over flat, grassy terrain that would make for easy running. Sound and sight blurred together as one as they lost their peripheral vision, only seeing what was directly ahead of them, the house. They put their heads down and ran, feeling Niko and Hazen gaining on them every step. Mara's braid had fallen out ages ago so she was very glad she and Leif were wearing protective battle gear. Her razor blades, normally woven neatly into the braid, just stuck out a random angles when her hair was down and were now rapidly flying everywhere. Because the wind was blowing her hair out like a sheet behind her she hadn't tripped on it, but once she slowed and it dropped back down here was a very good chance she'd step on it and faceplant. Having hair that reached the ground was useful, but it was also a hazard.

The large tree that shaded the manhole cover over the sewer entrance came close, closer, and then they were flying past it. A few seconds later Niko and Hazen also flew past it, making the leaves spiral down to the ground despite the fact that it was spring and the tree had just grown its new leaves for summer. The tree almost seemed to wilt in sadness after losing that bright green spring growth.

Mara, slowing down while still quite far from the glass side door so she'd have enough time to fully decelerate, felt her hair starting to fall back down against her back. Waiting till it was almost there she used her momentum to launch herself high into the air and flip around several times, trying to get as much distance as possible in the air before coming down hard and landing in a side drop, slapping the ground with her arm as she came down and holding her neck up to break the fall. Leif was far past her at this point and was slowing down to a stop right in front of the glass side door. Pumping his fists in triumph he made a show of waiting for Niko and Hazen to breeze in. They flew past Mara, blowing her hair everywhere, and stopped right in front of Leif. Mara's dark brown hair was now tangled as hell and spread out all around her like a large picnic blanket. By jumping and falling she had avoided tripping on it, but now she had to face the horrors of brushing it out. *This is why I always keep it up*, she reminded herself.

Even though the circumstances had been dire, almost everything had gone as planned. Kat was okay, or going to be okay, and they had had a blast racing each other home. Hazen and Niko deposited Kat, still out cold, on the porch leading up to the door. Mara held her hair up over her shoulder with one hand and ran the last few meters to the door, stopping next to Hazen to give her a high-five. Then they each bent down to grab one of Kat's limbs. Mara and Hazen took her arms and Leif and Niko her feet, and they carried her like a hammock through the door and down to their in-house hospital. They plugged her into a large, scary-looking machine with a lot of wires, switches, and sensors. By the time they were done and she was covered with a blanket and beginning to heal Kat looked like a person who had been used as a crash test dummy. Wires and sensors were stuck on her forehead and her arms, an IV drip was going, and several wires protruded from her abdomen. Attached to the ends of these wires were small robots called nanobots that were sewing her up inside. Her eyelids fluttered slightly but she was still out cold, having made only a few groaning sounds since they found her in the clearing. She was flushed, the kind of red that would have looked pretty had she been awake, and her hair was twisted off to one side so the sticky part of the sensors wouldn't get in it. On a large screen to Hazen's left there was an image of Kat's brain, constantly morphing and changing to show all angles. Technically, Kat wasn't supposed to have the resonance sensors on her face, but she had been unconscious for so long that Mara had decided that they needed to know if Erros had given her anything that was affecting her brain. So far her brain activity had seemed normal, as if she were very deeply asleep, but she was clearly not. Every attempt to wake her had failed.

"He seriously did something to her," Hazen said, shaking her head in confusion. They were the three top students at the Academy and a two hundred plus -year-old vampire and they still couldn't figure out why Kat was unresponsive. "If she doesn't wake up in the next hour she'll have been out for half a day. Mara, that's the limit for keeping someone at home in critical condition. If she's unresponsive for more than six hours we're bound by Council law to bring her into a real hospital."

Out of options, Mara sighed, resting her head on her fist. "Then we'd have to explain." She lifted her head up and waved her hand helplessly. "Is she *really* in critical condition, though? Isn't there some exception for people who are unresponsive but otherwise fine?" She gestured to the screen displaying the robot's process and then to the brain scan, emphasizing her point. "The bleeding is almost stopped and the nanobots should extract themselves in about ten minutes when they're through with regrowing the last of the tissue. Her brain is completely normal and our sensors aren't picking up any significant levels of pain or discomfort. She's fine and yet... she's not." Mara sounded helpless, confused, and defeated. They'd tried everything, gone over every possible theory of the attack by Erros, and researched every kind of poison and sedative that existed. Nothing made sense.

"In every remotely likely scenario Kat would have either awakened by now or died hours ago," Leif said. He had even run over to his dad's house and picked up one of the books on whatever type of illness he had, but it was a long shot and had yielded nothing. Niko had been quiet the whole time, just staring at Kat and narrowing his eyes like he did when he was thinking. They all sat in a circle around the bed, hands cupping their chins, waiting for the six hour mark that would force them to take her to one of the nearby walk-in hospitals.

CHAPTER 18

"*W*hat are you guys doing?" Etta asked in her impossibly high-pitched five-year-old voice. She smiled, her short blonde bob bouncing up and down slightly. She had fair skin, large brown eyes, and a *very* persistent smile. She always wore bright pink lipstick and way too much mascara.

Mara sighed, not in the mood for having to deal with a parent, but she plastered on a big smile and said in her perkiest voice, "We're just going out, Mom. Nothing you need to worry about. I just need to fetch something from my friend who lives pretty far away." Etta still thought Mara was the same girly-girl that Kat sometimes was, and Mara wasn't able to shake that image. Despite being a good fighter and a promising Warrior, Etta had married Mara and Kat's adoptive dad, Aerick, while quite young. She hadn't really had a chance to experience the real world before Aerick became a big name in the blowers business and swept her into a land of pink hearts and impossibly good things paid for with his money. As a result she had no idea that evil people even existed at all, let alone that they lived in Atherian, and she still thought Mara wanted baby dolls for her birthday.

"Oh, honey, that's great! I can't wait to meet your friend. I'll come with you!" Etta sounded very excited, her ever-present smile growing wider and her eyes lighting up. She had started for the door when Hazen threw out her arm and caught her in the stomach.

"Oh, sorry, Mrs. Cyania," she said, adopting the overly happy tone she'd learned to use through years of being around Etta while at training sessions or just hanging out with Mara after school. "I just wanted to say that before we go out I think you should, um, redo your hair," Hazen said, looking at Mara with the word "help!" written all over her face. Mara jumped in.

"I think while you were, uh, *baking* you got something in it." Mara had no idea if her mom had baked at all that day, but Kat had once calculated that their mother spent 78% of her time baking, so the odds were good. Etta turned to look at Hazen for confirmation and Hazen smiled widely, pointing at a perfectly ordinary spot on the back of Etta's head and nodding convincingly. The one advantage of having a very ignorant mother was that she couldn't recognize a lie if it smacked her in the chest. Mara could say she and Kat were going to try and turn guinea pigs into alligators on the dining table and Etta would reply with a cheerful "Well, have fun, girls" and another large smile.

"Oh, thank you, darlings. If I didn't have you I'd make such a fool of myself," she said, reaching back to try and find the 'thing' in her hair while she walked up the stairs to her bathroom.

"Yeah, we certainly do stop you from doing *that*," Mara said, grimacing. She turned quickly towards the door. "Okay, we have about four hours before she realizes that we left without her. Think we can make it there and back?"

Leif scoffed and smiled, his eyes lighting up. "I don't know, Mara, I think we'll be *really* pressed for time." They all laughed.

Leif and Hazen both grabbed onto Mara's hands and they took off as fog, a light gray streak against the evening sun. Mara watched the houses flash by underneath them, people's whole lives coming in and out of her field of vision in a split second, each of them looking so small and insignificant on their own. She stopped and pulled up, hovering as a cloud for a few seconds over her neighborhood. Everyone who lived near her was fairly well-off, and their large houses made all the yards and the land beyond seem small. Even though she couldn't shake her head while in fog form as she normally would have done, she turned away from her musings and shot off again. If they were going to make it to their uncle Tom's place before she ran out of power, they had to keep going.

Landing hard on her feet but trying to deposit Leif and Hazen gently Mara bent her knees and dropped one fist to the ground, collapsing into a crouch, ready to spring up if there was someone to fight. This movement came naturally even if there was no one to attack. She had had years of practicing how to "land right and ready to fight," as her rather annoying teacher Mrs. Graciet always called it. Pushing back up to her feet she was surprised to see that Leif was standing. Hazen had been traveling with Mara as fog since she was four, and had mastered the landing years ago, but for Leif it had only been about ten months. Mara gave him a look that said "Okay, fine, that was pretty good" and grinned at him.

"What? I'm just naturally awesome," he said, shrugging and looking as innocent as he could while trying not to laugh.

"Your face is turning red and it doesn't match your outfit," Mara said quickly, holding up her hands to fog up the air around his head. Since fog was made of water it naturally cooled people down. The fog completely obscured his face so he looked like one of those faceless demons in children's books. The fog condensed quickly and Mara admired her handiwork. Leif's entire head was dripping wet, his hair flattened, and rivulets of water trickled down his cheeks. The neckline of his shirt was darkening with dampness.

"Yeah, I know he's evil, but Erros was right. You *suck* at the basics," he said, wiping his hand along his hair and dramatically shaking it, sending water droplets flying.

"Well, you're not red anymore," Hazen said emphatically. "Come on, Tom isn't expecting us. It'll take ages to get him into gear and out the door, and then we have to get to the hospital in time to see if Kat's awake. And we have to do all that before your mom realizes we left without her."

Mara laughed. "Oh, trust me, if she actually finds something in her hair that's an extra two hours for us." As they started towards the modest house Mara swung her hair behind her without thinking. Leif barely managed to dodge her razor blades as they sliced through the spot where his left arm had been. Mara instantly realized what she had done and sighed with relief when she saw Leif was okay. She motioned for them both to go ahead of her. Walking up the steps to Tom's front door Hazen pulled back on the door knocker and let it clang back down several times. Almost immediately the door opened and there stood Tom, a middle-aged man with curly dark brown hair and the beginnings of a beard. Once he had told them he needed to shave several times a day because of his increased hair growth as a werewolf but they didn't believe him because most traditional rumors about werewolves weren't actually true, and Mara, Kat, and Hazen suspected this was one of them. Tom looked surprised, but happy to see them. He was a naturally happy person despite the fact that if anyone found out he was a werewolf they would either imprison him or just kill him on the spot. Werewolves could fit into society better than vampires because of their lack of immortality, but they still were in a great deal of danger. He motioned for them to come in.

"Mara, what are you doing here?" he asked as she walked in, closing the door behind her. He was shorter than Mara by quite a bit but it wasn't common for werewolves to be very tall. However, despite not even reaching Mara's chin he still managed to seem like the fatherly figure who would take care of you no matter what. Mara leaned down and hugged him. When she gave a nutshell story of where Kat was and what was wrong with her he looked very worried and motioned for her to sit down on the couch and tell him everything. Mara, Hazen, and Leif all looked at each other, dreading having to tell the whole story and relive it, but Hazen started and quickly told Tom everything they knew about Erros and what he was trying to do. Without Kat the story was incomplete because she had no doubt learned many things during the four days she spent as his prisoner, but they knew quite a bit and relayed every little detail to Tom, with no pauses for questions. Fortunately he didn't seem to have many; he just looked shocked and slightly queasy and stared at Mara, waiting for the rest of the story. Mara obliged and told of their time spent in the woods and how they found Erros and a small portion of his demon army. He smiled when she told how she and Leif fought off the demons and how Hazen destroyed all of his equipment.

"That's my evil-busting niece!" he said proudly. Tom was a trained fighter and had complete control of his transformation into a wolf so he was plenty dangerous on his own, but he had always loved hearing stories of the girls' success. Leif snorted softly and turned it into a nicely disguised cough when Mara elbowed him in the ribs. She continued about how Erros had gotten away, then turned to Leif. He immediately told of finding Kat, getting her back home, and the horrible luck they had in finding out what was wrong with her. He told Tom that Niko had taken Kat to the nearest hospital and that they needed to go there now.

"We won't know what Erros is planning until Kat wakes up, so we need you to change into gear super-fast and come back with us so we can all be there. If we're going to stop him from destroying this planet we need all the help we can get," Leif said, looking over at Mara. "Mara's already recruited several of the smarter students from the Academy who questioned what Erros said and who didn't take the pills. They're waiting at the house." Mara nodded and pushed herself up from the couch. It was a very low couch made of a squishy green material and it was very hard to get out of. Hazen struggled up after Mara. Leif, whose limbs were simply too long to make any use of his leg muscles, had to have Mara grab his hand and pull him upright from the position where his knees were obscuring his eyes. He started towards the door.

"Uh, Leif, why are you all wet?" Tom asked. Leif reached up guiltily to his hair and realized that it was still fairly wet and stuck to his head.

"Mara encased me in fog and soaked my head," he explained, looking at Mara out of the corner of his eyes.

"Ohhhh," Tom said. "Yeah, she did that to the DJ at one of her parents' parties a few years ago to try and block out the music. He was drenched, too." Tom and Leif laughed and followed the girls out of the house. They all joined hands as Mara vaporized, rising above the roof of the highest house before heading off in the direction of the hospital.

Kat's body felt limp and light in Niko's arms, her face slack and expressionless and her eyelashes dark against her cheeks. Her arms and legs dangled as he hurried her through the hospital doors and up to the check-in desk. The AI device came to life and emitted a soft purring sound. A smooth female voice came out of the small black cube that sat on the desk. WW couldn't spare people to do such mundane jobs, but they had plenty of AI sophisticated enough to send people to the right room or make an emergency phone call.

"Welcome. How may I help you?" the voice asked, in not quite a monotone but something close and just as disturbing. All the AI's were female now because studies had shown that both men and women responded better when talked to by a woman's voice.

Niko lowered his head to speak into the box. "I have a sixteen-year-old girl here who's unconscious and I don't know what's wrong with her. She's not waking up." He spoke in a loud, clear voice. The AI technology was impressive but it still couldn't recognize words that were said fast or with a strange accent. The machine whirred slightly louder, signifying that it was loading a room number and a medic for them. Niko took the time to examine the building. He had never been in a hospital before and, frankly, he found it quite interesting. The lobby was called a waiting room but there was no one else in it. It had color but in a way that seemed very forced. Pastel greens and purples covered the walls in strange designs, and the ceiling, floor, and desk were stark white. Several chairs had been set up around a few tables, all white and looking brand-new. The desk in front of him was small, just a table for the AI box to sit on. On either side of it were several doors leading down into the bowels of the hospital, a complicated maze of tunnels and rooms that confused everyone except the medics. It said on the information panel outside the door that only four medics manned this hospital; the rest of the work was done by small nanobots that could repair damaged tissue, stop bleeding, dislodge a blood clot, and a lot more things that Niko didn't know. The medics were only used for really serious things that were beyond the nanobots, which didn't happen very often.

Most medics were field medics, brought out during battles to heal the wounded on the spot.

"Please proceed to corridor 3-B and take door 7 into room F-16," the AI said. "Bots will attend to you." A small light above one of the doors started flashing red, a beacon to guide people who were not accustomed to hospitals. Niko hefted Kat up onto his shoulder and used his free hand to open the door into a sterile white corridor. Doors branched out to his left and right but they were all labeled with "Staff only" or numbers that weren't 7.

"Fourteen, three, staff only, eleven, two, twenty-nine, staff only, eight," Niko whispered as he passed doors. "Hospitals have *no* organizational system." He shook his head in exasperation. When he walked past some of the doors he could hear small, robotic sounds coming from them, but others were perfectly silent. Hospitals also served as morgues. Niko was glad he hadn't walked by any of those doors yet. Finally, he saw a door identical to all the others with a small placard reading "7" in black paint next to it. Upon entering he saw a large bed with white sheets and several machines surrounding it. The mechanical wires with the nanobots on their ends stuck out from a mechanism that was directly over the bed. Shifting Kat gently off his shoulder he laid her on the bed.

"I assume you'll be wanting my help," a female voice said from behind him. Niko spun around, almost revealing his fangs before remembering where he was. A middle-aged woman in a cream-colored lab coat and sterile gloves stood before him. Her gray-brown hair was tied up and pushed under a hair net, and she had kind hazel eyes. Silently walking forward she placed a hand on Kat's shoulder. Niko quickly moved out of her way. She was not imposing, but somehow commanded respect without saying anything.

"Tell me what you have already tried," she said, turning back around to face him. Niko immediately told her all the things they had done, the bots fixing Kat inside and the brain scan showing nothing. Although he didn't know as much as she did, he was definitely not ignorant about the workings of the WW body. She nodded periodically, but never corrected him even though he was sure he had gotten a few things wrong. When he was done she stood there for a few seconds before flying into action, occasionally speaking to explain what she was doing. When she turned on the bots machine the wires inserted themselves into Kat, but not in the abdomen where she had had the internal bleeding. They sought out the major blood vessels in her neck. Each bot's microcamera feed came up on the master screen as soon as it was in her bloodstream. The medic explained that if Kat wasn't responding and her brain seemed fine, then someone (Niko hadn't included Erros's name for the medic's own protection) had given her a poison that was preventing the stress signals from the rest of the body to get to the brain and tell it to wake her up. The brain thought everything was fine which was why it wasn't responding to anything, and it couldn't feel what the body was going through. She stuck a needle so fine you could barely see it into Kat's arm, injecting a liquid before pulling it out again and putting it on a tray.

"I just gave her a blood thinner. That usually helps flush out a poison or a blockage from the bloodstream, but it doesn't always work. Sometimes, if we can find the actual blockage, we have to remove it remotely using the bots," she said, looking up briefly at Niko before focusing back on her work. "You care for her?" she asked simply while punching more codes into the bots machine. The cameras showed them all moving, searching for any sign of foreign matter in her blood. Her sudden remark took Niko by surprise..

"Uh, well, yes. She's my niece," he said. The medic waved her hand, not satisfied by his answer.

"No, no, not that kind of care. A different kind. If I've read you correctly, and I have, you know what I mean," she said, this time looking at him a little longer before returning her gaze to the screens. Niko stayed silent, knowing what she meant but not sure of its meaning. The medic smiled, knowing she had unlocked something in him that, if he let it, would occupy his thoughts for many days to come.

CHAPTER 19

Mara threw open the door, striding purposefully into the waiting room and leading the group up to the AI box. The motion sensors all around the room picked up their presence and the AI promptly spoke.

"Welcome. How may I help you?" it asked. Mara leaned forward and spoke into the box.

"We're here to see Kat Cyania. She was brought in unconscious," she said urgently, almost forgetting to speak loudly and clearly. The AI whirred, running back through all the previous visits to find one that matched.

"Please state the number in your group," it said. In the middle of the sentence the AI glitched a little and the voice said "number" twice. It happened sometimes, not because of their inferior technology but because there were so many of them countrywide that Atherian was struggling to produce enough energy for them.

"Four," Mara said loudly, the sound echoing off the circular walls. Again the box whirred and after several seconds of anticipation the voice spoke again.

"Please proceed to corridor 3-B and take door 7 into room F-16," the voice said, and a small red light began flashing above one of the doors to the left of the AI box. Mara turned to reach for the door handle but Hazen, one step ahead of her, already had the door open and was holding it for the rest of them. Leif and Tom strode in followed by Mara and Hazen, who let the door slam shut loudly behind her. As each quietly whispered the numbers of the many white doors they passed they all noticed that none of it made sense.

"There is no pattern at all to these doors," Tom said, sighing loudly. "We've already passed nine, eight, and six, and there's no sign of seven." Slightly ahead of him Leif took off into a jog, reaching a door with the number 7 painted in black next to it. A small window with blinds pulled tightly closed was at head height. Leif pushed the door open quietly. Niko's head snapped up as they entered but he relaxed as soon as he saw who it was. Getting up from his post next to Kat's bed he briefly embraced Mara and patted Tom on the back.

"They say she's going to be just fine. The bots had to do a minor operation but she's healing from it right now," he said reassuringly. They all broke into smiles and sighs of relief, the tension and anxiety that had been building up for hours finally breaking. Mara and Hazen approached Kat's bed on one side, and Mara fingered the barely visible cut on her neck which she presumed was the site of the operation.

"What was it?" she asked, turning back around to Niko.

"Well, the medic told me that Erros must have given her a poisoned substance that created a blockage between her brain and the rest of her body. She was unresponsive because her brain couldn't feel that the body was telling her to wake up, and it thought everything was fine so it showed no abnormal activity," he said in a rush. He didn't quite understand it but the medic had showed it to him after the operation and it definitely smelled like poison. She had asked him to throw it away for her, and even though it was wrapped in gauze Niko had to focus all his energy on keeping his fangs retracted. With over 200 years of practice Niko knew he wouldn't attack anyone just from smelling their blood, but sometimes his fangs popped out when he didn't mean for them to. Mara and Kat knew that it happened and didn't really care, but people who had never met him often thought that he was threatening them. Carefully keeping his upper lip over his teeth he dropped the thing in the trash can where it was promptly incinerated. For health reasons anything thrown away in hospitals was immediately destroyed, so you had to be really sure that you had no use for whatever you were throwing away.

Hazen looked over at Mara with an expression that said, "Why didn't *we* think of that?" It was a fairly obvious solution and Hazen, for one, could not believe that they spent six hours at home without it occurring to them. Leif shook his head too, agreeing with the girls.

"Well, how long before she wakes up?" Leif asked, changing the subject.

"About thirty minutes, the medic said," Niko explained. "So, around 6:45." Leif nodded and pulled over several more stark white chairs from a corner so everyone could sit. They all took their places around her bed, watching the sleeping figure. Kat looked the same as she did while she was unresponsive, but there was more warmth in her complexion and her eyelids didn't flutter. She actually looked healthy.

"The medic told me something," Niko said abruptly. "Nothing about medicine, but about..." His voice trailed off, leaving the rest of the sentence unsaid. They all looked at him curiously, Mara and Hazen's eyebrows inching up higher the longer he sat in silence. Niko just shrugged and murmured something under his breath that not even WW or werewolf enhanced hearing could make out. They all leaned in with confused expressions.

"No, no, never mind," Niko said, waving his hand dismissively up and down in front of him. He was trying to keep emotion out of his voice and was doing a pretty good job, but instead he just sounded vacant, like something else entirely was occupying his thoughts. He got up quickly from Kat's bedside and awkwardly stood for a second before speaking. "I've been away from food for a really long time. I need to go hunting," he said, sounding almost embarrassed. They all relaxed their postures, relieved that nothing was wrong with Niko. Mara realized that he was right. They had kept him from feeding ever since they found him in the woods, and that had been well over a day. She suddenly felt guilty for forgetting the basic needs of her uncle.

"Be back by the time she wakes up, okay?" she said, and he nodded confirmation. He didn't look very happy, but Mara knew that was because of the stress of trying not to drink *their* blood in his hunger. He managed a smile and then walked briskly out of the room, greatly resembling someone who had to go to the bathroom really badly. Mara heard him take off running, vampiric super-speeding, down the hallway and out of the building. *Maybe he didn't eat while looking for Kat either*, she thought. *That would make six days without food for a vampire.* She shook her head. *No, that's impossible. He would have eaten us all or died by now.* The longest Mara had ever seen him go was a little under two days, and that was when he had to be her chaperone for a special WW training camp. He was constantly surrounded by WW so of course he couldn't feed. After two days he was finally able to get away and he was fine after that, but Mara remembered how stressed he had been, like a sheet getting stretched increasingly tighter over a splintery piece of wood.

She suddenly became aware of an annoying beeping sound by her right ear and she looked up, catching herself just before her head hit one of the complicated machines surrounding Kat. The large screen on the machine had just lit up, random lights and buttons flashing on the lower portion and a brain scan image on the top.

"Guys, look," Mara said, pointing at the brain scan. A few parts of the brain were starting to light up, the blank gray-blue color of deep sleep turning into the healthy green of wakefulness. "She's coming back." They all gathered around the machine, watching in anticipation as more and more of Kat's brain lit up. The frontal cortex was still in deep sleep, but Mara was sure that it would wake up soon. She looked at the white clock mounted high on the wall. 6:39 PM. Kat was waking up early. Hazen's long fingernails were clacking away noisily at the keys on her Device, probably sending a message to Etta that they'd be home very soon. Mara stretched her neck over Hazen's shoulder, proofreading the message before Hazen sent it. Her long, red fingernail hit the send button. Hazen had always had long nails that she kept painted. They were kind of like claws for her; she sometimes used them to cut things. A stray strand of her blonde hair flew into

Mara's eye, causing her to blink and bat it away, but Hazen didn't even look up.

"Look!" Tom said excitedly. "Her frontal cortex is lighting up!" Green was starting to spread into the front of her scan, quickly turning into a bright, neon light.

A gasp came from the bed behind them. They all spun around to see Kat sitting up, eyes wide and mouth in a large 'O', gasping for breath. At first she looked around frantically, seeing nothing but white hospital walls, but her face relaxed and her breathing slowed back to normal as she saw Mara, Hazen, Leif, and Tom standing over her with expressions of worry and joy on their faces.

"I'm really happy to see you guys, but where the hell am I?" she asked, pushing herself up out of the bed. Since she was completely fine now that the poison had been removed none of them tried to stop her; they simply stepped back and let her get the feel of her feet again. Hazen was the first to speak up.

"You're in the hospital, the one closest to your house," she said, smiling at her. All of them were smiling now, and the mutual feeling of good luck was felt throughout the room. Kat visibly relaxed a bit more. Leif reached forward and began pulling the sensors off of Kat's head and arms. She tried to raise her arm to do it herself but Hazen stopped her. Kat satisfied herself with looking at all of them, scanning up and down for any injuries. She turned her head to look around the rest of the room.

"Where's Niko?" she asked, becoming worried again. "Is he okay? Have you guys found him?" Her voice grew in volume and urgency. Mara put a hand on her arm.

"It's okay. He convinced Venus to let him go, then ran around the forest for days trying to find you. We found him after we rescued you and brought you back here. You were unresponsive for hours at home, so we had to bring you here. He was here; he just had to step out for a feeding break. I'm sure he'll be back in no time," she said in as soothing a voice as she could manage. Kat nodded. She glanced down at what she was wearing.

"Ugh, you guys couldn't even change me out of my muddy, dirty gear that's covered in pine needles," she asked, faking exasperation. They all laughed, including Kat.

"So you feel fine. Totally normal?" Tom asked, looking up at her with concern. She nodded.

"I'm fine, Uncle Tom," she said, continuing to smile before turning back to Mara and Hazen. "Can we *please* get out of here? Hospitals give me shivers." Mara laughed and patted Kat lightly on the back. Normally that would have called for a playful punch in the arm, but now didn't seem like the right time. Hazen started towards the door, followed by Kat and Mara. Leif fit in behind her and Tom took up the rear.

"Aahh!" Hazen gave a small shout from the front of the line as they rounded a corner into the main hallway. They crowded up behind her to see Niko, looking much healthier than he had half an hour ago, standing in front of Hazen and wearing a shirt that was slightly rumpled from their collision. They all started laughing. Niko spotted Kat and quickly strode forward to give her a gentle hug. She squeezed him back very hard and Mara saw his eyes bug out a little bit. Stepping back Kat looked apologetically at him.

"Sorry for tying you up," she said casually. Niko shrugged.

"Eh. Sorry for not being there when you woke up," he replied. Kat waved her hand, laughing softly. Mara, Hazen, and Kat linked elbows and walked off down the corridor towards the large white door that led into the waiting room.

"Catch up if you can, boys," Mara shouted out behind her. Kat started as if she had just remembered something and looked at Mara conspiratorially.

"I almost forgot to ask. While I was gone, did anything *happen* between you and Leif?" she asked eagerly looking back and forth between Mara and Hazen and smiling. They both reacted with looks of disgust, although, Kat noticed with delight, not as much as they had the first time she suggested it.

"Ew, Kat. I think I liked you better unconscious," Mara said. Hazen nodded her agreement but the second Mara looked away caught Kat's eye and winked. Kat mouthed a question to her and Hazen mouthed back.

"Not yet, but it's something." Kat smiled giddily and Hazen copied her. They turned their attention back to Mara to see her looking at them suspiciously. They both laughed and Hazen rolled her eyes from behind Kat's head.

Mara felt a tap on her shoulder and turned to see Leif walking quickly behind her, barely keeping up with their rapid pace. His long legs gave him an advantage, though, and Hazen pointed this out.

"That's no fair, Leif, you have weirdly long legs," she teased, also glancing behind her. Kat was the only one who kept looking forward so they wouldn't run into a wall. Leif took mock offense and threw up his hands.

He joined the line on Mara's side so it went from tallest to shortest. Without thinking he linked his arm with hers. He was surprised when she didn't resist at all, just ran slightly faster than everyone else. Kat matched her speed exactly as only a competitive twin sister could do. They broke their connections when Kat pushed the door open, passing the AI box on her way out the door. The motion sensors detected them and the box promptly spoke.

"Thank you for coming. We hope you have a wonderful rest of your day," the smooth female voice said.

"Boy, the resemblance between the AI and what Mr. Rosten said desk people sounded like in the old days is *really* creepy," Mara said. Several years ago she and Kat had taken ancient history with Mr. Rosten, and the subject was what life was like between the defeat of the demons and the creation of Gone, that short period in WW history that was close to peaceful. They all snorted, looking back at the AI. The boxes were programmed with almost every phrase in the language, and what they said was controlled by their algorithms. Mostly they just gave directions or answered questions, but occasionally you could really insult one, and they had a temper. You wouldn't hear the end of it for a week. *Insulting a* box! *This is what our culture has come to*, Kat thought, inwardly shaking her head.

"We *have* enjoyed our day, box, and we will *not* be coming back anytime soon," Hazen told it. The box didn't respond. "We need to go straight home, guys, get more provisions and organize. Oh, and explain all this to your mom." Hazen snickered at Mara and Kat's identical expressions of exasperation and annoyance.

They pushed the main double doors open and Kat tilted her head back and took a deep breath.

"Finally, I'm not smelling demon blood or fire," Kat said. "The air seems normal again."

Mara chimed in with a grin.

"And now that we're out of the forest we can all travel how we like. The boys won't keep vomiting every time we land," she whispered with an eye roll.

"We'll all meet back home," Niko said from behind them. They nodded confirmation. He gave them a crooked half-grin before he left, looking a bit stupid but cute just the same. His body was a blur; he ran so fast that Kat could barely tell he was a boy. His super-speed put him out of sight in a split second, leaving behind a light breeze that just barely ruffled Kat's hair.

Tom was next, dropping down onto all fours and taking off, careful to stay in the shadows. He didn't turn into a wolf, but werewolves could run extremely fast on all fours even when in human form, and he wasn't about to take any chances of people seeing him as a wolf. The remaining four looked at each other and simultaneously turned into their traveling forms, Kat's skin replaced by glossy orange and black fur and Hazen sizzling out of existence and replaced by a lightning bolt with that disturbing smell of cooking meat. The glowing white bolt took off, zipping around the corners of houses, always moving and crackling like a white-hot fire. Kat took off running at her enhanced speed, almost as fast as Niko, her muscles rippling beneath her shiny pelt. Leif had already taken Mara's hand and now she shot off too, leaving a breeze behind her, expertly navigating obstacles. Leif watched in wonder as the world flashed by below him, trying to look at individual things but only able to see blurs of color and faint shapes. He had once asked Hazen if Mara ever moved slow enough as fog that you could see things clearly while traveling with her, but she had only looked confused by the question. When she couldn't answer Leif just assumed that Mara never did. Secretly he wished she would, just once. He had always wanted to fly, to see the whole world from way up in the sky. But it was Mara's fog and Mara's specialty, and Leif had no right to tell her how to use it.

He could see the tall house with huge windows about half a second before they reached it and descended to ground level. Mara deposited him as lightly as she could, condensing back into human form a couple inches away from the ground and dropping the rest of the way, leaning down into her ready position on instinct before standing up again. Hazen and Niko were already there and she could see the speeding forms of Tom and Kat racing each other towards the house. Kat was winning, but that was probably because of her longer legs and all the built up energy she had after waking from a coma. Kat skidded onto the lawn a second before Tom did, remaining a tiger for several seconds after she stopped running. Sometimes Kat paraded around as a tiger just for fun. It didn't sap any of her energy to simply be a tiger and not exert herself as one, so she didn't see a downside. Tom pushed himself upright and held his hands out in front of him, careful not to touch anything. Running with his bare hands didn't hurt because of his very tough skin, but it did make his hands absolutely filthy. Once, after a run, he had touched Kat's vanity table without washing his hands. The dirt and old chewing gum stain still hadn't come off five years later, so the sisters had forbidden him to touch anything before thoroughly scrubbing his hands. Looking disgustedly down at his palms he cringed. Everyone stepped out of his way as he walked towards a small building on the lawn that he knew contained a sink. His palms were literally black... not gray or brown, but black.

Entering the small washroom Tom went to work scrubbing with the special strong soap that Kat had bought just for him. Soon the thick coating of dirt and grime was wearing thin and Tom could see the palms of his hands again. After taking a toothpick and working it under his fingernails he examined his work and saw not a speck of black grime. Pleased with himself he exited the washroom and made his way across the yard, noticing with dismay that not one of his friends had waited for him. Jumping up the steps two at a time he pushed open the doors and took the well-traveled route down to the painting of the seven-legged gazelle. He lightly knocked on it. Almost immediately it swung open revealing Niko who held it back for Tom to enter. The hole behind the painting didn't reach the floor; so you had to step over a two foot tall section of wall to get into the room. When the girls had first revealed this secret place to him and Niko, he had tripped over the wall and face-planted on the hardwood floor. Now there was a thick, plushy red carpet to cushion any future falls. No one else was in the room, but voices and clanging sounds were coming from the kitchen. Closing the painting behind him, Niko explained.

"They're cleaning up and searching for stuff in the weapons cache. Most focused teenagers I've ever met," he said casually. Tom nodded in agreement and walked into the kitchen. Hazen was at the sink scrubbing the blade of a curved knife with all her might. The lower part was clean and shiny but the upper curve and tip were still caked with dried black demon blood. Hazen was using extra strong soap and an abrasive cloth, which was working, but it looked slower than with Gone blood.

"Demon blood dries *hard,* harder than Gone blood," Hazen said when she saw them, gesturing to the several knives and Mara's double sword that were still to come. Both swords were out and both were covered in the black stuff. Niko rummaged in a cabinet to find another cleaning cloth. Hazen glanced at him gratefully before returning to her work. As Niko started rubbing back and forth along the blade of a short throwing knife he was thankful that scientists had come up with a super-strong alloy a few years ago to make weapons that were impervious to the new cleaning cloths. Only blood would be scraped off by the abrasive cleaner; the blade would remain smooth and shiny, free of the scratches it used to accumulate. Tom proceeded to the next room where he found Mara, Kat, and Leif knee deep in all sorts of weaponry, extra gear, shields, and random tech. Pushing the thick door to the weapons cache open further he carefully waded into the pool of sharp objects.

"Are we sorting?" he asked. Mara looked up and nodded.

"Yeah, just put gear and tech and shields on the back shelves, and all the weapons, in order from most to least used, on the shelves on the side walls," she said, pointing out each area. "Blowers go in the boxes in the corner. If you're not sure about something or if it seems too small to be put on a shelf just ask one of us. We need to have this whole thing organized fast before Erros starts making more trouble." Tom grunted to show he understood and leaned down to start picking things up and sorting them. Kat was at the back of the cache and

Leif was tossing things, mostly extra gear, to her. She would shove it back in on the shelf before spinning around to catch the next thing. Mara's hands were whizzing back and forth at high speeds, filing weapons where they were supposed to go. She picked up a shiny silver boomerang and, instead of putting it in the back where it usually went, she moved it up near the door for easy access. Tom picked up random things, sometimes tossing them to Leif if they were meant to go in the back but usually putting them somewhere on the side shelves. The walls were rapidly filling up with weapons packed neatly in orderly rows. The back wall was all filled up with gear, a few small shields which no one ever used, and many small devices that were supposed to do one thing or another. Leif and Kat had moved on to packing weapons as tightly as they could. When they first had the cache built it was ridiculously large for what few weapons they had, but over the years in the Academy they had built up quite a collection and now they were almost out of room. They hadn't resorted to taping anything to the ceiling… yet.

Their hands were all moving at super-speed now, urgently working to get everything organized and accounted for so they could go to the Academy to find the few students who weren't demons and get them to safety. Erros was no doubt regrouping his demon army and sending search parties out to look for the unfortunate students as they spoke. Their only hope of recruiting enough WW to have a chance of beating Erros was to get to the unchanged students first. Those students had received the pills, of course, but hadn't taken them for some reason. *They must have known somehow that Erros was up to something. It won't be hard to convince them of what he's doing and to get their help,* Mara thought as she fitted curved hunting knives onto the bottom shelf.

"Done with this wall," Leif said from behind Mara. Giving Leif a quick thumbs up she returned to her work, picking up the last knives from the floor and slipping them into their slots. They all stood there for a few seconds, looking around at the walls that appeared to be made out of weapons. Mara and Kat nodded their approval. As they left the room Mara sealed the cache.

Returning to the kitchen they saw Hazen and Niko working on opposite ends of Mara's double sword, holding it over the sink as they scrubbed, black blood dust falling down onto already large piles. Several other knives were on the edge of the sink, shiny and polished. Hazen and Niko turned when they heard everyone enter the room and stopped scrubbing for just a second. Mara patted Hazen on the back gratefully and began handing the cleaned knives back to the people they belonged to. Leif stepped forward and put his hand on Hazen's arm.

"You want me to finish that?" he asked. "You could go see the cache and stock up again; it's all reorganized." Hazen smiled and thanked him, handing over the cloth and walking out of the room. Kat followed her to open the cache door, and punched her in the arm a second before they exited the kitchen.

"Don't go stealing Mara's guy," she warned, looking at Hazen like she was a disobedient child. Hazen threw up her hands in protest.

"I'm not *stealing* him, I'm having him scrub demon blood," she said, trying to sound cool and unconcerned. Kat stared at her.

"You know what I mean," she said, looking meaningfully at Hazen. "That smile you two exchanged was *so* not okay. Mara has a guy for the first and

215

probably last time in *history*. If he falls for *you* my romantic movie plot will totally fail!" Her eyes widened and she looked desperately at Hazen. After a moment of total silence they nodded at each other and tiptoed back to the door, leaning their heads down to listen near the crack on the side. Mara's voice came from the other side, loud and clear.

"I can hear you guys. You sound like a traveling sorority circus with a *seriously* messed up idea of romance," she said sarcastically. Kat stayed silent for a moment, then decided to admit it and run.

"Not sure if that's a good thing, but we're gonna go now," she said, grabbing Hazen's hand and pulling her down the hallway that split off leading to Kat's side of the house.

Running on a hardwood floor with Xtreme gloss finish in four-inch stiletto-heeled boots was not an easy thing to do, but Kat had chosen that kind of heel on her battle gear boots for a reason. Ever since she was a girl she had loved trying on heels, and she had developed a taste for stilettos. Once she had mastered walking, running, kicking, jumping, and killing with the spike heels, Aerick and Etta had let her request them for her custom gear boots. Mara, being her usual boring self, had chosen three-and-a-half inch block heel for her battle gear boots, still high and good for killing but not nearly as hot as the stilettos. Of course, Kat had done everything she could to convince her sister to walk on the wild side, but to no avail. Hazen, also in her gear boots, had run these hallways in heels so many times that she had no problem keeping up with Kat, who swung them around a door and kicked it closed behind them.

"Wow!" Hazen said, never ceasing to be impressed by Kat's enormous walk-in closet no matter how many times she'd seen it. A full restaurant kitchen, a master bedroom and bath, and a large pantry could all fit in Kat's closet, which used to be the family ballroom until she took it over. Rows and rows of tops lined one portion of the wall, then dresses organized by color and brand, then pants, then skirts. On the back wall was stacked shoes, boots, slippers, anything you could possibly put on your feet. The opposing wall was adorned with accessories and a huge vanity table and mirror. Large boxes and drawers were filled to the brim with makeup, cleansers, and face masks. On a hanger right near the door and easily accessible was a change of warm weather battle gear, and on a shelf next to it was her cold weather battle gear and several extra changes of different items of gear clothing. WW always had to have gear ready in case of an emergency. On a large hanger at the front of the dresses section was a beautiful, tight, berry red sleeveless knee-length dress that Aerick had gotten Kat several years ago. It was dress gear, a line of clothes that were fit for royalty but had many hidden pockets for weapons. WW could wear these special gear clothes when going undercover at a fancy night out. They could look the part of whoever they were pretending to be but still be ready for the Gone attack they had been sent to prevent. Shaking herself out of her reverie over the dress Kat closed the closet doors and sat down on the shiny black floor. Hazen raised her eyebrows.

"*This* is where we're hiding from Mara?" she asked incredulously. "She's probably not even mad that you said Leif was her guy. I'm sure she likes him just as much as he likes her." Hazen raised her hands, about to say something else, then dropped them.

"I'm *right* here," Mara's voice said from behind them. Hazen spun on her heel and Kat whipped herself back to her feet to see Mara standing there, arms crossed across her chest, looking very annoyed. Her hair, perfectly rebraided in a single long French braid, lay over her shoulder with the edges of many razor blades glinting dangerously in the light from the overhead chandelier.

"So, you've been here the whole time?" Kat asked, not really a question but a hope.

"Yeah. When I'm fog I can follow you *anywhere*," Mara said, tracing her finger around in the air then pointing straight at Kat. "I just wanted to hear if Hazen actually liked Leif. I could never tell." Mara shrugged, as if disappointed. "I guess not."

Kat and Hazen both stared at her. "But it's obvious that he likes *you*," Hazen said, coming over to stand next to Mara. "We're just waiting…"

"And hoping," Kat added with a smile.

"… that something will happen," Hazen finished. She grinned at Mara.

"Look, Leif comes over to teach me and so I can give him money. What we have is basically a business arrangement. How many times has *that* resulted in romance in all of your plots, Kat?" she asked sarcastically.

"Well, let's see. Around, oh, three hundred," Kat retorted, trying to adopt a neutral expression. "Mara, look, we all think you and Leif are perfect for each other, but you're right. We shouldn't be talking like that. Just, don't push him away so much. Romance isn't all bad, even what I have with Chase." Mara and Hazen both smiled, assuming that she meant it as a joke, but Kat's face suddenly looked horrified.

"Oh my God! Chase! We have no idea if he's a demon or not. We have to find him," she cried, motioning for them all to leave the closet and get going. Mara grabbed Kat's arm, pulling her back.

"I sent Niko, Leif, and Tom to the Academy and all around the neighborhood to pick up any students that aren't demons and bring them back here. Niko told me that the Academy had been shut down by High Chairman Kurth, so they're out searching houses. I'm sure if they find Chase they'll bring him here," Mara said reassuringly. Kat's expression calmed a little.

From behind them Hazen scoffed. "Erros said he was taking *promising* students. Chase is fine," she quipped, but immediately realized what she had said and regretted it. Mara threw her a warning glance and punched her in the arm. She secretly agreed with Hazen, but now was not the time to antagonize Kat.

"I mean, I'm sure he's okay. We can go out and search for him now," Hazen corrected herself. Kat pushed open the closet doors and walked out, followed by Hazen and Mara.

"I think Niko and Tom are taking the south side. We can go east," Hazen suggested, grabbing a few extra butterfly knives on the way out. Kat strode into the entryway and stopped dead in her tracks.

"Hey guys. How's it going?" It was Chase, extending his arms for a hug.

"Oh hey, Chase," Mara said casually. "*Chase!*" she half-yelled, realizing who she was talking to. "You're… you're okay." She brightened her tone, forcing a smile to please Kat. Hazen did the same, acting glad that the fourth member of their team had showed up. Kat ran forward a few steps and hugged him, though not with as much vigor as Mara had expected.

"So, where's my bro, Leif?" he asked, looking around as if Leif would just materialize out of thin air. Kat just smiled and brought him into the kitchen.

CHAPTER 20

*A*bout five minutes later Chase had finished telling his story, which had nothing to do with Erros, a pill, or demons. Apparently his parents had given him money for a week's vacation in Dankfirtè, a large city in the Human world, and he had no idea that one of his professors was trying to turn the whole planet into burnt toast.

"So, did I miss anything over here?" Chase asked excitedly. "What's the latest gossip?" All three girls stared at him for a long moment before Kat finally spoke up.

"Uh, well, Professor Erros got fired from his job. He's been acting really weird since," Kat said weakly, trying to inform Chase that his life was in danger in a way that someone with his IQ could understand. Mara and Hazen nodded in confirmation. None of them were trying too hard to come up with believable lies – Chase was the *worst* at detecting falsehoods. He grinned and nodded his head as if this was everyday news.

"So, any big scary fights you two were in? Anyone die recently?" he asked, laughing as he did so as if in their line of work no one ever died. Mara clenched her fists in frustration, both at his lack of understanding and at his annoying habit of starting every sentence with 'So'.

"Well, Chase, Professor Erros is trying to turn us into demons. You too. He's trying to turn you into a demon..." Hazen began to explain, but trailed off when she saw Chase's blank expression. "Okay, forget that," she said quickly. Chase had no problem doing that, and his expression returned to one of confused happiness. "Professor Erros is bad and we have got to stop him before he does something, uh, bad," Hazen said, speaking louder and more deliberately. Chase held up his hands.

"I'm not deaf, Hazen," he said, laughing at his own 'joke' but stopping when he noticed the girls were just staring at him. Mara was surprised for a second that he actually remembered Hazen's name. "Anyway, you said something about Professor Erros being bad? Don't worry, ladies, I can help with that." Chase smiled his winning smile and assumed an air of superiority. Mara and Hazen exchanged eye rolls before turning back to him.

"Chase, I'm sure you can help," Kat said hopefully. "We're gathering the few students that haven't been affected by Professor Erros yet, like us. We must form an army so we can defeat him." They had learned over the years that with Chase it was best to spell things out, leave nothing to the imagination, and pretend that they really needed his help. He smiled when Kat finished speaking and readily agreed to help them find the other students. *Works every time*, she thought, grinning to herself and keeping up the façade up that she was grateful. She smiled and put her hand on his arm.

At that moment the painting opened and Leif stepped through, followed by Niko. After him came several flustered but determined looking teenagers. Tom brought up the rear of the strange procession, closing the painting behind him. Mara thought she heard one of the students whisper "nice place" but she wasn't sure. Quickly getting up from the table she walked over and gave Leif a fist-bump. He grinned at her.

"We found them in houses all around town. Most of them had gotten the pills and figured the situation out, but there's one who hasn't and is pretty freaked out." He pointed to a twiggy, timid looking boy who was being comforted by Tom.

"All right, everyone, can you all please make your way to the sitting room directly adjacent to the kitchen," Mara called out to the students. She pointed to an arched doorway and the students filed through it into the sitting room. Immediately some of the teenagers began to ask questions, and Hazen went around speaking individually to them, answering them the best she could. Tom held the timid boy back and Mara glanced at him gratefully. It wouldn't do for someone to start crying while she was explaining. She and Kat stood together, not sure of what to say. Kat began.

"You all know why we're here, and hopefully you know that we don't have much time," she said. Everyone nodded.

"He's turning our classmates into those black things. They're demons, right?" one of the girls asked. Kat nodded. "How do we stop them?" the girl asked, appearing ready to do battle.

"We had to fight our way through some of them to get to Erros a little while ago. You can kill them just like you kill Gone, but it's harder. You *really* have to kill them," Mara said. "Their true form is the black smoke things that you all saw come out of your pill, but they can transform into the students they once were. The only difference is that their eyes are liquid black. They may look like your old friends, but they're not," she warned. "They aren't Gone, either. Gone are dead and their WW souls departed when the demon soul is inserted, but these students were still alive. They have two souls, but the demonic energy claims superiority. These altered students remember everything that they learned at the Academy, including fighting techniques. The demonic energy inside of them has blocked all their WW magic, but they are still deadly. *Do not* underestimate them." The students looked at each other, then back at Mara and Kat. One boy finally spoke up.

"My best friend is gone," he said, sadness and loss filling his tone. "Erros took him from me and turned him into something horrible. I don't care what we have to do, he is not killing anyone else." All the students nodded along with him. Most of them had probably lost someone they cared about to Erros. Determination and anger showed on their faces. There were no tears in their eyes, only fire. Mara and Kat nodded gratefully. Hazen stood up and signaled to Mara that the students should go to the weapons cache.

"Okay, we have a weapons cache down the hall. Kat will open it for you, I want you all to stock up with as much as you can reasonably carry of all the things you're good with," Mara said, pointing in the direction of the cache. Kat went to unlock the door. Mara did a quick headcount as they walked past her. *Thirteen, plus*

Kat, Hazen, Leif, Niko, Tom, and Chase. And me. It definitely wasn't as many as she had hoped for, but they were all smart and near the top of all their classes. After all, only the best would have figured out how to test the pill.

After Kat had given them a play by play of everything that had happened and everything that Erros had told her while she was his prisoner, they thought it over and estimated that he had at least one hundred and thirty demons under his control. The details from the power circle Kat had witnessed confused them. They knew how power circles worked, of course, and this one was no different from the norm, but when Erros started controlling them without the energy they gave back he must have been extremely weak, and in the short period of time when the demons were transferring energy back to him *they* were weak. There were so many flaws in his plan, so many moments of weak energy transference that made taking out the demons and Erros that much easier, that Mara was sure there was something they still didn't know. The type of magic that Erros was using was so advanced, so unknown, it had to be into completely uncharted territory. There must be something else that only Erros knew, some secret shortcut that he could use to his advantage because no one else knew anything about the type and magnitude of magical control and rejuvenation he was attempting.

Mara shook her head, focusing back to the present situation, and noticed Hazen waiting for her at the doorway. She smiled absentmindedly and followed her to the side door. The students, already decked out in battle gear and weapons, were waiting by the door with Kat, Niko, Tom, and Leif. Chase was also in gear but was trying to corral the students into a circle as if he were a sheep dog. Kat laid a hand on his arm and gently guided him away.

"Ok, everyone, I'm sending you the battle plans," Mara announced, touching her temple with two fingers to activate one of her neural chips. Connecting with all the students she mentally sent out directions, battle plans, and related information to all of their corresponding neural chips. Their expressions changed after they had scanned and understood the message. They all nodded and headed out the door, led by Kat and Hazen while Niko, Leif, and Chase merged into the group. Mara was about to follow when she felt a tap on her shoulder. She turned to see Tom still holding the hand of the timid boy she had seen earlier.

"What should I do with him?" he asked. The boy looked terrified, as if he was about to cry.

"Uhh, just put him in the purple guest room and lock it. He'll be fine," she said. Tom raised his eyebrows but walked off anyway, guiding the boy and whispering words of comfort. Mara jogged out the door and super-sped up to the front of the group, taking her position between Kat and Hazen. Kat's hair had been pulled up into a high ponytail and was hanging down her back in silky ash brown waves. Hazen's hair was loose and fell down her back just past her waist in beach waves. For once it didn't look electrified; it actually flattened onto her head and wasn't floating around with static. Razor blades lined every inch of Mara's braid, sticking out at deadly angles, their sharp edges glinting in the afternoon sun. She had tightened it just before Chase had showed up, and she was confident it was good for at least ten demon heads before it began to fall out. Kat was wearing four inch heels while Mara's were only three-and-a-half inches. Mara was acutely aware of the reduced height difference between them; she had always prided herself on being the tallest member of their family, and Kat had gotten the highest heels possible to try to lessen that.

Kat shook her head dramatically, making her ponytail fan out. They had entered the forest by now and were advancing quickly. Somewhere between the house and the birch tree that shaded their sewer entrance the whole group had switched from normal walking to their special WW speed-gliding, their feet barely touching the ground. None of their heads bobbed from walking anymore; they just advanced as if they were on a moving walkway. Trees flitted by, their trunks rough with ivy vining around them. Leif had sneaked up behind Mara and now leaned down to whisper something in her ear.

"There are auras everywhere, and they're not good," he said softly, worry in his voice. "They're just hovering in the air all around us." He looked about him and shivered. Mara sometimes wondered what it would be like to actually *see* evil, not just fight it. She assumed it wasn't easy.

"Tell me if it darkens significantly. Anything out of the ordinary we'll stop and move in in teams," she whispered back to him. She felt him nod against the side of her head. His heat moved away slightly, but she could feel him still behind her. She thought back to the conversation in Kat's closet with her sister and Hazen, suddenly not so sure of the steadfast responses she had given. Leif was just her friend… right?

She decided that now was not the time to be thinking about things that would become completely irrelevant if she died in the upcoming battle. Just as she was taking her mind off him Leif spoke to her again, this time with undisguised determination.

"Stop," he whispered loudly, turning around to face the group of students. "Stop." Mara looked at him questioningly. He pointed forward and to the right.

"It's up there. I can feel it. All the auras spreading throughout this area go back to about five hundred feet up that way," he said, looking into Mara's eyes for confirmation. In the fraction of a second that she held his gaze she tried to convey as much as she could with only her eyes.

"Everyone split off into groups of three or four and surround the area that Leif maps out for you," she commanded. "Be very quiet and very careful. You all know what to wait for, but please, be careful." They all nodded and smiled, ready for the battle ahead.

CHAPTER 21

*M*ara teamed up with Tom and another student, a tall girl with platinum white hair cut in layers just past her shoulder who was carrying her weight in nunchucks and knives. Mara didn't know her, but by the way she carried herself she could tell the girl was a good fighter. Mara guessed she was around fourteen, young for an experienced fighter. Earlier Mara had taken count of all the specialty and talent magics, and she hadn't been disappointed.

"What do you do again?" she asked quietly. The girl leaned over slightly, not taking her eyes off the terrain ahead of them, and answered.

"Frost," she said. "And my name's Lissa." Her tone wasn't angry, simply informative. Mara nodded. Frost was a good specialty and would work particularly well against the demons who seemed to run on heat. Tom thrust his hand out, stopping them in their tracks.

"I can smell them," he said. "They reek." Wrinkling his nose he sniffed some more. Mara could see Lissa stiffen when she realized what Tom was, but she didn't say anything and didn't move away. Tom advanced slowly, pulling back the thorny bushes that were growing among many of the trees in this section of the forest. Bending down to see over his shoulder Mara left room for Lissa's head, too. Despite Tom's status as an illegal werewolf Lissa moved forward to have a look. Stumps littered the clearing just as they had in the place Erros had kept Kat captive. That demon hideout had been large, but it was nothing compared to what they stood on the edge of now. Keeping her eyes on the colossal clearing Mara held her arm out behind her and made a soft trilling sound with her throat. A second later Mamba landed on her lower arm, folding her wings in and ruffling her feathers. When Mara brought her forward so she could see in the clearing too, she saw Mamba's eyes widen slightly indicating that she was becoming very uncomfortable. The clearing, which would have accommodated Kat's entire walk in closet and then some, was teeming with the bodies of demons, all in student form but with those black eyes that showed the worst of all evil souls deep inside them. Lissa gasped quietly, covering her mouth with her hand. When Mara looked out of the corner of her eye to make sure Lissa was alright she saw the girl staring at one specific point in the crowd of demons. Following her gaze Mara saw a girl, slightly shorter and younger than Lissa but with the same smooth platinum blond hair and defined, almond shaped face. *Oh God. She has a sister.* A wave of pity swept over Mara as she imagined what it would be like if Kat had fallen for the trick and taken the pill. She didn't say anything to Lissa but fervently hoped that she would remember that her little sister wasn't human anymore and that there was nothing she could do to save her.

Mara began to see slight movements on the edges of the clearing all around her. Faces were looking cautiously out between trees. She saw Kat over to her right, and Hazen with another student, a boy whom she didn't recognize, off to her left. Looking over to where the demons were thickest, presumably where Erros was, Mara couldn't make out anyone between the bodies and the trees. Leif probably hadn't sent anyone over there because of the likelihood that they'd be discovered quickly and killed. Knowing that it would be awhile before anything happened Mara sat on the soft ground cover and set Mamba down next to her, motioning for Lissa and Tom to get down, too. They both dropped into comfortable sitting positions and tried to get into good spots for observation.

Mara had had Hazen check earlier for any significant uses of power in the area and she had come up with nothing, so Erros clearly had run out of tech to use after they had fried his last set. He had nothing except for his senses and his demons to tell if someone was watching, and neither was strong enough to detect them as long as no one used magic. Mara ruffled Mamba's feathers absentmindedly, something she did a lot when she was nervous.

Suddenly she felt her pet tense under her fingertips. Mamba was staring straight ahead into the clearing through a gap low to the ground, staring at something Mara couldn't see. She stood up and saw that the demons had formed a clump on one side of the clearing, leaving only about a foot of space between each one. She still couldn't see Erros but she knew he was in there somewhere, just waiting for the right moment. Looking to the right and then to the left she spotted Kat and Hazen's faces with identical looks of worry on them.

Venus and Kaeli must have sensed something too, Mara thought.

"I know you're there, Kat," a voice said from the clump. Slowly the demons parted like a great sea making way for Poseidon, and Erros stepped out in front of them. "I can feel you." He was unchanged from when Mara had last seen him, the perfect face that harbored a mind overrun with madness. Although his voice was soft it carried across the clearing, easily heard by all. Mara looked over to where Kat had been standing, seeing nothing at first but then catching a streak of movement out of the corner of her eye. Kat was suddenly only a few feet from Erros in the middle of the clearing, arms crossed with an expression of anger and determination on her face. She stayed put as Erros walked towards her and leaned down to whisper into her ear. Mara strained to hear what he was saying but she couldn't; she wanted so badly to run out and get Kat away from him. Against all her instincts she stayed put, knowing that whatever Kat was doing was part of a plan. Tom was staring at his niece too, horrified. Kat finally took a step backward and said something, still not loud enough for Mara to pick up. Erros shook his head in response to whatever Kat had said, opening his mouth and saying something that changed Kat's expression ever so slightly. She was looking everywhere she could without Erros noticing, sending a message with her eyes. *Get ready*.

"Oh, no, you're *all* out there somewhere," Erros shouted. Mara was sure all the students positioned around the clearing had heard that. She sensed muscles tensing, readying for battle. Erros moved lightning fast and grabbed Kat's arm. She flipped him over her head, but he landed on his feet and pulled Kat in, twirling her around as people did in those old dances from hundreds of years ago. One of his kamas magically appeared at Kat's throat and his other arm wrapped around her waist, holding her tight. Mara seethed more at this infraction than at the fact he was threatening her sister's life. Without taking the time to let her brain work through the battle plan Mara transformed into fog and shot out from behind the tree as fast as she could go, careening towards Kat and condensing to human a split second before slamming both fists, at the speed of sound, into Erros's rib cage. The human body instinctively lets go of things when it knows it's going to be thrown backwards, and Erros's arms flew out, releasing Kat. Erros soared through the air, landing in a small crumpled heap a good fifteen feet away from Mara and Kat, but he was back up on his feet in a second and starting towards them. They super-sped away, reaching the treeline in under a second but knowing there was no going back now. They had no idea where everyone else was but Mara knew they hadn't left the area.

Erros was now standing, tall and strong, in front of his legions of demons, all waiting for his command. "Come out, come out, wherever you are," he said in a singsong voice, though his face was anything but playful. Mara and Kat looked at each other. Their battle plan may have been ruined but there was too much anger in everyone's hearts to stop now. The battle *would* happen. Mara was just less sure of its outcome.

CHAPTER 22

*D*emonic eyes stared them down as they stood in front of Professor Erros, hair blowing in the wind and weapons at the ready. Mara had called all the students out of hiding after rescuing Kat, and they now stood in a small group facing Erros and his legions of demons. Mara, Kat, Hazen, Leif, Tom, and Niko all stood in front, protecting the students as much as they could. Erros had a hungry look on his face, leering at them as if they were chickens he had just roasted for dinner. Kat's fangs were out and she was hissing, claws out and itching to dig into flesh. Ice blue sparks were flying over Hazen's skin, gathering in her palms and lighting up her face with a deadly glow. All the students behind Mara had their weapons out, magic boiling, or both. Lissa, giving her sister an agonized look, held up a glowing blue hand of frost. As if on cue, everyone's eyes lit up. When WW channeled their energy, their eyes lit up in different colors. Each WW had a different magical eye color depending on their specialty, but all their eyes glowed brightly like stars. Erros laughed at them with derision. Leif was holding two shiny boomerangs and his eyes glowed especially brightly, his face taking on the placid, handsome expression that he used when breaking down mental barriers. Several of the demons' faces went completely slack, and they moved like robots over to the side of the students. Erros growled angrily at Leif. Kat hissed loudly and moved forward several steps. Erros held up his hands and opened his mouth to speak.

"It's no secret that none of you will survive this battle. I see no point in wasting good Witch Warrior blood so I'm offering you a choice. Stand down now and join my grand army or else I will have no choice but to water the trees with your blood." He spread his hands wide in an attempt at appearing to be welcoming. It was Mara's turn to laugh.

"You flatter yourself," she said icily. "None of us would ever join you, imbecile, and we *certainly* don't plan on dying." Erros looked apologetic as he shrugged.

"At least I offered. Clearly you don't recognize progress when you see it," he said, shaking his head before reaching behind him and motioning for the demons to advance. "Oh, and Kat?" he said, seeming to remember something very important. "I enjoyed that kiss we shared earlier in the year. Pity it was our first and last." Kat bared her fangs at him, looking ready to explode in anger and frustration.

"You *kissed* him?!" Mara said, outraged. Kat looked only mildly apologetic and mostly like she wanted to tear someone's head off.

"It was *before* I found he was trying to turn the planet into stir-fry and kill everyone we care about," she said defensively. Turning back to Erros she snarled before speaking. "You want another kiss? Come and get it." Erros smiled and laughed at her, shaking his head.

"You know, I really do care about you, Kat. I don't want to hurt you. That's why I agreed to take you instead of Mara and your friends," he said, sounding truly sincere. Mara was honestly not surprised that Erros still needed to feel that someone cared about him, but she couldn't believe that he thought *Kat,* of all people, would be the one to do the caring.

"Wait!" a shout came from the back of the group of students. Chase stepped in front of Leif and Mara, glancing back with a look of defeat. Turning back to Erros he clenched his fists, then let them hang loosely at his sides. "I will join you," he said, refusing to turn around when Kat and Leif both gasped. Erros smiled and held his hand up, stopping the demons in their tracks.

"Very good. Someone has common sense," he said, smiling at Chase. He beckoned Chase towards him. Mara and the rest watching in horror as Erros placed his open palm on Chase's forehead and closed his eyes. Chase's body gave a mighty jerk; he fell to his knees making soft grunting noises. When Erros let go of him he fell motionless to the ground. Against her instincts Kat ran forward and dropped to her knees beside Chase. Leif and Mara followed, with Hazen close behind.

"Look," Mara said, pointing to Chase's arm. "That symbol, I've seen it before." Darkening by the second was a mark that looked like some sort of ancient brand. "That's the symbol of death. He's gone," she said.

Mara looked sympathetically at Kat. Oddly, her sister didn't look all that sad, just disappointed. Leif was looking at Chase's body with a strange mix of anger, betrayal, and pain. Mara could only imagine how he must be feeling; Chase had been his only friend back at the Academy, and Leif must have believed that he would fight beside him till the end. She placed a hand on his arm and he looked at her distantly.

From above them Erros asked, "You see how well your little friend did. Some, the weaker ones, don't survive the process of turning. Do you really believe you'll do better?" Without warning Kat swung around and knocked Erros's feet out from under him, landing on his chest and putting her claws around his throat. Erros held up his hand and demons instantly surrounded him. Kat hissed once while looking at Mara who understood the message and stood up. She pulled everyone away from Chase and gave Kat her space.

Flipping to her feet Kat spun into action, slicing this way and that, disposing of demons left and right. The students took this as their cue and ran in. Erros did too, letting loose the demons who charged full power at the oncoming students. Mara, Hazen, and Leif jumped in. Mara caught a glimpse of Tom, now fully transformed into a wolf, snarling and slashing. His glowing green eyes, the werewolf trademark, flashed among the falling demon bodies. Niko, near him, was using his fangs to fight in the traditional vampire way – his amazing speed allowed him to rip the demons' heads off with his teeth. In a flash Kat was next to him, using her own fangs and claws to dismember demons right and left. Mara herself was fighting next to Hazen, whose butterfly knives were flying and who was electrocuting anyone within reach. With her double sword out Mara was spinning on her heels, swinging the sword and ducking when the demons came at her. Black blood splattered everywhere. A large explosion roared in one corner; Mara caught a glimpse of Kat smiling with her hands still outstretched towards a blackened crater littered with demon parts.

All kinds of magic were being thrown along with the silver flashes of blades. Mara felt a hand on her back and the sharp sting of a blade on her arm. Spinning around, her hand automatically went to the blowers in her sleeve cuffs. Picking one at random she sprayed it at the demon's face. A stream of fire shot out, cooking him where he stood. Shaking out her razor-bladed braid she used super-speed to spin around. Small cyclones of black blood followed her as she moved. She could feel the blood dripping from her braid but didn't care. Leif, a few feet away, was throwing boomerangs, then punching, kicking, and watching as they sliced through demons on their return trip to his hand. Across the clearing Mara saw Lissa approach her sister, brandishing a long sword. With a horrible expression Lissa drove the blade through her sister's chest. Mara felt a wave of admiration sweep through her for the young warrior, clearly so caring and yet sacrificing so much for the good of the planet.

Turning her attention back to the battle at hand she kept on killing, finding more demons where the ones she had just disposed of had fallen. By now the ground was littered with bodies, mostly demons but Mara noticed several students bodies among them. This battle would not come without casualties. Taking poison darts out of her dart cuffs she flung them at the oncoming horde of demons, watching them fall in place the moment the deadly substance took effect. As Mara ran her double sword through four demons at once she caught a glimpse of Erros fighting one of the students that she remembered from the briefing. His specialty was regeneration. As long as his heart and mind were connected he could grow back any damaged part of his body in a matter of seconds. Every time Erros sliced at the boy's arm Mara saw the skin simply grow back to normal.

When a large group of demons came running at her Mara launched herself high into the air. She took the opportunity to scan around the clearing for her sister and friends and saw them all fighting hard. Hazen was clinging to a tree branch with her sticky Glukon glue before she pushed off and landed behind several demons, running them all through with one movement. Coming down hard Mara swung the sword around her head, decapitating several demons before skidding on her knees toward the last one. Pressing the hilt of her double sword to its gut she hit the button on the end and felt the blade slide out straight into the demon's chest. It doubled over, black blood spilling from its mouth. Punching the demon off her sword she got a splatter of demon blood on her face. She spun around and began throwing knives and spinning her sword again, noticing that Erros seemed to be slowly running out of demons.

Mara disengaged from the battle and called everyone out of the fray. Surveying the clearing she saw layers and layers of bodies beginning to disintegrate into fine black dust that floated up into the air. Demons, when killed, were truly destroyed, and their mortal bodies quickly disappeared. What remained was Erros standing with about fifty demons and a few bodies of students on the ground. Six students were dead so far, but the ones that were left seemed quite ready to continue fighting. Erros roared and motioned the demons forward, leading the charge while swinging his kamas around as a protective shield. Mara yelled right back, charging to meet them.

The students followed her, Kat, Hazen, and Leif, yelling loudly. Blades began slicing, disgusting noises of blood being spilled filled the clearing, and demons were again falling and turning to dust. Mara saw Lissa fighting hand to hand with one of the demons; Lissa threw it several feet in the air, then launched herself up higher and came down with her sword through its chest. Another demon grabbed her shoulder from behind. Its hand glowed on her skin. She cried out in pain and slapped her own hand over the demon's. She channeled all her power into her hand, attempting to freeze him off. She glowed an unearthly ice blue but was fading by the second. Mara started to run towards her but her path was blocked by more demons. Defending herself from their blows caused her to drop her double sword, but she saw a sturdy tree branch lying nearby on the ground. Grabbing it she swung hard, slamming into the demons. More blood spurted and the branch flew off to the side of the clearing. Mara picked up her double sword. It felt satisfying to have it back in her hand. Walking confidently into the battle she looked for Lissa. What she saw was terrible.

Lissa's body was almost completely surrounded by the demon's bright red glow. Her hand was no longer glowing blue and her frost power was gone. It looked like all the moisture was being sucked out of her. When Mara thought about it that made perfect sense; the demons harnessed heat energy which meant they could draw all the moisture out of a person fairly easily. She watched in horror as Lissa's body slowly shriveled and crumpled. Then the demon released his hand from her shoulder. Furious, Mara leaped high into the air and came down with the tip of her sword pointed at the demon's head. He looked up and knocked the sword off to the side, avoiding the blow but not avoiding death. The second he pushed the blade off course Mara began to turn, flinging her braid around to slice through his throat. His head thumped onto the ground, the evil light leaving his black eyes. Pure anger was controlling her movements as Mara looked for more demons to kill. Turning into fog she flew around, punching and kicking the remaining evil beings before landing hard on the other side of the clearing. She slammed one fist into the ground with all her strength and channeled every bit of energy she had into it. The ground rippled, changing into fog as waves of her power radiated out from her fist. All the demons were caught in mid-leap or mid-strike, but the students, especially her sister and close friends, knew how to handle being turned into fog. The whole clearing, even the trees that stretched up to the sky, had become dark gray fog, completely under Mara's control. Changing and holding this much substance as fog took an immense amount of power and Mara soon had to let it go, standing up again as the fog rushed back and the world returned to dirt and flesh. The students landed perfectly, aiming killing blows at the demons they were fighting. The demons, startled and unable to deal with being turned into fog and back again, lost their footing and stumbled, making it that much easier to kill them.

Mara rejoined the battle to see Erros again attacking the regenerating student. This time, though, it seemed he had figured out the secret of regeneration. As Mara watched he swung his kamas around to build up speed, and struck lightning fast at the boy. For a split second it looked as if nothing had happened, but then the boy's body separated cleanly into three pieces – his legs, his torso, and his head and neck. Lavender and white blood flowed freely from the sections, making large puddles on the dry ground. Erros had cut the connection between heart and mind, and the boy could no longer regenerate.

Looking pleased with himself Erros finished his killing swing by sticking the kamas into the ground and pulling on them, flipping himself high up into the air. Mara looked beyond him and saw Kat, with a murderous expression on her face, staring directly at Erros. Clenching her hand she jumped into the air and flew towards Erros's unguarded rib cage. Using super-speed for extra power she rammed her fist into his gut, causing him to fly to the side and smash into the ground, sending up clouds of dust and dirt. Kat landed a few feet away from him and started towards his prone form, but he was faster. Pulling his kamas from their hold in the dirt he swung them around parallel to the ground, bringing them up at the last moment and cutting deep into Kat's arm. Wincing, she hissed and morphed into a tiger, leaping onto him and sinking her teeth deep into his neck. Scrabbling at her shoulders he got a good grip and threw her off ten feet to the side. She skidded, getting back up immediately and returning to human form. Her gear shirt sleeve was torn and wet with purple and white blood where Erros's kama had ripped her skin open. Her irises glowed bright purple, the same color as her pressure waves. Noticing a large group of demons attacking several student to her right she threw her hands down to load the ground under them with pressure. Immediately the ground exploded in a cloud of fire and flying dirt. The boom from the explosion rippled out over the clearing, shaking the ground like a small earthquake. Only small bits of black-stained flesh littering the ground indicated where the demons had stood. One of the students gave Kat an appreciative nod before heading back into battle. *Demons may be strong, but they don't have blast-resistant battle gear*, Kat thought.

Grinning she re-entered the fight, swiping left and right with her claws and blocking blows. One tall girl came in at her from behind with a long hunting knife raised over her head. Unaware, Kat dispatched another demon by pulling its striking arm behind it, breaking it easily. Then she placed her hand on his back and loaded him with pressure causing him to explode in a shower of black blood and innards. Kat wrinkled her nose in disgust before turning just in time to see the girl's hunting knife slicing downward toward her head. With super-speed she grabbed the attacker's wrist and pulled her off to the side. Going into the dead side, Kat sank her fangs deep into the girl's neck, jerked her head sideways and pulled the girl's head off. Kat dropped the limp body to the ground and began spitting desperately. She tried using her hands to wipe off her tongue but found that they too were completely caked with the viscous black blood that had the worst taste of anything Kat had ever experienced. Spinning around to hook-kick a demon in the head she gave up trying to clean her mouth, figuring that there was a time and place for everything and this was not the time to find a water fountain.

Using mostly kicks Kat cleared the area around her of demons. She tried to rest her arms enough to be able to keep throwing blasts of killing pressure. It had been at least ten minutes since the battle started and Kat had been using magic nonstop. Exhaustion swept over her. Once again she turned into a tiger, utilizing her most powerful weapon at the time – the muscles that her tiger had that her human body didn't. Leaping high into the air she came down hard on several demons, ripping them limb from limb. Suddenly, something large and furry came crashing into her, throwing her off the dead demons and crushing her into the ground. She pushed off with her powerful back legs and threw off whatever was on top of her. Baring her teeth she snarled at it until she realized who it was.

Tom's eyes, glowing bright green, stared back at her. His fur was tangled and coated in sticky black blood, but otherwise he seemed fine. His mouth was slightly open as he panted and Kat could see the black-coated teeth beneath his dark gray muzzle. Growling softly as if trying to tell her something he ran back into the crowd of moving bodies. Kat did the same, glad to have had some contact with her family. She hadn't seen Mara in a while but was sure she was okay because she had seen many demon bodies on the ground with cleanly cut heads, clearly the result of Mara's deadly braid. There were frequent blasts of lightning from various places around the clearing, so Kat was sure that Hazen was still up and fighting. She was worried, though. During her battles around the clearing she had seen many of the dead. There were, she estimated, probably over a hundred and fifty dead demons now, but the number of student bodies she had seen was alarming. Mostly they were either dismembered or shriveled beyond recognition. Kat had seen a demon do this, drawing all the moisture out of one of the younger students and harvesting it for itself. The student had simply shriveled up and collapsed, dead before he hit the ground. Kat was trying to count the number of non-demon fighters left and came up with only Mara, Hazen, Leif, Niko, Tom, herself, and two remaining students. Of the original twenty only eight were left, but the demonic forces had decreased by at least twelve times as much. The clearing was significantly more open. Kat estimated that only around thirty demons remained alive.

Through the greatly-thinned crowd she saw Niko, his mouth covered in black blood, looking disgusted as he ripped another demon head off with his fangs. Throwing it clear out of sight, a distance of almost forty feet, he moved on to the next foe. A demon with a short sword and another with a long, deadly-looking dagger were charging at him from opposite sides. Ducking at the last moment Niko grabbed both of their hands and shoved their respective weapons into each other. They both fell onto him, splattering more blood everywhere, but he shrugged them off. Noticing Kat through a gap in the bodies he grinned crookedly and started towards her. A demon appeared behind him, raising a long blade to sink into his back. Before Kat could call out a warning Niko whipped his hand back in a backfist, slamming the creature in the forehead with vampire strength hard enough to smash its skull. Speeding the rest of the way to Kat he asked breathlessly if she was okay.

"I'm fine, but the death toll is high for both demon and student. We need to get everyone out of here and regroup," she urged. He nodded and sped off, grabbing people by the arm and pulling them along with him. Dodging blows from some especially fast demons he found the two students that were still alive and brought them to the edge of the clearing. Mara got the memo when she saw Niko and the students leaving the battle, so she sped to the side of the clearing as fog. Hazen joined them a split second later as a blinding lightning bolt; when she sizzled back into human form she looked as excited as Kat had ever seen her. Hazen was also splattered with blood, but she had a knife in each hand and looked totally riled up and ready to finish off the demon army.

Erros, seeing that everyone had withdrawn, slowed his kamas down and wrapped them casually around his body. Taking his place in front of his group of demons, now thinned to about ten, he seemed just as confident as ever despite the fact that he was flanked by only a few protective guards. The demons behind him snarled, spittle flying from their mouths, their fluid black eyes swirling dangerously.

"You have to get out of here. Both of you," Mara whispered to the two students. They both shook their heads violently, but Kat had already grabbed them by the shoulders.

"Go!" she said. They looked down for a second, before offering their remaining knives to Mara and Kat.

"Promise us you'll kill them," the girl said. Mara nodded, taking the knives and sticking them in her gear. Casting one last glance at the demon army, the students sped off in a flash.

"You're giving up?" Erros asked the warriors, laughing at his own question. "Who am I kidding; you're all too dumb to realize the pointlessness of your cause. I will kill every last one of you and then I'll go to your houses and kill everyone you care about." His voice deepened and he sounded deadly serious.

Mara shook her head slowly, wiping a smear of purple blood, her own, off the side of her mouth. "Not today," she growled. Erros twisted his mouth into an expression of fury, his perfect features contorted beyond recognition. Swiping at her with one of his kamas he brought the deadly blade down through the air so fast that it was almost invisible. Mara, always anticipating, threw herself sideways just as the kama sliced down where she had been standing. As he swung the kama back around himself Erros's upper lip twitched. He snarled a few mangled words in a rough, demonic voice. He was speaking in Yyuligian, but somehow he had managed to turn the language inside out; it no longer sounded like the beautiful, seductive tongue of the ancients, but more like words created to cause harm and summon destruction. The more Mara thought about it, the more she began to realize that that was exactly what Erros was using Yyuligian for – the summoning of demons.

Moving as one hyper-fast unit the demons came forward. A flash of silver on her right caught Mara's attention and she looked just in time to see Leif's wrist flicking out and a boomerang slicing through the ranks of demons with deadly grace. There was a long, bloody cut on the side of Lief's leg and he was hobbling. Several demon heads fell to the ground with sickening squishing sounds, black blood flowing freely. Erros resumed swiping side to side with his kamas, engaging Niko in a super-speed battle. The vampire hissed angrily at Erros, showing long, bloodstained fangs that ended in razor-sharp points. Erros paid Niko's hostility no heed; he simply laughed, and tried to fit words into his fight patterns.

"So, you're the vamp that lives at the Cyania's," he taunted. "Bet the girls don't appreciate having a monster for an uncle." He grunted as Niko dodged a kama and came in lightning fast with a rising palm strike to Erros's jaw. The blow sent Erros flying backwards several feet. Niko strode forward to put his boot on Erros's throat, leaning down to hiss something in his ear.

"You're right. I *am* a monster," he said in a deadly soft voice. "And you should know it's best not to make a monster like me angry." Erros laughed, his grin twisted from pulling at the spots of dried purple blood on his face. Niko growled and slammed the heel of his boot down harder onto Erros's windpipe, causing Erros to make a pathetic choking sound. Flicking the fingers of his right hand Erros unwound his kama and swung it up, driving its blade into Niko's back. Erros pulled on the kama with all his might, causing the blade to rip sideways along Niko's spine. A cry of pain escaped Niko's lips and his boot involuntarily lifted from Erros's throat. Mahogany blood coated the blade of the kama and soaked Niko's shirt, pulsing out of the deep wound. Erros was already on his feet, having spun his legs around and used the momentum to flip himself back upright, and he was coming at Niko again. Niko clenched his fists, snapped his head back up, and dodged Erros's blow just in time. Flashing from place to place as only a vampire can Niko rained fists down on every soft spot that Erros possessed. Erros arched his back in pain and fell down to the ground. Lightning fast Niko was at his ankle, sinking his fangs deep into Erros's flesh. Vampire bites, despite coming from only two fangs, cause immense amounts of pain for the victim. Erros screamed loudly, swinging his kamas around behind him, trying to dislodge Niko who scrambled backwards, letting go of Erros's leg in order to stand up again. Refueled with fresh blood Niko formed two fists and directed his vampire healing power to his back and neck. The cuts began to stitch themselves together, the blood slowly drawing back into the wounds. In ten seconds there was no sign that the deep slices had ever been there.

Meanwhile, Mara, Kat, Hazen, and Leif were fighting hand to hand with the demons that were left. Because so many demons had died Erros was able to channel all the energy he had given them into the remaining few, strengthening them greatly. Only two had died since the fighting had resumed, and both deaths had required several previously fatal blows. Mara was battling a large male demon with spiky hair who was proving very difficult to kill. Her double sword was way across the clearing and she couldn't free up a hand to bring it to her, so she resorted to using smaller hunting knives and her own fists. Hooking the demon around the neck with her leg she slammed him down to the ground, punching him hard in the jaw bone as she did. His head snapped to the side and blood flowed, but he brought his foot up and drove it hard into Mara's knee. He regained his footing and came at her with a longsword in his hand. As he brought it down Mara rolled out of the way, letting the sword get stuck deep into the ground. Whirling her legs around she hit his rib cage with both of them, causing him to stumble sideways and lose his grip on the sword. Launching herself into the air she spun around so her back faced the demon and struck with the knife-edge of her left foot. She connected with his temple, sending his head turning at a disturbing angle. Throwing his hands out he braced himself, pushing back up into a standing position. Mara landed squarely on her feet several yards away from where the demon was now standing.

With demonically-enhanced speed he charged at her, ready to bring his fist down on her nose, but she ducked and slid between his legs, flinging her arms backwards and arching her back as if she were doing the limbo. Pushing up off her knees and ready to spin around and attack, Mara suddenly felt a hand on her shoulder, its incredible strength forcing her back down to the ground. A white-hot pain exploded in her shoulder and raced throughout her body. She screamed silently, not wanting to distract anyone else. She saw that her fingers were beginning to look as if she had spent too long in the bath. She had seen the same thing happen to Lissa only minutes ago, the moisture of the human body sucked out by the unrelenting demonic heat energy harnessed by the creatures. She made a fist and jerked her elbow up to slam into the demon's groin. She felt him buckle and the hand released her shoulder, but she knew she hadn't hit him very hard; he would be back any second. She was now seriously dehydrated. Her muscles felt like lead balls dragging her down. Struggling back to her feet she turned just in time to see a foot flying towards her. Before she had a chance to block it the foot slammed into her chest, sending her staggering backwards. Throwing her hand out behind her Mara let gravity flow downward from her palm.

This allowed her hand to remain steady about a foot above the ground. She leaned all her weight on the suspended hand, put more energy into holding the opposing gravitational force, and kicked off the ground with both feet. Tensing the muscles in her holding arm she pushed off hard, adding an extra shove from her self-created gravity so she could get high enough to slam her heels hard into the demon's chest.

The demon crashed down and Mara landed on top of it, holding out her free hand as she flew through the air. Searching for a second she found her double sword with her mind and pulled hard on it. The gravity around it swelled and became unbalanced, making the sword swing upright and fly towards her outstretched palm. Just as the demon landed flat on his back Mara planted her feet firmly on his chest as she felt the hilt of her double sword slam satisfyingly into her hand. She raised it over her head and thrust it down into the demon's chest, right between her feet. He arched his back as the sword went through his heart; then his body fell back down with a sickening thump. Black blood splattered all over Mara's gear boots. Stepping off the demon she watched it disintegrate before her eyes, ending up as a small pile of black dust.

Swinging her double sword around her a few times just for show she caught Kat's eye and nodded ever so slightly. Kat had recently dispatched her demon and was moving on to the group that surrounded Hazen. Mara followed, striding across the clearing. She could barely see the shiny blonde of Hazen's hair through the swarm of three or four large demons that encircled her. Two of them were missing limbs, the wounds so neat that they had to have been caused by a blade. Hazen was fighting fiercely, but for some reason the greatest number of demons had come to attack her. Kat had already made it to her and was sinking her claws into one of the demons, getting a good grip and flinging him high into the air. The demon disappeared through the treeline, its faint cry fading into the forest. Another one of the demons spun to face Kat, engaging her with a short hunting knife that Mara recognized. As the demon slashed at Kat from every angle Mara threw out her hand and drew the knife towards her. It took a great deal of pulling but finally the knife came out of the death-grip of the demon and flashed into Mara's hand.

"This is mine!" she said angrily. "No one touches my stuff!" Drawing her hand back she flung the knife at him, purposefully aiming too far to the left for it to hit him. The demon, not bothering to look to his right, leaped away from the knife speeding towards him. Instantly the tip of a blade poked out of his chest as his eyes died and his body fell limp. Kat, standing the whole time on the demon's other side with her knife at the ready, had simply let him jump onto the blade as he tried to avoid Mara's strategically thrown dagger. Pushing him off her sword in disgust Kat reached out toward the demon's body. Purple waves of pressure emanated from her hand. Before releasing them she took several steps back. The ground exploded in a small, controlled blast, not designed for death but simply meant to prevent the demon from disintegrating.

A mushroom cloud blossomed up from the blast site, briefly obscuring Mara's vision, but she transformed into fog and flew around the smoky area to come to Hazen's aid. Momentarily turning her hands back to flesh she grabbed one of the demons and swung him around her body, spinning an extra time as fog for maximum propulsion. Using all her strength she hurled him, watching as he soared up like a large ungainly bird, through the canopy. The momentum from her throw had sent her speeding towards the ground; at the last second she turned back human, slamming down onto the hard dirt in a right front roll, using her shoulder and upper back to protect her head and neck from injury as she rotated back up to her feet.

"Mara, duck!" Leif cried from somewhere to her right. Snapping her head around Mara saw small glints of silver flash between the two demons remaining around Hazen. Leaning far back and throwing her arms out behind her head, Mara watched as the boomerang sailed over her face, both edges covered in black blood. It disappeared from her field of vision and Mara snapped back upright. She felt the air around her ear stir as the boomerang whipped by her again, returning itself as always to Leif's waiting hand. Both demons were now decapitated and lying lifeless on the ground next to Hazen. The remaining one, seething with anger at the death of its fellow fighters, came at Hazen fast with a side kick and an attempt to grab her arm and bring her around into an armbar. Hazen, raising her leg to knock his kick off course, grabbed his fist with hers and simply stopped his swing. She could hear the tiny bones in his hand crunching as she pushed back on his wrist with all her strength. Her eyes crackled with lightning, the small sparks flashing all over her body giving her a blue-white glow. Hazen wrapped her free hand around his neck, squeezing with electrically charged fingers. The smell and sound of sizzling flesh tainted the air as the demon cried out in pain, an inhuman sound that evoked no pity. Summoning a large lightning bolt Hazen let go of his fist and neck just in time for the bolt to come crashing down straight through the demon's head. He was already a small pile of black dust before he hit, or rather, floated to the ground. When Mara and Kat's eyes recovered from the blinding flash of white lightning they saw Hazen standing over the pile of demon dust, hair wild and full of static, hands clenched at her sides.

Tom skidded to a halt a few feet in front of where Mara and Kat were standing, several long lacerations down his sides and across his back. He was panting heavily but still he looked at Kat and Mara, checking them for any serious injuries. They were all bloodied and bruised, weakened and exhausted by the prolonged exertion. Sweat gleamed on every forehead including Niko's. Erros was looking around him, searching for his demons and finding only one. The sole remaining demon, a girl, was standing next to Erros; she seemed to have a glowing aura of orange-red light that surrounded her, making her look almost ethereal despite her horrific eyes.

"That's the energy I saw him transfer when I was prisoner," Kat whispered to Mara. "He's giving it all to her." Erros smiled as if he could hear them, as if he were glad that they knew what he was doing.

"You may have killed my army, but I have killed most of yours, too. Even with only one of my demons left you will never win," he declared contemptuously. "My power grows stronger with every passing day, while yours only weakens." He held his hands up, orange-red pools gathering in his palms, glowing with a deadly supernatural light. Letting the light fade and the glow dissipate he lowered his hands again and looked challengingly at Mara and the others as if to say, "I'd like to see one of *you* demonstrate such power." Standing beside Mara, Kat scoffed, raising her upper lip in a sneer.

"Well, are you sure you still have one demon?" she asked innocently, widening her eyes and switching her determined expression to one of honest questioning. Erros turned, suddenly alarmed, to the glowing demon standing next to him. For a second his fears were unjustified. The demon was standing there looking completely normal. But then something flat and silver shot out of her chest, flying so fast it was a blur, and stopping only a few inches from Kat's nose before turning back around and speeding back into the hand of its owner. The demon fell forward, a clean hole cut right through her chest, draining black blood down onto the dirt.

"No!" Erros screamed, rage raising his voice to an unbearable volume. His head tilted upwards and his arms extended out, palms opening towards the sky. The orange-red light that had surrounded him, almost blindingly bright, was now funneling up off his body and slowly disappearing. He continued to scream, this time in pain instead of anger, and his body began to twitch and shake uncontrollably. The light continued to fly up off him, leaving less and less of an aura around him until there was none left. Dropping his head back onto his chest and lowering his arms he stopped screaming and stopped shaking. There was no longer any light, any power, around him; he looked drained of color and life.

Raising his head with effort to look at the group of haggard, shocked people standing in front of him, Erros's face began to turn red with fury. Suddenly he whipped around, blindingly fast, and clenched his fist around Leif's throat. Leif had been hiding behind Erros waiting for the right time to strike, but Erros moved so fast that even Leif couldn't see it coming; his feet rose several inches off the ground as Erros squeezed his windpipe tighter and tighter. Leif's face turned red as he struggled to get out of Erros's choke but Erros, in his unbridled rage, was far too strong.

Seemingly by magic, a long curved blade appeared in Erros's free hand. Pulling it behind him he readied it to be sent forward into Leif's gut, but Kat's hands were faster. Waves of purple pressure flew out, reaching Erros in a split second and exploding in a large, uncontrolled blast around the hand holding Leif's throat. Erros's face showed pain but his hand did not let go. When the smoke cleared Mara saw in horror that his whole hand was charred black, but his grip was just as strong. Blood was running out of his hand onto the ground but that didn't appear to concern him.

"You've lost your power," Hazen said suddenly in a provocative voice. "Now that your demons are dead, you're just the same as you were before you made the first pill, before you started this sick crusade. You're just a fallen idol." Erros growled in fury at her, forgetting for a second about the boy he was about to run through.

"I was always more than they thought I was," he said softly. "They couldn't understand what I did, they didn't see my greatness until it was too late for them. They are caught in the past, while I am years into the future." He seemed to have forgotten all about the WW standing in front of him, and was talking only to himself.

"I *will* be victorious, and there's nothing you can do to stop me!" he yelled, bringing his head back up to face them with a maniacal grin. "You should be honored. You are giving your lives for a great cause, and your deaths will contribute to building a new, everlasting society." He directed his attention back to Leif.

"How would you like to be first?" he asked so quietly that none of the others could hear him. The blade moved, coming in as a blur towards Leif's exposed chest. Leif's leg moved too, swinging up towards Erros's head, trying to wrap around his neck and throw him to the ground. Stopping his strike for a second, Erros blocked Leif's leg. He no longer possessed demonic power but he was still one of the best fighters in the country. Leif had been out of air for too long and was turning purple. His arms and legs moved feebly but he was too hurt and suffocated to put up much of a fight. Erros's blade was only centimeters away from Leif's abdomen.

They all started moving at the same time, Kat throwing out her hands and exploding large chunks of air around Erros's sword hand, Tom taking great strides with his long wolf legs towards Leif, and Hazen pulling lightning from the clouds and aiming right through Erros's head with one hand and flinging several butterfly knives with the other. Niko began to blur towards them with vampire speed. Mara, shouting as she did so, rippled smoothly into dark gray fog, moving in a thick line as if having been shot through a fire hose towards Leif at her absolute top speed. A large boom sounded, and what looked like a quickly moving shadow expanded off of Mara's fog as she reached top speed, breaking the sound barrier. The ground shook beneath her but Erros didn't stumble, never losing his balance despite the rocking movement caused by the sonic boom that seemed to reverberate through the ground. He jabbed the sword forward so fast even Mara couldn't see it move. A scream filled the clearing.

CHAPTER 23

*B*lood spurted from Leif's mouth as the shining blade slid through his gut like soft butter. Mara's hand was outstretched, her fingers reaching desperately towards the sword. She could see it, almost feel the metal on her skin, but her fingertips were millimeters away. The second the tip of the sword penetrated his body her senses blacked out, leaving her blind and unaware of the world around her. Hearing, sight, smell, touch, and taste were all gone, leaving her in a silent black void of nothingness. Like a rubber band being stretched too far and breaking, her senses snapped back to reality as suddenly as they had gone and she could once again witness what was happening. Leif's body curved in pain as the tip of the long sword poked out of his back, completely coated in blood. Trickles ran out of the corners of his mouth and dripped down onto his shoulders; his hands clenched into loose fists at his sides before falling limp.

Mara silently screamed, still as fog, as she saw his eyes change. Once lively deep emerald pools of knowledge, strength, courage, and determination, they were now the portals of death. On the outside his eyes remained the same as they had always been, but Mara looked deeper and saw blank emptiness, unseeing and unliving, a soul jarringly removed from the mortal world.

Mara solidified as she fell to the ground on her knees, arms reaching out just in time to catch Leif's falling body before it hit the ground. Around the area of the wound his shirt was soaked with blood, like a river had overflowed its banks. Behind her she could faintly hear the explosions and the lightning brought on by Kat and Hazen, and she felt a gust of wind as Niko and Tom skidded to a halt a few paces away from her.

Leif was gone. Mara could tell the second she looked closely at him that he was already dead. On the inside of his lower arm a mark was slowly appearing. Mara had seen it before, when Chase had died. The symbol of death darkened into a horrible, black curse painted in cruel writing on Leif's tanned arm. Looking at that mark, the sign that the soul had left the mortal body, time left Mara. The moment stretched, a rubber band with no limit, into eternity. In her mind she knew Kat and Hazen should have come by now but they hadn't, and her brain wasn't functioning enough to care. No tears left her eyes, no sobs heaved; she just stared at the broken body lying in her arms, careful not to let it touch the ground.

The flash of silver was the only thing she saw. The kama pulled back just as quickly as it had come, leaving a thin line of blood on Leif's leg. Without thinking, Mara flew into action. Setting Leif's body down as softly as possible she spun, twisting her feet around and feeling her hair fly out behind her as she did so. The world was a blur of green and brown, but she saw one thing very clearly – Erros, standing directly behind her, covered in blood and blackened burn spots, holding his kamas with a provocative expression on his vain and arrogant face. He barely had time to register what was happening, let alone duck, before the razor blades sliced cleanly across his chest. He staggered back a few feet, blood spurting out of the wound, but Mara could see that it was shallow and would not kill him. Finishing her turn she planted her feet and threw her hands out in front of her. All the knives remaining in her gear flew out of their pockets as she adjusted the gravity around them and sent them speeding towards Erros's exposed body. Sinking deep into his shoulders and legs the knives drove Erros further back. He landed hard on his spine, sending up a puff of dust.

Mara ran to stand over Erros's body, bending her knees and leaning over his face. Gripping two of the knives that were stuck in his shoulders she twisted both of them, digging deep into his flesh. His face contorted in pain as he screamed, a sound like sweet music to Mara's ears. Blood pulsed out of his wounds in sync with his heartbeat.

"Why not just kill me? Why not end it?" he asked in a strained voice, trying to meet Mara's eyes. "You're capable. But you won't." Mara growled in rage.

"You will feel all the pain he felt. You will feel all the pain *everyone* you ever hurt felt," Mara said in a controlled, venomous voice. "There's no way for any of them to forgive you now. How are you ever going to be able to forgive yourself?" As Erros laughed a bit of dark lavender blood came up with the spiteful sound and splattered on his stubbly cheek.

"You talk about forgiveness, but you know nothing of it. You have no purpose in life, whereas I am fulfilling a great dream. I need no forgiveness from anyone," he said, raising his head so his nose was inches away from Mara's.

Mara gazed down at him with something that could only be described as hateful pity, a strange and rare mix of emotions. "You're sick, and twisted, and dark," she said. "*You* of all people don't understand forgiveness."

By now Kat, Hazen, Niko, and Tom were all standing in a reverential semi-circle around Mara and Erros. Tom had morphed back into a human, Niko and Kat's fangs were concealed, as well as her claws, and Hazen was no longer covered in blue-white sparks.

Erros seemed to have no more words for Mara. Instead he looked past her to the figures standing around his prone form. "We could have been gods, Kat, and yet you choose a weak, mortal life? Living in this hell hole?" He looked at Kat with wonder and pity in his eyes. Mara suddenly pushed herself off Erros's chest and strode back to join everyone else. Kat took her place immediately, crouching down next to Erros and grabbing the two knives that were stuck deep into his thighs. Erros didn't even try to stop her as she twisted the hilts viciously and watched calmly as blood poured out of the holes. Clearly some vital nerve endings and muscle connections had been severed by the knives because all he did was twitch his fingers and gasp in pain.

"If you ever cared about me, something I'm seriously doubting, you'd know that love doesn't mean blindly following the object of your affection. Maybe I *don't* know what love is, maybe I've never felt it, but it sure as hell isn't that," she said softly, leaning down and bringing her face close to Erros's. "You need a soul in order to love, and that is something you are sorely lacking."

For once Erros didn't seem to fight the statement; he just lay back and stared up at the sky. Slowly Kat removed one hand from the hilt of the knife and held it off to her side, outstretched as if expecting to catch something. A hunting knife slid smoothly out of the sheath hidden beneath her sleeve and fit neatly into her palm. Her fingers closed around the hilt and she began to lazily twirl the knife around her fingers as if she were a magician and the knife was a gold coin.

Mara stepped forward, stretching her hand out towards the knife in Kat's hand and preparing to alter the gravity around it to send it away, but she felt a warm hand grasp her own. She turned to see Hazen, blond hair charged with static, looking meaningfully at her with her distinctive ocean blue-green eyes.

"Let her," Hazen whispered, her eyes conveying more than words ever could.

CHAPTER 24

*K*at's mind was a flurry of activity, confused, two halves of her personality fighting over her next action. The knife shook in her hand, deadly silver tip quavering a half-inch away from Erros's gear-covered chest. Closing her eyes for a moment, quieting her mind and banishing the anger-driven thoughts that swirled around her consciousness, she let out the breath she didn't know she had been holding and slowly lowered the blade.

"You don't deserve what I'm giving you," she whispered to Erros in a broken voice before smoothly rising to her feet and turning her back. When she walked past his legs she made sure the diamond-tipped stiletto heel of her gear boot scratched his ankle, leaving a thin line of dark blood.

Kat slid her arm around Mara's shoulders as they walked away from Erros. On her other side Niko was coming towards them with Leif's long, limp, bloody body draped over his arms. He carried the body as easily as if it were a feather, trying his best not to let

Leif's head bump up and down. He kept his distance behind Mara and Kat, not wanting to remind them of the price of their victory.

"Aaahhhh!" A yell sounded from behind them, short and sharp, a sound as much of madness as it was of desperation. Just as the noise reached them a huge, concussive blast hit their backs, throwing them all several feet into the air. Niko twisted in mid-air and landed on his back, throwing one arm out to keep Leif's body from hitting the ground. Mara, Kat, Hazen, and Tom all slammed into the ground, oriented so their hips and shoulders took the blow instead of necks, spinal cords, or faces. Mara's arms instinctively went up over her head and chest, guarding her vitals as she had been taught in bomb detonation class. Dust and dirt swirled in the air, blocking any visual of what caused the explosion. Kat climbed back up to her feet, too exhausted to do a flip. She could feel the bruises forming where her body had hit the hard ground. Mara and Hazen were getting to their feet. Niko had taken a hard hit to the head while shielding Leif's body from harm and was unresponsive, lying motionless on the ground. Tom staggered over to him and lifted Leif, gently placing the body over his shoulder before leaning down again to grab Niko's feet. He began to pull Niko off to the side of the clearing, away from the blast crater and out of harm's way. Mara squinted through the dust as a light began to grow in front of them, an orange glow that lit up the whole clearing. The source of the glow stepped into a patch of artificial sunlight. Hazen let out a small gasp as she saw the face that stared back at her.

He was barely recognizable; his eyes, mouth, and hands had turned into pure orange light. His face was twisted, now more than ever a true monster. Mara and Kat simply stood there, shocked, staring at the being that was in front of them. Erros's eyes were pure orange light, as if his eyeballs had been replaced by magic. When he opened his mouth to laugh Mara saw with horror that his insides, too, were glowing with that unbearably bright light.

"Why won't he *die*?!" Kat whispered angrily. Erros staggered towards them, his arms stretched out sideways and his palms open to the sky. His hands had been consumed by the light and now there was just a ball of raw power on the end of each arm.

"He's unstable, Kat," Mara said, loudly enough that Hazen could hear too. "Look at his veins, they're glowing with power. If we don't kill him he's going to detonate." Kat nodded, a sick expression on her face. As he got closer, his steps uneven and jerky, Kat saw what Mara was talking about. Everyplace that a vein, capillary, or artery ran was emitting an orange-red glow indicating the magic had taken over; pretty soon his mortal body wouldn't be able to contain the power.

Mara's double sword was immediately in her hand, both blades out and glinting in the late afternoon sun. Faintly she heard the telltale sounds of Kat's fangs and claws unsheathing themselves and Hazen's lightning crackling into existence.

"He's not human anymore. He doesn't deserve mercy," Hazen stated coldly. Erros's head snapped around to look at her with his blinding eyes. Hazen, eyes watering slightly from the overexposure, stood her ground and looked straight back at him. With a flick of her finger she sent a deadly bolt of blue-white lightning towards his chest. His movements were slow and disconnected, as if his brain was having a hard time telling his muscles what to do. He wasn't fast enough to dodge the lightning. It struck his chest with a boom and then stopped. The electricity fizzled out and Erros continued to stand there, unfazed. A black burn mark grew quickly across his chest, his shirt all but gone where the lightning had struck, but still he was unconcerned. He jerked forward several more steps.

"What the hell?!" Hazen whispered.

Mara vaporized and shot like a contrail around Erros, finding her footing once she was directly behind him. He noticed she was gone and tried to twist his head around to see her, but couldn't turn it far enough. Kat took the opportunity to throw her hands out and shoot spears of pressure at him, glowing purple spikes that were as deadly as they were beautiful. This time he moved, stepping aside just before the spears would have hit him. The spears continued, pointing at Mara's chest instead, but she immediately turned to fog and the spears passed right through her. Only after the spears had crashed into a tree behind her and the tree had gone up in a mushroom cloud did Mara return to human. Erros's right hand began to amplify its glow, forcing Mara, Kat, and Hazen to raise their hands over their eyes to shield their vision. He shot a ball of pure power out of his open hand. Hazen dropped to the ground like a marionette with its strings cut in order to dodge the flaming ball. The power hit Kat as she was dropping, searing along her leg as she bent down. While it was not a direct hit Mara could see where the magic had burned a large hole in Kat's gear pants, and there was freely flowing blood underneath. Kat cried out in pain, pressing her hand hard over the open wound.

Without warning Erros shot a ball of power out of his other hand, aimed behind him, straight at Mara. Throwing her body to the side she just managed to avoid being hit, but the ball continued on its path and cut through the trunk of the tree directly behind her. It began to fall. Hazen cried out; it looked like the tree was going to come crashing down on Mara, but it stopped an inch above her head, suspended in midair. Mara's mind held it there, morphing the gravity around it so that it would neither fall nor rise. Not a muscle twitched on her face as she made the tree fly away from her, crashing it down to the ground in a cloud of dust twenty feet away. Erros was now looking at Mara, his body turned to face her and his eyes blindingly bright. She noticed that his veins were now glowing even more brightly. There wasn't much time left before the power inside him would blow. He began to walk towards her and she towards him.

Mara's feet began to lift from the ground, her hands opening at her sides. Soon she was four feet off the ground, one leg slightly bent. Kat and Hazen stared at her in wonder. Their hands were raised as well, magic pooling in them, but neither made a move. Erros, for the first time, showed some degree of worry when he saw Mara floating slowly towards him, her feet equal with his chest.

"So? What's your move?" she asked, loud enough for everyone to hear but clearly directing her question at him.

Erros looked momentarily conflicted as to what he should say, his mouth slightly open and letting a sliver of orange light out. Finally he opened his mouth wider, casting a circle of light up and onto Mara's chest. "I killed your friends. I killed your boyfriend. I will cleanse the whole planet of the WW disease if it's the last thing I do."

"Wrong. Move." Mara whispered. Glancing down at her hands she closed her eyes. Snapping her head back up she opened them again, not knowing what she was doing but feeling the pure power in her veins. Kat and Hazen gasped as they saw Mara's face. She was crying, tears dripping slowly out of her eyes and falling to the ground. Her eyes, however, were what horrified Kat and Hazen so. They were black. Pure, oily black, a perfect yet terrible imitation of the demons they had just slaughtered.

"Mara!" Kat cried out desperately, but there was no response. Not even a flicker of understanding showed in those black eyes. Her mouth opened suddenly and she screamed, an inhuman screech that rang out and forced Kat and Hazen to clap their hands over their ears. Mara's head tilted back until her eyes faced the sky. Her body began to twitch as if she were having a seizure. Erros was staring at the spectacle before him with a mixture of confusion and fear. Suddenly Mara's screams stopped, their echoes hanging in the air before quiet began to settle again.

The brief moment of calm was just that. Brief. Mara's hands, which had been hanging limply at her sides, opened up wide with her palms facing Erros. A black substance Kat couldn't identify twisted out of Mara's hands and moved quickly towards Erros, surrounding him in black tendrils of what looked like extremely condensed smoke. Soon he was no longer visible; the black stuff had created a wall around him. Kat and Hazen watched in disbelief as they began to see orange bursts of light through the blackness. Erros, panicking inside the swirling tornado of black magic, was desperately firing blasts of his own power at random. Kat could see that every time an orange blast hit the wall it became more transparent, but when she focused her eyes on Mara it was clear that the magic pouring out of her hands would not stop and would keep on rebuilding the wall. Meanwhile, the wind around Mara had picked up significantly even though there was no wind anywhere else. Her hair, previously in a braid that was covered in dried demon blood, was now flying loose around her head, the silver razor blades flashing when the light caught them. The blood was all but gone, blown away by the strong winds that Mara had conjured. Leaves and dirt had been swept up in a cyclone around her, making it increasingly hard to see her features. Her eyes, though, were horribly clear. The blackness was moving as if it were liquid, swirling just like the growing typhoon around Erros's body.

Hazen gripped Kat's arm, looking at her with fearful blue-green eyes. The twisting black mass that was Erros had begun to move towards them, and so had Mara. She was floating purposefully through the air, hands out and moving the magic that surrounded Erros. Kat's eyes watered as the wind blew into them but she kept looking straight at Mara. The expression on Kat's face was clear. Desperation. She knew that if the twister containing Erros moved too close to them it might very well consume them, too. The blasts had grown less frequent but no less strong, and Kat was not eager to be stuck in a vortex of deadly black magic with a very angry and unstable man.

Mara's eyes flicked up, for the first time showing some sort of feeling through the bottomless blackness. Kat thought she saw some small part of her sister surface in those eyes and convey something to her, some old trick they had come up with back when their lives were still reasonably normal. She grinned despite herself. Taking out the long blade that one of the remaining students had given her, she held it out to Hazen, who wasn't quite sure what was going on but who had trained with Mara and Kat so long that she knew they could communicate without words and surely had some sort of plan. Hazen put her finger on the blade, lightning crackling down her arm and covering the blade in a web of blue-white sparks. Kat motioned for Hazen to stand back, then took a position behind Erros.

Mara waited a second before springing into action. The black magic flowing from her hands stopped as suddenly as it had started, and the wall around Erros began to quickly deteriorate. Giving a yell Mara propelled herself forward, moving the tornado of wind with her. Erros and the remaining magic around him moved too, faster than before. A blast of orange power split the black magic barrier and sheared through a tree to Kat's right, leaving a hole in Mara's wall. Mara's expression darkened, her yell growing louder as she leaned forward once more, forcing Erros back.

Kat swung the electrically charged blade a few times to gain momentum, aimed for where she knew Erros stood, and plunged it forward. The lightning surged forward when it touched the greatly diminished energy shield, bolts spreading out and encasing the black wall like a spider web, eating through the black magic and allowing Kat to get a clear shot at Erros. She barely glimpsed Erros's face, a mask of fury and fear, before striking. Her blade, no longer covered in electricity but just as deadly, sliced easily into Erros's side. She felt the tip come into contact with his spine.

She pushed harder, feeling his spinal cord snap beneath her sword. His face tipped back in agony, mouth open wide but emitting no sound, only orange light. The black magic had now completely disappeared, giving Kat a clear view of Mara past Erros's broken body. Her sister was back on the ground and the howling wind had died, but her eyes were the same soulless black. Her double sword was in her hand, only one of its blades out. She spun it in a circle once before plunging it into Erros. The tip came out a few inches away from Kat's abdomen, covered in muddy purple and white blood. Kat could tell by the placement of the sword that Mara had punctured his heart. This time he did scream, letting loose his agony before falling to his knees, unable to hold himself up any longer.

"This is for *everyone* you ever hurt, all the lives you ever ruined," Mara spat.

"And this isn't just *them* getting *their* revenge. This is us getting ours," Kat snarled. She began to slide her sword out of Erros, but stopped and leaned down towards his ear till her lips were almost touching it. "Bye, luv." Just as much venom was in her voice as in her previous statement, but she also let the pain through. She and Mara yanked their blades out of Erros simultaneously, and he fell to the ground, dead before his body thumped onto the dry dirt. Blood poured from his mouth, no longer emitting the eerie orange glow. His eyes and veins appeared normal again. The unstable power had left him the second his heart stopped beating.

"What happened to you?!" Kat asked. Mara shook her head, a blank and distant expression on her face but no longer in her eyes. They had turned back to their original deep green.

"I don't know," she said, looking disturbed and confused as she said it.

CHAPTER 25

*Q*uiet choral music filled the hall, growing louder as the church's lead soprano hit her high note. People wearing fancy dress gear sat uncomfortably in the small hard pews facing the priest. At the far end of the church lay the object of the gathering – the coffins. Thirteen of them, white with ornate decorations, the style varying depending on the wealth of the families of the deceased. The priest stood solemnly in front of the two neat rows.

The church itself was beautiful, with an intricately tiled façade and tall stained glass windows. The vaulted ceiling was high with a distinctive Gothic look, and above the coffins was a large, decorated wall. In the middle of the wall, painted specifically for funerals and covered up for any other event, appeared three symbols, denoting the WW, death, and the angels.

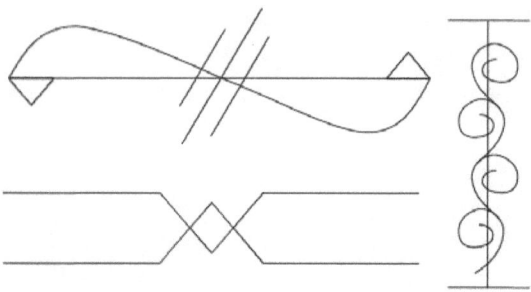

The inside walls of the church were pristine white with details in gold, silver, and other precious metals and stones. There were engravings of animals, people, and words, mostly in Yyuligian. A large stained glass window dominated the right wall. It was done in a mix of blues, greens, and golds and it depicted an angel guiding several WW on the path to protecting the world.

The church's enormous double doors were constructed of a nearly indestructible metal alloy, which had been painted over and richly decorated with mother-of-pearl and lapis lazuli. The two large iron door handles had been left unpainted. They were shiny, obviously polished, with not a speck of rust on them.

Mara, Kat, Hazen, Niko, Tom, Etta, and Aerick occupied one of the shorter front pews, only a few yards away from the coffins. A priest was pacing back and forth in front of them, waiting for the funeral to begin. With a nervous expression on his face he positioned himself in front of the coffins and cleared his throat softly. The room went from being filled with music and soft chatter to deadly silence. Mara took Kat's hand on one side and Hazen's hand on the other according to tradition when the priest began to speak about the value of life and the honorable cause of death. Mara wasn't exactly sure what he was saying but she could hear his soft, strong voice as though it was passing through water before reaching her ears. Instead of focusing on the air of death that hung over the congregation like a dreary cloud, Mara focused on the intricate patterns on her dress gear. For an important event everyone was expected to wear their nicest clothes – for most people this was their dress gear. Mara's dress had short sheer sleeves and was made of a silky soft black fabric that reached to her ankles. An intricate design of shimmery gold strands was woven into the bodice, sleeves, and down each side past her hips. She could feel the knives, blowers, and her double sword, cleverly hidden from view, pressing against her legs.

Kat was wearing her favorite dress gear outfit, a tight cherry red dress that came just past her knees and black four-inch stiletto heel ankle boots. She leaned forward slightly and looked past Mara to Hazen in order to examine her dress, a deep purple beaded garment with a v-neck and sheer, flowing sleeves.

Suddenly the preacher's words became louder and Kat could tell he was beginning the formal service. Pulling her focus away from clothes and back to the priest Kat tried to make sense of what he was saying. He was clearly new, inexperienced and prone to stuttering. Some of his words were coming out funny – warped, as if they had gone through a time/space continuum portal. He was just finishing the mandatory part of the speech that addressed how the deceased had died and how honorable it had been. Kat was sickened by the words he used to describe the horrible things that had happened. The phrases "felled fighting the righteous battle" and "deaths were for the greater good" were uttered several times in the monologue. Kat's mind was reeling from the events of the past few days, and listening to this man proclaim that the deaths of these righteous students were *necessary* to ensure the safety of Atherian, like the deaths of cattle in a slaughterhouse are necessary for food, only made it worse.

Mara, meanwhile, was having a much tougher experience as the priest called out the names of the fallen students and read a short paragraph about their virtues and how he hoped they would find their rightful place in the afterlife. Every time he uttered a name that she recognized the world around her became devoid of color and sound, then disappeared. Suddenly she was back in the battle, back watching those innocent students die, ripped apart by demons. She could see herself, too, fighting off black-eyed creatures. It was as if she was watching the battle all over again, only this time she was standing like a ghost at the edge of the clearing, witnessing the horrors but not lifting a finger to stop them. Her mind focused on the particular student the priest had just mentioned, saw them fighting for their life and losing, and then feeling the pain they must have felt. Then, as suddenly as it had appeared, the scene inside her mind disappeared and her senses returned to the church and the sound of the priest's voice, finishing the paragraph and moving on to the next student. On and on the funeral went, and each time Mara relived the deaths of the people *she* had persuaded to follow her. There were tears forming in her eyes but she refused to let them fall. Instead, she worked on retaining a calm and sorrowful expression.

When she heard Chase's name Kat's grip tightened, her long nails digging painfully into Mara's palm. His eulogy was flattering; it left out his repeated failures to graduate and his rather useless specialty. Kat thought that it did a good job of highlighting what was good about him, the small strands of gold woven into a fabric made mostly of burlap.

"I'm sorry," Mara whispered. "I know you cared about him." Kat turned her head to look at her sister.

"It's… it's okay. Losing him actually made me realize that he was never the one for me," Kat said quietly.

To Mara's surprise Leif would not be remembered and then buried in the church graveyard that day, but would have to wait until his funeral in the Human world was complete. Since he still had Human family who would no doubt wish to hold a proper service for him, the government of Atherian could not yet legally bury him. Mara had been told that he was in one of the back rooms being prepped for travel to a Human church. The woman who had told her of Leif's whereabouts seemed very disapproving of Mara's desire to see him, but she planned to ignore the woman's disapprobation and sneak back after the formal funeral was over.

Hours had passed since the depressing funeral had ended and still neither Mara nor Kat showed any signs of wanting to leave the church. An hour earlier Hazen had been escorted out by her father, a harsh-looking man with platinum-blond hair and cold brown eyes that didn't match the rest of his complexion. Niko and Tom had stayed for the first hour but then left, expressing an unspecified need to do something. Mara stood solemnly over one of the coffins, the one that had a small removable tag on it that read "Lissa."

"They had their whole life ahead of them. So much they hadn't done that now they'll never get a chance to do," she said, only loud enough for Kat to hear.

"I'm not going to say that it's not your fault. You won't listen to me even if I do," Kat sighed. "But they died fighting. That's all anyone can ask for. If you die knowing that you shrank from every challenge you faced, then you die a coward. A coward whose heart is filled with sorrow and regret. And that's the *worst* way to go."

Mara shook her head, keeping her eyes trained on the coffin in front of her. "Maybe it wasn't my fault, but they trusted me to lead them and I failed," she said, finally turning to face her sister. "Never again. I'm leaving."

Kat's expression took Mara by surprise; it was one of resignation, suggesting that she knew this was coming. "Fine," she said simply, staring Mara down. Surprised and confused that Kat wasn't opposing this, Mara began to turn away.

"*But* you take Hazen and me with you," Kat added.

Mara stopped in her tracks for several seconds but refused to respond. Finally, she walked away silently towards an unmarked door that she assumed led to the back room where Leif's body was being kept.

His face was placid, pale white, an expertly done mask of what it used to be. Someone had closed his eyes and smoothed his hair so that it looked clean-cut and sharp. Mara reached out and ruffled it back into his usual style. There was not a speck of blood on him, and he had been changed out of the black battle gear he died in. Instead, he was wearing a brand-new white gear outfit. The lack of color washed him out, making him look even more pale and lifeless.

Out of instinct Mara placed her hand gently on his chest, trying to feel some movement that would indicate his heart still beating. The second her hand made contact with the rough material of the white gear she couldn't move, held in place by some invisible force. An eerie golden light began to glow at the point of contact, growing so that Mara could no longer see her hand. She desperately tried to move her feet, to lift her hand off Leif's chest, but neither worked.

Without thinking she wished that Leif was alive, standing right next to her. He would know what to do when anyone else would simply panic and leave her alone.

As the thought flitted across her mind it was as if the invisible force had moved from her feet to her throat, wrapping itself around her neck and squeezing with all its might. Mara could feel her heels lifting off the floor until only her toes remained lightly touching the tiles. She choked, opening her mouth wide and straining to get air into her body. Black spots were dancing around her vision as she tried to focus on something, anything, that might help. Her hand stayed stuck to Leif's unmoving chest, the golden light growing stronger by the second. Her free hand was groping at the air in front of her neck but it found nothing, nothing that indicated what was choking her. The black spots grew, slowly taking over what was left of her vision and plunging her into darkness. Only when her eyes were rendered useless could she begin to feel something tugging at her arm, pulling hard on her fingers. Desperate for anything that might help she pulled back, entering into a tug of war with whatever resided in Leif's chest that was trying so hard to drag her down.

To her surprise the thing stopped its insistent tugging the moment she began to fight back and slowly, very slowly, she was able to lift her hand, a millimeter at a time, away from Leif's chest. The farther her hand got away from Leif's chest the more the invisible choke hold released, finally letting Mara take in a great gasp of air. Almost immediately her vision returned. In shock she saw her hand rising out of the bubble of gold light with something in it. She wasn't even aware that she was holding it but there it was, clear as day. A sphere, about the size of a softball, made completely of fog. Not just any fog, Mara's fog. She held it cupped in her hand, staring at it in wonder. It looked ordinary enough, but there was something about it that seemed enhanced, as if it had gone through vigorous cardio exercise while inside Leif. Mara remembered the sphere, of course. It was the one she had implanted in Leif in order to save his life when the demon took control of his mind.

Her other hand moved without her telling it to, rising up above the ball of fog and spreading its fingers out over it. Mara stared at it, not afraid anymore but dying of curiosity. She knew very well that her brain was not sending commands to the hand that was extended above the fog, and she had no other reasonable explanation for why it was moving, but she did have an unexplainable feeling that the hand knew what it was doing.

Golden light, the same as she had seen moments earlier surrounding Leif, pooled in her open hand. A tendril separated itself from the mass of light, stretching down tentatively like a vine towards the ball of fog. Many more followed, making a sort of woven wall around the fog constructed completely of light. Mara could no longer see the fog at all, but just felt it in her hand. She could see through the glowing wall enough, however, to make out a brightly lit object traveling slowly down through the corridor of woven light and towards the top of the sphere of fog. As it got closer Mara had to turn her head away because her eyes could no longer bear to look at the mysterious object. It was small, no bigger than the tip of her pinky, but infinitely bright.

Suddenly the light disappeared and Mara hastily turned her head back to look at the intertwined golden magic stretching between her hands. The tendrils that formed the wall were retracting, coiling back into the mass of gold light in Mara's palm. It was disturbingly similar to what she had seen Erros have in his palm when he channeled the power of his one remaining demon.

What interested her more, though, was the fog. It was still a sphere but at this point it was lit up, glowing brightly. Now Mara understood. The bright object had implanted itself into the fog, giving it an otherworldly glow that emanated off her hand. Narrowing her eyes and looking closer, Mara saw something that gave her a burst of hope. It was pulsing. Ever so slightly, the light was pulsing, remarkably similar to a heartbeat. More sure of her movements Mara took one step closer to Leif's body and lowered her hand down towards his chest, a few inches off to the left where she knew his heart was. She had a strange feeling deep inside that she had done this before, that perhaps this was a common procedure. Shaking off her worries and praying that whatever her body was telling her to do would work, she lowered her hand into Leif's chest. Her hand passed through the solid surface as if it were also made of fog.

She felt the connection the second she let go of her hold on the fog. Inside her she could feel some sort of power that allowed her to feel what was happening to the fog inside Leif's body. She withdrew her hand quickly, letting the fog do its work. It was latching onto something, reaching its golden tendrils deep inside and giving it a jumpstart. Mara could then feel it transporting the bright gold object into whatever it was connected to. Then suddenly, and rather painfully for Mara, the fog disappeared.

Mara could see the movement before she heard the sound of a heart beating. Leif's chest rising and falling ever so slightly, the almost imperceptible twitch of his right hand pointer finger. It took several seconds, several unbearable seconds that felt like years, but eventually his eyes flicked open. Mara smiled widely, letting out breath that she didn't know she'd been holding. Leif turned his head just enough so that he could see her and cracked a crooked grin. His eyes, instead of the bright and energetic green they used to be, were now a dull, lifeless muddy-green. Mara's smile faded as she saw this and she reached forward instinctively, touching the tip of her finger to the corner of his right eye. Leif looked momentarily worried, too. Flattening his palms on the cold marble surface of the raised table he was lying on he attempted to push himself up into a sitting position, but immediately groaned and flopped back down.

"Ow... yeah, I'm not going anywhere," he said weakly. He tried to raise his arm to take Mara's hand but abandoned that, too. "That twinges!"

"You lost almost all your blood. It's going to take a long time to replace it," Mara said soothingly, remembering the reason for his weakness. "You were also dead, so that might contribute a bit." Leif laughed, a soft chuckle followed by a wince of pain.

Mara's fear that he had come back only half-alive was soon alleviated when she saw color quickly returning to his skin, eyes, and hair. Instead of dull muddy-green his eyes were in the process of returning to their normal emerald. She reached down and wrapped her arms around him, resting her head on his shoulder. She could feel his muscles tense as he painfully lifted one arm and draped it over her back, grasping her left shoulder.

"How?" he whispered in her ear. She shook her head. Leif wasn't sure if she meant that she didn't want to talk about it, or that she didn't know at all, but he decided not to pursue it. If he had died and miraculously come back to life he wasn't about to challenge it. Instead he lost himself in Mara, her slim strong arms wrapped tightly around him. He could feel the heat of her cheek on his neck and her rapid heartbeat on his chest.

Without warning he slipped his hand under her chin and moved it up so her face was inches from his. Closing the distance between them he pressed his lips to hers. She was still, utterly still, and Leif was immediately worried that she would hate him for this. He was about to pull back when he felt her fingers sliding up the back of his neck and into his hair, ruffling it gently. Finally she responded to the kiss, moving her mouth against his, sending pangs of relief and joy through Leif. Not surprisingly she tasted like blood, but Leif, who hated the taste of blood, thought it was perfect. She drew away first, unwinding her hand from his hair.

"Sorry," Leif whispered, unsure of what would come next. Mara shook her head, giving him a small smile.

"It's okay," she replied softly, looking directly at him without remorse. Leif smiled back, thinking he probably still looked horrible from being dead but not caring, knowing that Mara was deep enough to see past his outward appearance. She put her arm around his shoulder, resting her other hand on his arm to help him up to a sitting position. He moved his legs slowly over the edge of the table. Knowing better than to try to stand while he still felt so weak he remained sitting, and occupied himself with taking in every detail of Mara.

The door burst open with a loud bang, swinging hard enough to seriously dent the wall. Kat appeared with a panicked expression, holding out her hands for Mara to see. They were glowing a bright silver, the veins highlighted just as Erros's had been the day before. Kat glanced down at her veins and then gave Mara a look that was both accusing and horribly afraid. Her face changed, however, the moment she saw Mara; her look turned into one of pure horror. She pointed at Mara's arms. Looking down Mara saw that she too was glowing, fainter than Kat but still glowing, her veins the same shade of shining silver.

"Did you do something? Anything?!" Mara asked, now just as panicked as her sister. Kat shook her head.

"I came in here because I thought *you* did someth... Ahhhh!" Kat stopped her sentence with a yell when she saw Leif, sitting up and very much alive, on the table. "See, I told you, you did something," she said, pointing at Leif. Kat's voice was raised and her eyes were wide. She had seen the mysterious thing that had happened to Mara on the battlefield and, frankly, she had had her fill of weird for the next few years. Now she was turning into the sort of monster that Erros had been. "Look, you're getting brighter now, too!" She moved her pointing finger from Leif to Mara, who was still staring at her rapidly brightening veins. Reaching down to the hem of her dress she hiked it up to her knees, showing that the glowing veins were not just on their arms.

"Uh, Mara?" Leif asked. "Now you have shiny silver markings all over your face and neck." She ran her hands over her cheeks and neck but felt nothing, as if whatever markings Leif was talking about were tattoos.

"Kat has them, too," she said, looking at her sister who had begun to develop exactly what Leif said *she* had. They were like the ancient runes Mara had studied back at the Academy, only painted on Kat's face and neck in glittering silver. Leif pushed up off the table and tried to walk towards Mara but stumbled and grabbed the sharp corner to steady himself.

"Ah," he gasped, holding up his hand where there was a long, thin cut. His eyes widened. Instead of purple and white WW blood coming out of the wound, there was a metallic brassy bronze color of thick liquid squeezing out. Holding his hand up for both sisters to see made Mara crack.

"What the *hell* is going on?!?!" she yelled at the top of her lungs. Kat could swear she saw sound waves resonate from Mara's mouth but she knew it was only her imagination. What *wasn't* her imagination was that Mara's eyes had begun to glow. No, not glow. They

287

were completely gold. Just like on the battlefield when her eyes had turned black they were now a moving, liquid gold. Without asking, Kat knew that her own eyes had undergone the same transformation.

"What *is* this?" Leif asked, examining the bronze blood with intrigue and fear. Calming himself just enough so that his voice sounded normal, he said, "This is *not* Witch Warrior blood." Mara shook her head, wincing as she did so. Her hands had squeezed themselves into fists and her knuckles were white from the force.

"No," she said, her voice strained and her muscles tense from pain. She hunched over, grimacing, and waited a bit before elaborating. "That's Fear Quirk blood. Something must have happened t-..." Her sentence was cut short by a scream of pain from Kat, who was also hunched over. Her back, more specifically her shoulder blades, looked like they were growing. She quickly resembled a very old lady with a spinal curvature. Leif was rapidly glancing between Mara and Kat, trying to decide whether to freak out about the change in his blood color or their disturbing change into... something. Leif knew all about Fear Quirks, and thought that if he had to be stuck as something other than a WW for the rest of his life, a Fear Quirk wasn't that bad. He got up from the table, adrenaline the only thing keeping him upright, and staggered over to Mara. She grabbed at his arm, fingers curling around his wrist and holding tight.

"Ow!" Leif cried, jerking his arm away and looking at the underside. Five bloody puncture wounds lined his arm. The same sticky bronze liquid was dripping out of them, too. Mara held up her hand and Leif stared at it. There were long black claws, elongations of Mara's fingernails and ten times stronger, on the tip of each of her fingers.

"I'm so sorry," she whispered.

Something large and strong hit Leif over the head, sending him sprawling down onto the floor. His hands went out just in time to prevent a badly broken nose, but not some serious bruises. Turning over onto his back Leif saw something wide and silver descending again and he raised his hands to shield his face. Scrambling back on his hands and knees Leif hoped he had gotten out of range of whatever had struck him so hard. His hope was short-lived, however, when what felt like the same thing smacked him on the back and sent him sprawling again. Getting back up to his feet Leif was shocked by what he saw.

Mara and Kat were standing looking at each other, expressions of mixed horror and curiosity on their faces. Neither of them paid any attention to Leif, but he was certainly paying attention to them, and he gasped as he identified what had been knocking him around.

Two large silvery wings protruded from each of their shoulder blades. They were at least ten feet in length and stretched from above their heads nearly to the floor. The silver markings had spread to cover each girl's entire body, but they had changed from being jarring silver tattoos to merely silver shimmers. Their eyes were the same – pure liquid gold.

Finally Mara turned to look at Leif and he noticed something else. Both girls were wearing an enormous amount of what looked like makeup but might well have been markings just like the silver shimmers. For Kat the dissimilarity from her usual look was slight, but Mara was almost transformed into a completely different person. Silver outlining emphasized the gold of their eyes. Elaborate twirls of makeup ran from the edges of their eyes all around their faces, giving them a distinctly celestial look. Both girls were breathing hard, their chests rising and falling rapidly underneath their gowns.

Leif got up and made his way over to Mara, placing his hand hesitantly on her shoulder. She didn't move, simply fingered the tip of one of the silver feathers on her right wing. Kat walked toward Mara, too, bumping her enormous wings several times against the walls of the room. She stopped when she was still a few feet away and reached both hands back, clearly annoyed. Grabbing the edges of her wings she pushed them together. Surprisingly they yielded without much resistance, folding neatly along her back and compressing to about four feet in length. Moving next to Mara, Kat simply stood there, completely at a loss for words.

However, she didn't have much time to come up with something to say. At that moment the ceiling cracked, showering dust down on the trio. Mara began shaking her head.

"Oh, not again. Not something else," she said wearily, turning to Leif for support. He gently pushed her wings to a folded position and awkwardly tried to wrap his arms around her. She laced her fingers with his, watching the ceiling suspiciously.

Boom! Dust and bits of sheetrock tumbled down on them as the entire roof blew off of the room. Mara extended her wings again, stretching her right wing up to cover Leif's head. A large, misshapen brick fell on the wing, but instead of breaking Mara's bones and continuing down onto Leif's skull, the brick shattered upon contact with the silver feathers. Kat had wrapped

290

her wings around her head and vital areas. Now she unwrapped herself in order to stare at the whirling vortex of golden light that was descending on the church through the now nonexistent ceiling. The light gradually condensed into the form of a woman. A very distinctive woman.

She was at least twelve feet tall and dressed in unimaginable finery, and she looked very similar to Mara and Kat. She had wings, just as large as theirs only gold instead of silver. Her pure gold eyes matched theirs, and she too had markings all over her skin. The only difference was that everything about her was gold – her hair, makeup, wings, eyes, markings, claws, clothes. Her face was fine-boned and had an elegant, regal look to it. Her high cheekbones emphasized by gold makeup gave her a look of unreal perfection. She smiled compassionately at them as someone might smile at poor, lost orphans.

Mara had seen pictures, illustrations of women who looked just like the one standing before her now. In Mr. Rosten's history class back at the Academy she remembered learning about the golden protectors of their world who had mysteriously departed hundreds of thousands of years ago. The pictures of such women had always been labeled "Angel." Directing her attention to Mara and Kat, the woman folded her wings delicately behind her back and opened her perfect mouth to speak in a silken voice.

"Greetings, my lovely daughters."

ACKNOWLEDGMENTS

As in any situation where someone has written a literary piece, there are rooms full of people who helped me come up with this. I would like to begin by thanking my wonderful family who supported me and helped with homework as I tried to balance school and writing. My mother Julie, father David, and grandmother Louise maintained a positive attitude when my writing hit a slump, and lovingly nagged me to get to bed earlier when I insisted on getting up at 6 AM to keep on typing. Louise, especially, edited constantly whenever I asked her, saving me from the embarrassment of many typos.

At school, I received great enthusiasm and positivity from my friends and teachers when I told them of this endeavor. Larkin Stephanos, Angeni Lieben, Catherine Vojta, Isabelle Lurie, Maia Drasin, Maya Armstrong-Azhar, Claudia Cruse, Molly Ransdell, Ella Thompson, and many more were always providing interesting new ideas and plot twists for me to explore, and sharing their own literary work. A particular thank-you to excellent artists Ella Thompson and Larkin Stephanos for their great ideas on design and fine-tuning the looks of my characters. And huge appreciation to Robert Grubbs for his phenomenal cover design.

A shout-out to my 8th Grade English teacher, Ms. Rachel Pledger, for allowing me to write during class most days. I'm eternally grateful for the support you gave me throughout the year and the feedback on the first ten pages. Thank you.

ABOUT THE AUTHOR

This is Lydia Osborn's first novel. She is thirteen years old and lives in the San Francisco Bay Area with her family and two cats, and spends every waking minute writing when she isn't in school, at swim practice, or doing martial arts.

www.ingramcontent.com/pod-product-compliance
Lightning Source LLC
Chambersburg PA
CBHW031659170626
46808CB00005B/1531